# UNDER THE BLACK BANNERS

K. ELLE MORRISON

This novel is a work of fiction. All characters and events portayed are either products of author's imagination or used fictitiously.

Cover Designed by: J M Steger Fantasy & Coffee

Kellemorrison.com

Print ISBN: 978-0-578-94330-5

Ebook ISBN: 978-0-578-94628-3

# CHAPTER ONE

His lips grazed my ear as his warm breath brushed against my cheek. "I finally have you all to myself."

I closed my eyes and tilted my head to rest on his chest to expose my neck to him. The palm of his hand slid up and over my shoulder; his lips moved along the sensitive crook where my necklace rested. A small wanting sound escaped my lips and a low rumble was his reply. A vibration from my skin, down through my tightening muscles, tumbled into a place deep in my stomach. I arched my back trying to will him into action, and my backside edged closer to his hips. The warm bulge in the front of his slacks pressed against me which answered my next question, but what kind of Temptress would I be if I didn't ask?

"Are you going to keep me waiting all night?"

He let out an amused hum as the hand at my neck tightened and his other hand rose to my hip, squeezing and bringing me closer. Turning me to face him, he held my chin firmly between his fingers, lifting so our eyes met. His pupils dilated in the dim lighting, almost completely eating up his warm brown irises. Our lips danced closer together, but waited for the other to make the first move. It had to be him to strike first, otherwise, I'd lose all control over this situation. I wouldn't let that happen.

The flickering of a candle in the dim room popped and spit, sounding like encouragement or a warning. Cool, summer night air filled the room with the scent of jasmine from the creeping vines outside the open window of the great stone walled hotel. I tried to focus on the breeze coming in and not the heat that was pressing in on me. Jaara smiled and lowered his eyes to my chest, gliding a finger over the top of my shoulder, threatening to slide the thin strap of my dress down. I moved my arm back behind me, feeling for the bed and pulling away from his curious fingers. His eyes flicked back to mine, and I knew what was going to happen next, but I gasped nonetheless. In one smooth movement, he entangled his fingers into my brown hair, grabbing a full palmful and pulling my head back. His mouth connected with mine, hard and deep.

I parted my lips to let his tongue in, coaxing at him with my own as both my hands pressed to his chest and pulled at his shirt. He stepped forward, forcing the back of my legs against the bed. His hands and mouth released me, the force of his body downward inviting me to sit rather persuasively. He stared down to me as I slid my hands over the smooth linen duvet and waited for his next silent command. I made to pull my high-heeled shoes off, but he grabbed my chin, tsking and shaking his head slowly. My eyes fell to his slacks then flicked back to his face. His full lips parted, his tongue pressed between his teeth, and I took it as permission and unclipped his belt, unbuttoned his slacks, and let the rich material fall and reveal his tight undershorts. Seeing the near-perfect outline of his excitement, my eyes widened.

I cupped him briefly, feeling him pulse in my hands before I slid them under his shirt and up his coiled muscles. His skin tensed beneath my touch from anticipation or the chill that had found my fingertips. I lifted my eyes to his, waiting. He unbuttoned and shrugged off his shirt, it found a place on the floor near his slacks, his gaze never leaving mine. He leaned down, curling his strong arm around my back, lifting and practically throwing us both to the middle of the bed. His mouth found mine once more as his hands explored the curves of my body—breast and hips lifting to meet his touch. The hem of my dress pulled up to give him a position between my legs where only thin layers of fabric separated us.

Blood rushed to my head and pounded in my ears. It was now or never because he was going to find my blade any second. I pushed his shoulder up suggestively to the side then threw my leg over to straddle him. His expression quickly turned to awe and confusion at my display of dominance. I reached to my inner thigh, pulling a thin, small throwing knife from its sheath, and before he could see the candlelight gleam off the tip, his throat was slit. He grabbed at his neck wildly as blood began pooling on the cream sheets. I could see his mind trying to work out what was happening, the wheels turning and connecting the dots, stringing together the evening.

Who was I?

Who sent me?

Then, he stopped thrashing, there it was. The realization flickering in his eyes. I leaned down, brushing my lips to his ear. It wouldn't be long now.

"Mr. Morganson sends his regards and is waiting for you in Sheol." I kissed his cheek before raising off his body.

I wiped my blade on the bed linens before returning it to the sheath and crossed the room to the small entry table to collect my clutch. I waited to hear the wet choking of his last breaths leaving his body. Looking over my shoulder to where the maid would find him in the morning, I couldn't stop the corner of my mouth from rising at my quick work. In the small mirror on the wall of the entryway, I took out the tube of red lipstick from my bag and dabbed it to my lips, touching up the smudged pigment, then gave my hair a shimmy before leaving the room.

In the light of the hotel hallway, I could see a damp circle of blood on my black dress. It was going to be hard to explain to the dry cleaner, but it was one of my most successful dresses. It hugged my body in all the right places and distracted the weak marks. When I reached the elevator and requested a lift, I checked the time. It had taken me thirty minutes to finish my assignment from the beginning of our "date". I could still grab a drink at the hotel bar before heading home.

The doors opened with a muted tone, but it wasn't empty. A tall man looked up from where he'd been watching the floor, his thick black hair parted to the side revealing smoke-filled eyes. His darker irises and pupils like a ring of stormy grey. An Incubo; a nightmare.

My spine went stiff, and I drew in a sharp breath as I stepped into the soon-to-be too small elevator and faced the doors. His gaze followed my every move as if he were watching for me to exhale. The relaxed posture he showed did little to ease me. His black suit jacket open to reveal a silk dress shirt embossed with golden thread that dripped with sophistication and wealth.

"Rough night?" He moved his eyes away from me and looked straight ahead at the distorted reflection in the elevator doors as he spoke in a smooth, playful tone.

"No more than usual." I drew in a shallow breath but didn't fully feel the air reach my lungs.

He inclined his head to me subtly, but it was enough to show that he had marked me as the Temptress I was posing to be. The lift's muted tone rang out as the doors opened again, and he took a step out and extended a hand to me.

"Shall we?" he said coolly, waiting for me to obey him.

His outstretched hand wasn't an offer, but a command. If I didn't oblige my cover would be compromised. I laid my hand onto his, and he gave me a small tug. He led me to his room

4

around the corner from the elevator, about ten doors separating it from the traffic of other patrons. The door opened and he slid behind it, inviting me into the dimly lit room. It was identical to the one I had left minutes ago, except for the missing newly-drained body on the bed.

I stood in the middle of the room for a moment, his body lingering behind me. I could feel his eyes scanning over my backside, possibly noting the throwing blades attached to my body which were not visible to the naked eye. But to his kind? I didn't know. The Incubo were said to have different abilities that weren't always easy to spot.

His hand flattened at my lower back as he approached my side and nudged me further into the room. The pressure was brief as he moved to the bed directly in front of me and sat down, crossing his ankle over top of his knee. His fingers inter-laced and fell to his lap as he looked up at me, his eyes rather unsettling, waiting for me to speak. But as a Temptress, I was supposed to only take directions, even when they're merely implied. I shifted my weight to one side and crossed my arms right below my breasts. I cocked my head to the side trying to give the impression that I was bored.

"Right then," he began, amusement in his voice, "where should we start? I've not had a Temptress in my presence in ages. It's quite the treat."

I've played this part many times. Posing as a Temptress often brought my targets closer quickly and gave me a reason to be alone with them without being questioned. However, this was the first time an Incubo had requested my services. They often kept to their own kind for good reason. Unlike most Fata, Incubo had Mortal features except for their eyes which varied in shades or hues of irises beneath the veil of smoke covering them. I had heard only rumors of their abilities—that other beings didn't possess. Each Incubo was said to have unique attributes such as telepathy, or inhuman strength, but more terrifying was that there didn't seem to be a limit to what they were capable of inflicting on other beings. Incubo were as beautiful as they were dangerous, which was almost tragic: otherworldly handsome, every single one of them. Lethal when Mortals or Fata stayed too close for too long in their small circles.

"It's been a long time since I've had the honor of serving an Incubo, but I am yours for the evening," I lied; I'd only ever met an Incubo once before in passing at a party.

I drug my sight over his well-tailored suit, from his pressed collar to his lux leather shoe planted on the floor. When our eyes met again, I searched for a glimpse of intention. He had no business with a Mortal Temptress. He could have any woman or man eating out of his hand in moments at any establishment in the city. He gave a sly smile that pulled a dimple from his cheek before looking at the ground again.

"You see, that is hard to believe."

"What's hard to believe?" My brows lifted at his remark.

He glanced back to me, and in one fluid movement that seemed to slow time, he was standing in front of me. An inch separated our chests; he was at least half a foot taller than me, even in my stilettos. He leaned in close to the side of my face and drew a long breath through his nose, smelling me.

Could he smell my previous companion? The blood on my dress?

"It's hard to believe that I am an honor to serve. You haven't asked how to address me. You also haven't offered me your limitations or payment expectations." His voice was clear but only above a whisper.

How could I be so stupid?

"I'm sorry, sir. I'm nervous." I turned my face away from him in an effort to appear coy as I internally cursed myself.

"You will address me as Talos." He traced the edge of my

cheek, jaw, and neck with the back of his slender fingers. "What may I call you, Temptress?"

I tried to swallow, but only struggled to form and push words out of my mouth as his touch grazed the sensitive groove of my collarbone.

"You may call me Isa, si—I mean, Talos," I corrected myself, but I needed to get myself together.

I gave him my real name and perhaps I shouldn't have, but I was having a hard time breathing and thinking of a fake name on a whim. If he had any suspicions, they'd be validated if I didn't calm myself.

"Good girl, Isa." He practically purred. The sound dangerous and tugged at a knot inside my chest.

He moved back to the bed, this time walking to the head of the right side, flinging the extra pillows to a chair nearby. He pulled the corner of the linens back and began to shrug off his jacket, folding it neatly and placing it on top of the pile of pillows. Casually, he inclined his head and swept his hand over the space on the bed as an invitation to sit. I tossed my clutch on a table near the door, a sense of deja vu hitting me as I made my way over to the spot Talos had indicated. I sat and waited for his next command.

Talos moved past me, his slacks brushing my knees as he did so. He sauntered to the foot of the bed and faced me, and I watched him closely. He seemed so relaxed, almost as if he'd known he'd run into me in the elevator. But how could he have known about Jaara?

I steadied my breathing, still staring and still waiting.

"Isa. That is a beautiful name. Have you had it long?" His hands busied themselves at his sleeves, uncuffing his cufflinks and rolling them up in smooth motions, exposing his forearms.

"Of course, Talos. All twenty-six years of my life." My voice sweet, but low.

"Of course." He echoed slyly.

Sliding his hands back into his pockets, I could now see a tattoo on the top of his forearm. A plump bird holding a branch of a plant, the leaves and flowers bright against his bronze skin. The wings of the bird looked almost animated, so realistic that I thought the tiny thing would, at any moment, start flapping.

"Would you like to join me on the bed, Talos?" I smoothed my hand across the open sheet.

He tilted his head to the side, continuing to stare at me for a moment longer before speaking in a velvety smooth voice. "There is nothing more that I would rather do than join you in that bed, Isa. But I worry that I wouldn't see the light of morning if I did, and I have many people to meet with tomorrow. They would be very disappointed."

I stood up and grabbed one of my blades from my thigh in a smooth motion. I let the blade fly, aiming between his dark eyes, but he simply stepped out of the path of the blade and it pierced into the wall behind him. Before I could blink, he was standing in front of me once again, only a heartbeat away. His body boxed me in between the bed and the wall, his hands quickly pinning my wrists to my sides before he brought me a little closer to him.

"Now now, Isa," he cooed, "That was not very subservient of you. What would your Mistress say?"

He knew I didn't have a Mistress; he knew I wasn't a Temptress. But what else did he know of me? Had he been following me all night? Was Jaara an associate of his? So many questions. I needed to get out of that room before I also became a mess for the maids to clean up in the morning. I twisted my arms in a cross, pulling his body toward the bed, then broke free of his hold by kicking at his shin with my stiletto heel. He cursed out loud as I darted to the door, but found it locked. I turned around to scan the room, but he was already blocking me...

In a fast motion, much too fast for me to anticipate, he bent

8

down and grabbed the back of my legs. He hoisted me up and slammed me against the door, pushing himself between my legs. I thrusted my upper body upward, wrapping my arms around one side of his head and neck. I pulled and he let go, dropping me to the floor between his parted legs. I kicked up towards his very sensitive undercarriage, but he was quicker. He grabbed my ankle and pinned it to the ground. He was practically sitting on top of me, putting his weight on my body to hold me still.

"I don't want to hurt you, but if you keep fighting, I will have to show you a side of me that not many have seen in a long time." The casualty in his tone told me that I hadn't even caused him to break a sweat.

I stopped fighting. He lifted his body off me and extended his hand to assist me to my feet. I hesitated for a moment but took it as a gesture of good faith that we wouldn't try to injure each other.

He reached up to where the blade was sticking out of the wall next to us and pulled it out with little effort. The small knife made a soft clunk when he set it down flat next to my bag. He made another sweeping motion over the bed, but I didn't oblige this time. There was no need to pretend to be obedient now. The door may have been blocked, but I needed to remain standing. I needed to find another exit route. I'd been stupid in not finding one before stepping into this room. It was as if I had gradually stepped into a fog, had adjusted enough, but was still disoriented.

"As you wish." He sat on the bed himself. "I'm sure you have questions about who I am and why I've requested your company. But first, your real name would make this conversation much more personal."

I narrowed my eyes. My name was no more personal than his body sitting on top of me or how close my blade had come to his face before that. I said nothing, he didn't need further information to continue this encounter.

"Very well, but I'm rather disappointed," he sighed.

He stood up and walked around to the minibar near a door that I assumed was the bathroom. The windows to the left of me looked out over several floors onto the street below, but there was no balcony to his spacious room. I doubted that the windows opened.

He opened a small bottle of clear liquor and drank directly from it in one gulp; he didn't so much as blink. He turned toward me offering me a second bottle from his hand.

"Could I interest you in a nightcap? Or do you only drink alone after a job is completed?"

That was a statement, and even though this meeting felt like a threat, it wasn't. Because if he wanted me dead, I wouldn't be standing with a dumbfounded look plastered to my face.

He held out his hand, a small whiskey bottle dangling from his fingers. I took it, but only toyed with it in my hands as I watched him open and drink another clear bottle.

"Your skills are impressive, Isa. May I still address you as Isa?"

"I didn't lie about my name. And you ask a lot of questions for someone who seems to have been following me."

A look of amusement danced across his face, tugging one corner of his mouth upward as he opened a third bottle, holding it in his hand out in front of him. He gave me a "cheers" motion and downed the bottle.

"I have not been following you, but I am in need of your services. Your true services." He paused and I thought he would go for a fourth bottle, but he set the empty one down and slid his hands into his pockets.

"As much as I think I would enjoy you as a Temptress," he scanned me from my shoes back to my face, "I find the need for your lethal qualities of more value, for now."

I shivered. Incubo rarely mingled with Mortals in their personal lives, including what he was insinuating. I'd only met a handful of Mortals who had been entangled with Incubo and they were not very talkative. They seemed to be in a trance or fucked into submission before vanishing for good. Not a terrible way to go, but not my preferred method.

"Doesn't your kind take care of your own misdealings personally? Why would you need my services?" The small bottle was starting to feel warm in my hands, but it grounded me.

"My kind? What an interesting choice of words." He considered that for a moment and looked as if he were going to comment further on that remark but decided to move past it. "Yes, the Incubo do tend to clean up our own messes. But certain circumstances have come to my attention for which I could use your assistance, if you could find it in yourself to help someone of my kind."

His last few words dripped sour-sweet; heat started to brush my cheeks with slight shame. I had nothing against Incubo personally; even if I sounded hostile, I had no issue with them.

"I don't doubt you could afford my fees. And, as I'm assuming you are aware of, I have just finished an assignment. What's the job?" I relaxed my shoulders, not realizing they had been so tense.

"Have one drink with me, and I will be happy to tell you all the details." He practically glided towards me.

With his body being close to mine once more I noticed his scent for the first time as my bewilderment had subsided. He smelled fresh, like cedar and white musk, but also warm like tea. He pulled a hand from his pocket, lightly taking hold of my hand that held my small whiskey bottle. Lifting the bottle right below my chin, I glanced down to its shiny top, but caught sight of his tattoo again.

There were symbols that I didn't recognize at the breast of the bird, following its curve below its beak that held the delicate branch. His other hand appeared to unscrew the top of the bottle and toss the small cap to the side. I followed his movement closely, then met his gaze again, I pressed the bottle to my lips and drank the harsh liquid quickly.

It burned as it slowly whirled down my throat, hitting my stomach as the warmth started to radiate through me. I hadn't realized how cool my skin had become, or how warm his hands were against my skin. He brushed a stray lock of my hair from my face, his fingertips tucking it behind my ear and running down my arm.

"I can see how your victims could become disarmed by your beauty." These words brought me back from somewhere far off. "They must be very welcoming once they have your full attention. I'm finding it difficult to focus now that I have you."

A quickening response in my midriff surprised me, and my lips parted, but I had nothing to say, nothing, instead shallow breaths passed through them. When he spoke again, I could feel my body moving closer to him and my insides starting to feel loose.

"Thank you for accepting my offer, it is terribly lonely to drink alone."

His head tilted and his eyes landed at my shoulder, reminding me that his fingers were dragging up and down the back of my arm bringing forth the image of his arms around me.

"I- you're welcome." Was all I could choke out.

"Talos."

"Uh… what?" My lazy vision was now coming back into focus.

"My name is, in fact, Talos. In case you have the need to use it." His smile was devilish, sending my stomach tumbling. He looked as if he had many ideas of how I would need to use his name here in this room.

"Right." I stepped back from him, against the protest of the rest of my body.

He didn't miss a beat, closing the space between us and

resting his hand on my lower back, pulling me closer. My legs and torso betrayed me as I leaned into his embrace. His eyelids lowered over the solid black that had engulfed every bit of his eyes, his mouth lowering to mine and pressing softly. A rush of sensations flooded through me: the taste of the liquor on our tongues as they touched, his hands roaming my backside and swimming through my hair. Below the taste of whiskey and vodka, something lingered. I pulled away, realizing it was Jaara. I was tasting the man I had dispatched no more than twenty minutes ago, who had also brought me to his room in the hopes of becoming entangled with me.

I turned away from him, hand to my mouth in my own disgust. I couldn't fathom what I was doing or why. Facing him I saw the utter horror on his face as he met the same realization I had before I'd stopped him. As the bathroom door behind him came into view, I ran for it without saying a word and locked the door behind me.

# CHAPTER TWO

I turned the hot water faucet on while I unrolled a washcloth from its decorative plate on the bathroom counter and waited for the steam to rise from the basin. I ran the palms of my hands over my face and through my hair, attempting to erase the horror of what just happened. I soaked the cloth in the scolding stream before wringing it out and using the rough material over my swollen lips in an unsuccessful attempt at erasing the memory of his mouth and face stubble against me. A light rapping on the locked door startled me, but I didn't answer.

I waited for him to speak, to rationalize my thoughts for me, but he was silent as death. After several more silent moments I heard the door to the room open and shut. Turning off the tap, I unlocked the door and peeked through a small crack. He was gone, the room completely empty. I didn't wait for a sign that he would be returning. I went to grab my clutch on the entrance table and found a business card laid next to it. A thin, silver-embossed, matte-grey rectangle. Perfectly centered in silver and gold text was:

*He can't be serious.*

*Could he?*

His title explained why he felt comfortable being in my presence, knowing exactly what my profession was. He seemed to know how to get a hold of me if he wanted to, but chose to make this initial meeting seem organic so as to not alert anyone who may have been passing by while I was in disguise.

But then why leave? Perhaps a better question was, why kiss me and then leave?

I didn't want these questions answered immediately. I slipped the card in my bag and left quickly, avoiding the elevator to use the staff stairway that gave a direct exit to the back of the hotel. I took my shoes off about halfway down the first flight of stairs. I could run faster barefoot if I needed to, and these were my favorite stilettos. Breaking off a heel would have been the cherry on top of this strange evening. The staff parking lot was secluded enough. I looked to the surrounding rooftops for any risk of being seen. I put my shoes back on my feet and stayed close to the building's shadows. I tried to look casual, but getting away was my main priority.

At the corner of the hotel, I quickened my pace down the alley to the busy sidewalk and stopped a few feet from the many beings passing along the walkway. Three blocks down, I could make out the illuminated entrance sign of the trainway through the crowd. Saturday nights were filled with street festivals and music performances. The theater across the street had let out a large group of beings that were now crowded around, hailing taxis and waiting for valets.

I started on my way, not a glance in my direction as I emerged from a dark alleyway. It helped that Cinder was full of life, but I was still under the guise of a Temptress who was possibly leaving a client. Most beings wouldn't stop to question a Temptress unless they wanted to deal with an overbearing Mistress.

Temptresses and Tempts were Mortal or Fata confidantes of rich and powerful beings in all circles. Most clients were too busy or repugnant to hold committed relationships. Through the Mistresses they were able to connect with beautiful companions for all matters— business dinners, vacations, galas, company parties, and so on. Clients paid a hefty price for them to be completely devoted to their every whim.

Becoming a true Temptress or Tempt took years of training and sacrifice. The invaluable, in-depth seduction tactics, social etiquette, and literature education had them held in the highest regard. They were often privy to private quarters and parties, which made posing as one worth the risk of being caught.

I was hired by Mr. Morganson's second in command. A deal they had struck went sour, taking close to a hundred pounds of street drugs and Morganson down with it. But the order on Jaara had been set in motion as a fail-safe. It wasn't my job to judge my marks or who hired me, but two fewer drug lords walked the beautiful streets of Cinder tonight.

When I reached the trainway, several other beings were standing around waiting for the next train to arrive. I surveyed every single one for darkened eyes. I wouldn't expect Talos to follow me at this point, but I still had no idea how long he had been keeping tabs on me. I looked into my purse and to the business card lying at the bottom of the shallow bag. My mind wandered for a moment, but I quickly snapped it shut as the train came clanking up the tracks. It slowed before the doors opened, letting riders off and new riders enter. I took the nearest seat and breathed a sigh of relief as the doors closed and the train began to move.

There were only three other beings aboard my train car, all engrossed in their own worlds: reading books or magazines or listening to music through small devices. Maybe leaving work to return to their homes or loved ones. I imagined it was a simple life to be one of them; completely unaware of the dark side of the city or of the woman sitting in the train car with them. It must be so blissful to be completely average.

I'd never known average; I was eight years old when I was sold to the Black Banners, an organization that, by all accounts, didn't exist. They raised and trained highly skilled assassins to be used in the politics of Mortals, Fata, and, I suppose now, Incubo.

My drug addict mother sold me to a man named Mr. Blue. I'd never heard a whisper of her whereabouts since I watched her drive away, and I had never asked. It wasn't the first time she had left me somewhere, but it was the first time she hadn't come back. I didn't cry. I haven't shed a single tear about her abandoning me in years. Lucky for me, Mr. Blue was kind and had been looking for children who wouldn't be missed, who wouldn't have family members to look for them.

I remember the day after the transaction better than most days in my life. The room they gave me had a real bed, not just a mattress on the floor. Ms. Green and Mr. Blue treated us like their own children, caring for every scrape, sniffle, and trauma. The morning meal was prepared by Ms. Green who asked me what foods I actually liked and then cooked in front of me in the large kitchen. She made a feast of eggs, bacon, and pancakes. I hadn't eaten the night before, due to anxiety and insecurity, so every single bite hit my stomach like a rock. When I finished my first plate, I was offered a second helping, then another after that plate was emptied. I had never eaten so much in one meal in my life and after my fourth plate was gone, I was offered a snack to take with me to my first day of training.

Ms. Green was the cook, house cleaner, and all-around den mother to all of us at the Black Banner 216 House. Each house had a code name and only housed twelve Banner recruits at a time. They scattered houses all over the country, usually placed in the middle of large cities to not draw attention. Hidden in plain sight.

Every day we woke up at six in the morning and trained for twelve hours. Our training wasn't only in physical combat or weapons, we were expected to be quick-witted, persuasive, resourceful, and well-educated; every lesson carefully modeled after situations that a former Banner had encountered. When it was time for our first assignments, we would team up with a more experienced Banner, and we either came back successful or in a body bag.

I have been part of the Black Banners now for eighteen years and have been taking assignments on my own for the last five. Since becoming an active Banner, my jobs have included taking down other assassins from rival organizations and small government leaders. My bread and butter, however, has been greedy businessmen trying to outlive one another. Which is what brought me to Jaara this evening and to the train I was sitting in.

The train slowed before the doors opened and I stepped out onto the platform, looking around to be sure I wasn't followed. I was more aware of my surroundings after a job, but the encounter with Talos had me more on edge. I needed to get home where I would be safe.

The Incubo were much smaller in their numbers, only about one fourth of the population, but they held powerful positions in the corporate and legal world. Mortals and Fata often worked alongside each other with little issue. Fata and Incubo, on the other hand, had scuffles amongst themselves every once in a while. The details were usually hidden from the public.

Cinder, where I lived and did most of my assignments, had a darker underbelly teaming with drug lords, gambling bookies, black market business dealings, and corrupt government officials. Often these beings found themselves in my family's crosshairs.

The man working at the train toll booth was a Fata. His skin was dark like the night, his eyes completely white and luminous which stood out in stark contrast to his complexion as if he could look right through me. He likely worked the night shift and rarely saw the light of day, allowing his complexion to take on the characteristics of its surroundings. This didn't happen to every Fata, many you couldn't tell apart from Mortals, but their tipped ears were a quick giveaway. I gave him a nod as I passed by, and he gave me a kind tip of the hat before returning to reading his book inside the booth.

The trainway stairs ascended out onto the street a few blocks down from my building door. The beautiful ivy-covered stone archway of the old building led into the pure-white marble floored lobby, and a crimson rug led to the elevator. The doorman, Rollins, summoned the lift for me and gave me a gentle tip of the brim of his hat as I walked past him. I pressed the penthouse button and the doors closed. A moment later, I was standing in my most favorite place in the world. My home.

As a young child living under bridges or in the back of cars, I had never imagined that I would live in such a beautiful place. The large open entryway gave an unobstructed view to my living room and to the balcony that looked over a large portion of Cinder's East End. Large stone buildings lining the streets could be seen, but the bustle of the living could hardly be heard from my home. Every building in the East End was required to have walls covered in vine plants, which reduced noise, but also made it the prettiest area in all the city. Other areas of Cinder were adopting this rule, including the hotel in which I'd left Jaara's body in.

I headed to my bathroom to rinse the last remnants of both men out of my mouth, setting my bag down on my bed as I passed on my way through the cream tiled room. I turned the shower on as hot as I could and let it run while I got undressed. Slipping my black dress off, I lifted the spot of blood up to the light. It had dried and was barely a hue darker on the soft fabric. I stepped out of my shoes before depositing everything into my walk-in closet. Most of my wardrobe was separated out into work related sections. Little black dresses and reconnaissance gear off to the left, while casual pants and blouses hung to the right, the wall dedicated to my footwear at the back center wall. I'd always loved shoes, even as a little girl I tried to keep the shoes I was able to have as clean as possible.

What I loved most about this closet was the hidden door behind the shelves of shoes holding my arsenal: knives, daggers, expandable batons, tasers, a crossbow or two, and a few handguns. I rarely had a need for firearms. Most jobs I accepted required that I appear to be as docile as a kitten, so having a gun strapped to my body would give me away in an instant. But my knives were an extension of my body, of my fingers and arms. Their razor thin blades could hide so beautifully in any lingerie or slim fitting dress that was required so often.

The knives I had used would be returned to their safe home after I cleaned them, but not before I cleaned myself. The hot steam and water were an instant relief. Washing the stress and stench of Jaara and Talos off my body and out of my hair felt like washing away years of invisible grime. I massaged soap over my arms and legs, then chest and neck, rinsing it all away as my skin became pink from the heat. So satisfying. But not as satisfying as it would be to eat a homemade meal and lie in my own bed.

My birth mother hadn't taught me how to survive on my own, she didn't get much of a chance, I suppose. I learned to cook from Ms. Green and books or TV shows. While we never had to fend for ourselves at House 216, we would often take turns helping in the kitchen when there was time. It was how we learned skills other than killing, and how we bonded with our new family. That's what we were. Family. Not all of us called each other "brother" or "sister," but we would all do whatever it took to keep each other alive. It was rare that we didn't get along because arguing with each other could lead to one or more of us in a morgue.

I tossed my used towels in the hamper and put on a relaxed tank top and a pair of worn-in sweatpants before heading for the kitchen that took up the whole left quarter of my home. At times of confusion or wariness I cooked to bring myself comfort, which would bring me right back to the image of Ms. Green taking us to the markets or standing next to me at the stove of the uptown Brownstone.

In my own kitchen the black cabinets reached the ceiling and the thick butcher block counter lined most of the far wall. From my kitchen island I could see the rest of the layout and my balcony that was laden with plants. The stone balcony walls had the building's ivy creeping in and out of every break in the wall and over the ledge. I ate most of my meals among the peaceful vines and potted plants.

I finished cooking—coconut milk braised fish stew over ginger rice—and took my plate out on the balcony, laying my plate down on the hard stone barrier between a few vines. I loved watching the city come alive late at night and into the early morning from this balcony. Fata and Mortals alike passed below me on their way to or from work, to run errands, or to meet their friends and families for outings. It all seemed so peaceful and, in a small way, I felt like my job made this possible.

My typical targets were small scale crime affiliates or crooked businessmen, but every so often I'd be hired to level the playing field in politics. Some would say my role wasn't the fair way or even the moral way, but it was the way money and influence were played. As far as I knew, there was a network of Incubo connected by rich, old families that intermingled and only bred when members died off, which wasn't often. Mortals and Fata don't know how to kill an Incubo, they merely exist alongside us as shadows.

Talos was likely an underling for a larger family that could very well be his own blood. Though if he was in the service of a higher ranking member of their society, he would no doubt be wealthy in his own right. Incubo kept their numbers small, but they needed their own kind in all aspects of their ranks. They relied on their seclusion to remain secure in their wealth among all other beings. As for there being some type of Incubo royal hierarchy, that was unheard of and Talos being the head of a royal family security made my head hurt. Our country had a high council, government leaders, and elected officials, not secret royal families.

Incubo were illusive beings, but they occasionally took Fata as lovers or close companions, but as partners they could not conceive. There were whispers about Incubo taking Mortal lovers, but it was typically frowned upon, their strength often broke our bodies easily and their cruel nature often ended lives. Newspapers often needed to find new editors after large scandals broke pertaining to Incubo involved in conspiracies or unexpected deaths. Fata and Mortals occasionally dated or married, but were cursed with infertility. Offspring between the two wasn't impossible, but it was rarely accomplished without intervention.

My mind went to the business card that he had left for me; accepting an assignment from an Incubo could be an extra dose of danger compared to my usual. That's not what worried me— I could handle complicated jobs. It was how he had found me. He had come to me in person, alone. I had a feeling if I didn't reach out to him, I'd find myself being found by him again and he might not be in such a nice mood as he had been tonight. I resigned myself to calling him in the morning, but tonight I would enjoy my solitude in my fortress, my home.

# CHAPTER THREE

I'd slept comfortably through the remainder of the night but was restless once the sun started peeking through my bedroom curtains. By seven o'clock, I was eating breakfast after a hard training session in the gym downstairs. I'd picked this building for many reasons, but the most useful was the large basement fitness center. I rarely saw other residents use it, but it was always kept clean and waiting for when I needed it. Often nerves or memories would drive me from sleep and training helped ease my anxieties for the rest of the day.

I sat with my coffee staring at the business card in my hand for what felt like the hundredth time. I knew I needed to get it over with. Maybe he'd changed his mind about hiring me after our encounter last night. But he wouldn't have left the card if he had any intention of taking back the offer. I paced the kitchen floor one last time before dialing. The other line only rang twice before it was answered.

"Hello, Isa." His voice rough with sleep. "What a pleasure to hear from you so early in the morning."

"You have an assignment for me?"

He gave a sigh that sounded more like a deep groan, and he was quiet for a moment before answering.

"I'd prefer to meet and speak face to face; this assignment is very personal to me and *my kind.*"

"Where and when?" I was trying to hide my annoyance. I didn't usually meet clients in person.

"I'll text you the address, and your first payment will be waiting for you upon arrival." He hung up and a moment later a text came through with the address and the amount he'd be paying me.

One million dollars. Twenty thousand upon our first meeting, just for my time. Why did this feel like a trap?

My services weren't cheap by any means, but this was double my typical amount for high profile assignments. Nevertheless, I'd be prepared. Most assignments started the same day so I would need to grab my go-bag and a few weapons. I would also make a call to my landlord to water my plants. She was always very kind to do me that favor, and I also paid her an extra percentage to keep my name off any of the building paperwork. As far as anyone knew, I was an accountant who traveled often and only worked with exclusive clients so my identity needed to be hush-hush. Which was as good as any other alias.

A half hour later, I was on my way out the door wearing casual black slacks, a white blouse, and a pair of sensible shoes. I folded my jacket over my large messenger bag that was crossed over my shoulder and packed with accoutrements. After I got to the ground floor, I slipped my key into the lock next to my penthouse button within the elevator to ensure no one would be able to enter while I was gone. I trusted our doorman to not allow anyone up, but I wouldn't want to risk it. The only other being with a key was the landlord.

The address Talos sent me wasn't far; I didn't have to get on the train to travel the eight or so blocks north to the line of brick bungalow homes that were all edged with summersweet shrubs. The bright white flowers danced in the slight breeze, cast against the dark green leaves. The flowers looked as if they were glowing in the shade of the trees along the other side of the sidewalk. The whole picturesque street could have been hung as a piece of art in a museum.

I found the door and knocked, but was left waiting for several moments with no answer. I checked the address again before ringing the bell. Suddenly, the door flew open, but no one was there to greet me. Instead I heard a call from somewhere inside the house, "We are in the lounge, please join us."

It was Talos' voice, at least from what I could recall. He had hardly talked above a whisper upon our first meeting. My gut was telling me that this was a terrible idea, but I entered anyway, the door shutting behind me on its own accord. I walked deeper into the house and down a hallway lined with large photographs and paintings from the wainscoting to the ceiling. Almost every inch of the walls on either side were covered with items that looked as if they belonged to a family who had owned this house for hundreds of years. They very well could have, this area of Cinder was one of the first residential areas and often these homes were passed down from generation to generation.

I came to a break in the wall that opened up to what I assumed was the lounge because there sat Talos with a young woman on a large, white velvet wingback couch. The low table in front of them had a whole tea service waiting for a company of four. Talos and his companion had half-filled tea cups and small plates nearby with triangle sandwiches that looked untouched. When I stepped into the room, Talos stood and walked around the table to greet me with a dip of his chin.

"I hope you weren't waiting on me?" I said, glancing down at the table.

"Of course we waited, it is the polite thing to do. Please have a seat, Isa." He gave a casual wave towards a large wingback chair that matched the sofa he returned to before offering me a cup of tea. I took my bag off my shoulder and sat it next to my chair. He turned slightly to the young woman at his side and put his hand on her knee. She looked up from her cup and with her ash, smoke-filled eyes, glanced at the two of us before finding her cup more interesting.

"Isa, I'd like to introduce you to Lady Althea of Cinder." He turned to me now, and his dark, smoky eyes found mine quickly and held for a moment. I wasn't sure if he was waiting for me to speak or bow.

I didn't do either. Aside from being blindsided with this awkward tea party, I had no idea what this young woman was Lady of. Mortals and Fata didn't have royalty ruling over our city. I lifted the delicate white and floral painted cup to my lips and took a small sip of the strong tea. I didn't drink tea often, but it was better than sitting in silence.

"My Lady, Isa is the young woman I was telling you about. She is very cunning and I suspect the two of you will get along quite well." He removed his hand from her knee and picked up his own cup to drink from.

The way he spoke to Althea about me sounded as if he were a very old man, but he didn't look a day over thirty-five. Sunlight streamed through the window beside us, brightening the room and allowing me to see him in full view. His handsome, warm bronze skin almost glistened in the golden rays, and his high cheekbones caused a light shadow at his cheeks. Heavy, dark brows caused his already dark eyes to seem more gloomy, like a stormy night. His dark hair was brushed up away from his face, but I would bet it was wavy when wet. He seemed to really like being dark and mysterious because it reflected in his choice of clothing. His suit looked almost identical to the one he had been wearing last night, but the shirt underneath was midnight blue with black embroidered detailing.

I knew I had been staring at him for too long when he looked back up at me from his cup and raised one of his brows. Blinking, I looked into my cup and took another small sip then returned it to the small saucer on the low table between us. He looked back at Althea and stood before saying, "My Lady, I think it is time for your next lesson with the Countess. She is waiting for you upstairs."

Althea's cup lifted from her hand into the air, and she watched as the fine teacup shook and trembled in the descent to its paired saucer. She gave a disappointed sigh as she stood and elegantly glided out of the room before I had thought to stand up to bid her goodbye. I watched after her as she left and was even more confused as to why I was there. Talos sat once more and crossed an ankle over his knee, reclining back on the sofa. I watched him for a moment, waiting for him to begin explaining the assignment he had called this meeting for.

"Isa. That truly is a lovely name," he finally spoke, but I almost wish he hadn't.

I said nothing.

"Please excuse Lady Althea, she is under a lot of stress for such a young woman, and I'm afraid she has forgotten her manners this afternoon."

"Why am I here?" I couldn't take this anymore, and it didn't sound like he was going to get to the point without some direction.

"Ah yes, that would be helpful. But before we talk about this job," he pulled an envelope from the inside pocket of his jacket and turned it over in his hands, "your deposit."

He straightened his arm out towards me, holding out the envelope with a gold wax seal in his palm for me to take. I reached over to grab it as he lightly brushed his long fingers along the underside of my wrist, and I slid the envelope off his hand. It felt purposeful, but he gave no indication of it being intentional. I broke the wax and opened the flap of the envelope to see a large sum of cash. I put it in the outer pocket of my bag, turning my attention back to him.

"Lady Althea is to be married next month and, to put it simply, I would like for you to keep her alive long enough to cut the cake," He said as he ran his thumb over the fabric of the sofa's velveteen arm.

I narrowed my eyes and couldn't help but cock my head at this casual statement. "Who has been hired to dispatch her before her blessed union? And why would you ask me to do what I'm assuming is usually your job?"

His eyes fell to his lap and one corner of his mouth lifted as he gave a sly smirk, flashing a glimpse of his too perfect white teeth. "My job is very complicated at the moment," he paused and lifted his gaze back to me slowly, "I would be indebted to you if you'd take this assignment." The deep tone in his voice sent my stomach tumbling.

"It isn't often that someone with my skill set is called upon to protect. I'm much more proficient at the complete opposite. I'm sure you know of many bodyguards who would be willing to babysit your Lady."

He lifted his brow again, surveying me. "You're not wrong. For this amount of money, anyone in the country would leap at the chance to watch over Lady Althea, but the threat on her life is more than most would be able to handle. If I am to do my job and deliver her alive to her betrothed, then I need an expert in more than just protection. I've heard many things about you and the Black Banners; word does travel fast in all circles in Cinder. And a young, beautiful woman who is as skilled as you are would be a great asset to my mission. I also think that aside from the wealth this assignment will give you, it will be a break from usual life and possibly cool some tension that I have heard is mounting at your heels."

I wasn't sure where he was getting that information from. The only beings who even knew I existed were my fellow

Banners, some past clients, and my landlord. It was very rare that assignments found their way to me organically, it was typically through the Black Banner network. You had to know somebody, who knew somebody, to get to a Banner.

"Why would your kind need me or my skills?"

"My kind? I'm starting to get the feeling that you don't much care for Incubo? Which would be a shame, I know a few that would find you quite appealing." His tone was playful but becoming increasingly venomous.

"I've heard plenty of rumors to know that Incubo have trust issues when it comes to their private affairs."

"What an interesting choice of words." He parted his lips for a fuller smile this time, reminding me of a jungle cat who was absolutely amused by his prey before pouncing.

"Am I saying anything that isn't true?" I crossed my arms at my chest, resting one of my hands on a blade I had hidden in the waist of my pants.

"I suppose you aren't. It is rare to meet someone so bold. I imagine you've had your fair share of private affairs? Maybe mine aren't that interesting to you?"

Ignoring his comment I moved on to more pressing questions. "How long does she need to stay breathing? And how many hits are active on her?"

Talos stood up and walked to the window and clasped his hands behind his back laxly. He looked out towards what I imagined to be a patio area by the opaque reflection of bright pinks and deep purples on the glass.

"She has one month before the union. As far as I know, which is usually more than others think, there are two beings hired to murder her. She is set to leave this home at the end of the week, hopefully with you by her side, and set off for Arta for the next three weeks to prepare for the wedding."

"And how does Lady Althea feel about this arrangement? She

didn't seem too keen on the idea moments ago." I glanced at the doorway she'd left through.

"Do you normally care what your commitments are feeling when you take an assignment?"

"Well, normally I'm not so involved with the concern of my targets breathing that long." I gave a sarcastic shrug, still feeling the cool handle of my blade at my fingertips.

He was quiet for a moment until turning to face me. He strode to where I sat, bending down low while placing a hand on either arm of the chair so we were at eye level to one another. The fresh and earthy smell of his cologne washed over me and it became hard to focus. His eyes weren't just the color of a smoky sky, it was as if I could see them shift colors and change shape as he searched my face. The slightly darker outline of his pupil moved back and forth over my brows, down towards my chin, and settled on my lips for a moment before meeting my stare again.

We had been swept up in this discussion for so long, and now that he was in such close proximity, I wasn't sure how much longer I wanted this conversation to go on.

"She is well behaved and would rather not lose her life." His statement was put rather simply, but the feel of his breath over my mouth displayed how close to me he truly was.

His mouth parted slightly, his hooded eyes falling towards my mouth, and my heart started to pound as if trying to hop out of my chest and into his hands. Before I could stop myself, I tilted my head and moved in closer, allowing his lips to softly press against mine before I closed my eyes and took in the full breadth of the moment.

He pressed in slightly harder and one of his hands found its way from the chair to the top of my shoulder and into my hair. I unfolded my knife-free hand and placed it on the nape of his neck. He swept his tongue over my bottom lip seeking permission, and I gave it. A rush of fluttering in my lower stomach caused me to release a small whimper, and in one swift motion he had pulled me up to my feet and encircled me with his other arm. Releasing my knife and inhibitions, I wrapped my arms around his neck.

A low sigh grew into a groan in his chest as he pulled me over to the sofa and sat down. He pulled my legs over his hips to straddle him, hands wrapped around my thighs before gliding up my backside, then higher. Catching my blouse with his fingers, he pulled it free of my waistband, and slid his hands underneath. He gave my waist a slight squeeze and a pulsating began between my legs. His palms brushing over my lace concealed breasts, and I leaned into him in encouragement.

He pulled away from the kiss as his hands slid from under my blouse to make quick work of the small buttons on the front. Once it was opened to him, he pulled me closer, his lips damp on my clavicle, then moved over my chest and down between my breasts. My hips felt the pressure of his fingertips digging into them as he began making small circular motions, pulling me closer into his lap. The erect length of him was hard against the layers of fabric holding us back. Pressure within me mounted as he reached up and pulled on one cup of my bra revealing my taut, bare breast. The tip puckered, he flicked his gaze up to me to give me a wolfish grin before he took me into his mouth, swirling his tongue and sucking gently. I pulled him in closer and held him still against me.

Every nerve in my body began to tingle as the tension started to peak and finally gave way to climax. I cursed as I threw my head back and felt, more than heard, his ragged moan against my skin and his hand at my hip, squeezing. I shuddered and looked back down into his face as he looked up at me with his chin still nestled between my breasts. Both of us were flushed and breathing heavily. He adjusted the cup of my bra for me and laid his forehead against my chest, taking in a long breath and then sighing.

My sensibility returned to me, shame blooming on my cheeks as I pushed against him to bring myself away from him to stand. I turned away to button my shirt as I questioned my sanity.

"I'm not sure what came over me," he said, still sounding very relaxed and not getting up from where he lounged back on the sofa.

"I should go. I'll be ready to leave when she is." I didn't look at him as I grabbed my bag and headed for the door.

# CHAPTER FOUR

I didn't allow myself to reflect on what had happened until I got back home. As I stood in my living room in shock, I dropped my bag and coat to my feet and turned my face up towards the ceiling, my eyes closed. Slow breaths in through my nose and out through my mouth. My lips slightly swollen and stinging from the gruffness of his facial stubble. I wet my lips with my tongue, the taste of him already fading away, letting go a deep sigh and rotating my head and neck from side to side before going to the kitchen for a glass of whiskey.

I took a large gulp from the glass and held it in my cheeks for a moment trying to erase every last molecule of him from my every nook. The burning sensation traveled through my throat and warmed my belly; calm swept over me, the heat from the liquor burning away the shame. Casual encounters weren't unusual, but I didn't get close to anyone long enough to develop a relationship. This, however, was so spontaneous and inappropriate. I'd never crossed this line with a client in the past. How did we even get to the boiling point?

I felt like I had missed a silent conversation our bodies had without us knowing. There were so many questions buzzing through me, but the only answer I had was another swig from my whiskey glass. I drained the remainder and grabbed my secure line, the phone Banners used to communicate with each other, knowing exactly who I needed to talk to. The other line rang as I filled my glass again, this time adding a few cubes of ice from the freezer.

"We do not shy away from the dark." Zaida's voice came through the phone, and I felt the calm after a hurricane.

"For we are the shadows," I answered.

"Hello stranger, how was your assignment?" Her mood lifted now that our family code had been met.

"Hey. Can you come over?" Taking in a sip. "I've had the weirdest day and I need a drinking partner."

"I'll bring provisions." And she hung up.

Zaida and I were brought into the Black Banners within a few months of each other. She had been there first and took me under her wing. She was a couple years older than me and as much of a big sister as I'd ever had, but our loyalty ran deeper than typical sisters. We were chosen for the Banners, but we chose each other as family. It's how we built our network and how we kept so secretive in the position we took up among the shadows of society. Not all of us were full-time killers for hire, some became government-only operatives or trainers for future Banners. We only took care of our own while on assignments which had often given us the reputation of being ruthless and cold to outsiders. But it gave us security. I always knew I could call a Banner if I were to find myself in a compromising position, or for a day of drinking after a rough assignment.

It only took Zaida a half hour. The doorman buzzed and sent her up in the elevator. She had two large, flat pizza boxes in one hand and a tote that clinked as she walked straight to the kitchen. I sat on the couch right off the kitchen with my third glass of whiskey waiting for her to get situated.

Her beautiful, tight black curls bounced slightly as she

unloaded the boxes onto the counter. She had always been the prettiest of our house with deep umber skin and a toned physique. If she hadn't been a Banner, I had always imagined she'd be an actress or model. Tonight she was wearing a white sundress that hugged her slim middle and showed her trained arms and legs. Often, when we met out for a drink, men would fawn over her, but she rarely gave them the time of day. Like me, and most other Banners, she didn't get deeply involved with Mortals or Fata. Some, like Mr. Blue and Ms. Green, found a partner within our ranks to grow an attachment with, but Zaida cared little for long-term companionship.

"You need more junk food in your cabinets for days like this!" she said into a bare cupboard, not seeing anything she liked then moving on to another door.

"As if we are ever home long enough for snack binges." I laughed into my glass and took another sip. "Check the freezer. I usually have an emergency stash of ice cream in there."

She opened it up and took the large tub of Rocky Road ice cream out to set on the counter to soften, then grabbed a couple plates and started piling them with slices of pizza and a few breadsticks. She brought me a plate and set hers down on the coffee table in front of the couch before going back to the kitchen and rattling her liquor bottle filled tote. She didn't bother pouring a drink in the kitchen, instead she grabbed my half-gone bottle of whiskey, a glass for herself, and a bottle of something clear.

Plopping down on the other end of the couch, she cracked open the top of her bottle and filled her glass before setting her bottle down without the lid and held up my whiskey to me, a silent offering to fill me up which I accepted. She leaned back, kicked her shoes off, then tucked her feet into the couch before grabbing up her glass and plate of food, turning slightly towards me.

She smiled. "Ok, go!"

I couldn't help but laugh, she truly was my favorite person. The appreciation I had for her in that moment was only amplified by the whiskey that had already gone to my head. I told her everything to the last detail of how Talos smelled and tasted. She took bites of her food and filled her own glass once after draining it while I talked for what seemed like too long, considering I'd only been around this Incubo for several minutes between two days.

When I was done, she gave a big sigh and swallowed the bite she had been chewing. "Wow. That is... Wow." She shook her head and took a drink.

"I don't know what got into me." I laid my head on the back cushion and took a deep breath.

"Well, to be fair, you didn't let him get into you." She winked and smirked.

"So funny. But with the way it's escalated, that might be what happens if I accidentally bump into him on the sidewalk." I turned my face towards her and we both giggled.

"Wouldn't that be a scandal! But the assignment sounds lucrative and almost too simple to employ a Banner. Why would this Incubo not protect her himself?" Her question was valid and one I had thought of as well, but still had no answer to so I shrugged in response.

She threw her head back, downing the remnants of her glass and refilling it before the next question. "This is an arranged marriage, right? And why now? I've not heard of any Incubo deaths. Don't they usually marry to breed when one of them passes?"

"That's what I thought, too, so I'm not sure if it's arranged, but there is so little known about their kind that isn't second-hand information. They could be trying to expand their numbers, or hiding a passing for whatever reason unbeknownst to the rest of us." This was my suspicion. Along with rarely having or keeping Mortal companions alive, Incubo rarely divulged information willingly.

"How did it feel being entangled with him? I've heard rumors that you can feel their energy when they're *provoked*." She hushed her last few words as if someone would hear us through the walls.

Talos hadn't felt any different than any other man I'd had an encounter with. Everything about his anatomy seemed slightly above average, but nothing more than that. The thought of the tightness in his pants against mine sent a shiver through me and I curled my legs up to my chest, wrapping my arms around them and laying my head on my knees.

"Maybe? I don't think so, but I was a little provoked at the time as well." I started to stand up, "I'll be right back, bathroom."

I heard her glass clink against the bottle as she refilled her glass. "Hurry back! I have at least twenty more questions."

In the bathroom, I turned towards the mirror and looked at myself closely. I looked tired, as if it weren't early evening. I went to unbutton my pants and felt the skin at my hips give a quick, sharp jab. I pulled my blouse up and my pants down to see almost perfectly round, fingertip-shaped bruises where he had held me, pulled me, rocked himself against me until I'd crashed in on myself. There was a tug at my naval as I smoothed my fingers over the spots. I finished up, pulled my pants up, but didn't tuck my shirt in.

When I came back into the living room, I held the side of my blouse up and stood in front of Zaida. She looked up at me, then her eyes found the bruises. "Now that's a bit arousing."

It was, and I blushed. "Am I going into dangerous territory taking this assignment? Not only will I be surrounded by their kind, but one of them seems to have an attraction to me."

"Isa. We do not shy away from darkness, for we are the shadows. We do not have fear, for we are the terror. We know no danger, for we are vicious," she recited; we'd heard the phrase daily growing up.

"We are the Black Banners," I finished for her.

I'd been stupid to let whatever mental ensnarement I felt towards Talos blur my judgement, but now, clarity washed over me. My assignment was to protect Lady Althea and get her to her wedding night without any issues, and that was what I would do. Afterwards, I'd swear off working for Incubo.

Zaida and I drank and laughed well into the night before we fell into a drunken sleep in my bed while watching old movies. Over the next week, I prepared for both my assignment and the time away.

# CHAPTER FIVE

By the end of the week I had gotten a message from Talos on when and where to meet. We'd be traveling by train to Arta in private quarters. I would meet Lady Althea at the station platform. I packed three bags: one for clothing and shoes, the second for comfort items, and the third for weapons. My weapons suitcase was specially designed to fool even the most high-tech metal detectors and security personnel. The false sides needed an extra key that I had on my key ring, but otherwise it looked like an overly sturdy case. I packed a camera, electronics, and power cords inside to further disguise the contents hidden within its walls.

I hadn't been given the address to the residence I would be escorting Lady Althea to yet, but I expected a full briefing before we departed. As I did before each away assignment, I tidied up the apartment and did a sweep to be sure everything was secure and inconspicuous. My landlord would be checking in for me every few days and watering the small forest on my terrace if it didn't rain enough. I took a final look around my sanctuary and sighed before summoning the elevator. Leaving so soon after an assignment wasn't abnormal, but the idea of a new type of mission felt exhausting already.

Deciding on wearing clothing that would be comfortable to travel in or that I could move quickly and easily in was a hard choice, but in the end I chose dark jeans, sensible shoes, a black blouse, and leather jacket. I brought a carry-on bag in which I'd put some knives in the concealed pockets after going through security along with some travel essentials. My three suitcases were checked after having no issue with security. After doing a full search of the station platforms surrounding ours, I waited for Talos to arrive and submit Althea to my care.

I took a black leather belt from my travel bag's hidden pocket; the middle of the belt held a four inch sheathed blade. I quickly looped it around my hips and clasped it in the front so that the weapon was sitting at my lower back, hidden by my jacket. The other three knives in my bag would be easy enough to get to, but having one attached to my body would give me better reaction time.

Arta was about 200 miles northeast. It had a cooler climate than Cinder and was surrounded by large lakes that often dropped in temperature. Unlike Cinder, Arta exported most of their goods to outside cities and most of the laborers were Fata working at the many mills and factories. The lands around were perfect for farming. Arta had engineered trees that grew up to fifty feet tall in a matter of months. Not many Mortals lived near or in Arta due to the high probability that they'd mysteriously disappear in the forests. At least, that was what the rumors were.

When I saw Talos and Althea approaching, I gave Talos a nod before giving the area one more check. Still clear. I waited for them both to get several feet away from me before stepping onto the train. I surveyed through every cabin, a blade tucked into the hem of my jacket sleeve as we passed. Althea was several steps behind me, Talos behind her. We got to our private quarters which were as large as three passenger cabins. The open space at the entrance had a coat closet to the left of the door, which I opened and checked for anything suspicious. I hung up my bag before looking through the other storage areas, the bathroom to the far right, and another door leading to a small room with a twin sized bed and hardly any walking space. All were clear, and I returned the blade to its sheath on my belt.

Althea walked straight to the bolted down couch against the windows that sat outside the bathroom door. Talos headed for the small bar area that was directly facing the entrance door. He pulled out several small bottles of dark liquor and two glasses. I locked the door and drew the drape of the small window in the middle of the door. I turned back to the cabin and waited, but neither Talos nor Althea said anything and I knew the train would be departing soon.

"I'll need the information packet before you go."

Talos didn't turn around, but I heard the bottles opening and liquid being poured. "I will be giving you the briefing myself, please take a seat."

I stood staring at the back of his head for a moment, then looked to Althea with her nose buried in a book already. She didn't bother to look up or acknowledge me as I sat to her left, facing the door on the L shaped couch. Talos came and sat next to her before he reached over to hand me a glass. I looked down into it but didn't take a drink. I needed to be fully aware in case anyone decided to take this opportunity to get the jump on us. I had run through any possible scenario if I were hired to kill a young woman on a train. There were at least five ways to do it, and I wasn't going to let the first day of the assignment be the last.

"No need to be so uptight today, Isa. I have men stationed in several places on this train, including the cabin across the hall, in the dining car, and in the boiler room. Your position today is

41

to observe and keep me entertained." He gave me a very wicked smile before taking a drink from his glass.

I furrowed my brow and looked him up and down. He was dressed in a pair of his usual black slacks and dress shirt, but like the first night I'd met him, he had taken off his jacket and had rolled the sleeves of his deep blue dress shirt up, revealing his strong arms and the intricate tattoo. His ankle crossed at his knee, seeming completely relaxed as if the woman he'd hired me to protect wasn't in as much danger as he had led me to believe. His dark, smokey eyes watched me, waiting for a response.

"I could have traveled alone if you had already decided on planting Incubo through the train. It may have been less conspicuous than the three of us boarding together." I leaned back and crossed my legs above the knee, letting my arms relax across my stomach.

"But then who would keep me company on such a long journey? I imagine My Lady will fall asleep any moment; she is utterly exhausted from anticipation." He glanced at her, but she didn't bother looking up from her book. "Do you perhaps play cards?"

"No, and I'd rather not be distracted." I stood up to take my glass to the bar counter, but he caught my hand.

"Have this one drink with me, and I will leave you to be the meticulous protector." His voice was smooth and deep, his fingers letting go of my hand slowly.

"It's a little early in the day for a drink, don't you think?" I said, looking down at him as he grinned into his glass as he took another sip.

"Perhaps, but what harm could it do?" He waved his hand towards the spot where I had just been sitting.

I had the feeling he would pester me if I protested anymore, so I sat and took a small drink. He watched me as I did and my senses perked a bit at the fleeting idea that he might try to drug or poison me.

"Is there a reason you are so adamant about me taking this drink with you?" I didn't expect him to tell me if he had poisoned me, but he seemed to catch my tone of suspicion.

"I hate to drink alone. And I rarely get to share a drink with someone so captivating." Something about his choice of words brought back the sensation of his mouth on mine and his fingers digging into my hips.

"I'm not sure how you've determined that I am so interesting when we've hardly spoken." I took another sip from my glass.

"Our few conversations have ended so abruptly but have been riveting nonetheless."

I glanced at Althea, but had the suspicion that she would neither hear nor speak to me. As if she were in this cabin alone and not with the two of us exchanging banter. I looked back to Talos and couldn't quite read his expression, but could practically feel his gaze on my skin. In an attempt to break the tension, I looked down into my glass and cleared my throat.

"I'm not sure what came over me during our last meeting, but I assure you, it won't happen again." The knot in my stomach wasn't so sure I was telling the truth.

"That's dissatisfying. I've enjoyed our meetings greatly." He drained his glass and stood to grab another small bottle from the fridge.

The train started to rumble as it began its departure. I heard footsteps in the hallway shuffle past as beings started to finalize their stay on the train. Althea's Incubo, smoke-filled eyes glanced up for the first time and looked out the window. We were slowly pulling away from the platform and she let loose a deep sigh before looking back to her book with the ghost of a smile.

"Is there anything I can get for you, Lady Althea? Do you need anything from the dining car?" She only shook her head in reply to my questions and I looked to Talos who was now settling back down on the couch beside her.

"Lady Althea is capable of tending to her own needs, Isa. But it is very kind of you to offer. Once you finish that drink, we can begin the brief." He lifted his chin up towards me encouragingly and I finished off my glass.

"Obedient. I like that," he said and my stomach dropped.

I swallowed hard and didn't look at him, instead got up and returned my glass to the bar. I turned towards him and leaned against the wall, crossing my arms across my torso. I needed distance or else I might very well end up embarrassed for a third time meeting with him. He watched me for a moment and must have decided not to comment on my new location.

"Lady Althea and her fiancé, Lord Cornelius Welp, will be staying at his family's summer estate until the wedding date. It is a very private property but is rather large. You'll be staying in her suite with her day and night until she's delivered to him at the wedding ceremony. I will also be within the grounds, as will the men I've brought with us. Lord Welp has also supplied me with security members to instruct, but I have not fully vetted them so I will be dismissing them and suggesting all unnecessary staff be removed as well. Your only duty is to Lady Althea's safety and you are to answer only to me. Here is the layout map of the estate, your contract, and a confidentiality notice. I do not need to stress to you how sensitive this assignment is to my kind and, in effect, to yours." He reached into the bag he had carried on with him and pulled out a thick black envelope embossed with silver lettering on the front.

He held it out for me to retrieve, but I didn't move from my place near the bar. I looked at the envelope, then back to his puzzled expression.

"We do not have Lords and Ladies in this country. Who exactly are they lording over on this estate?" I narrowed my eyes and held his stare.

"They are the Lord and Lady of the Incubo," he simply stated as if that were all the answer I needed.

"Since when do Incubo have royalty?"

His face became stoic. "We have always had important families, surely you know that. We do not typically advertise how our world works, but I assure you that this threat on her life is real."

"Who among you would set a bounty on her head? If this is such an important union, why is it being opposed?"

A look of surprise and bewilderment crossed his face. He thought for a few moments before responding in a low tone.

"That information is worth much more than what I am paying you to complete this task." He sounded almost angry that I would question him.

"I will have no problem keeping my word," I assured.

Secrecy wasn't just part of my employment, it was how I was raised within the Black Banner. We rarely spoke of assignments after they were carried out aside from the money we'd earned and our new body count.

"I have no doubt, I know this confidentiality agreement isn't required, but I can not leave any loose ends. I'm sure you understand." He raised his arm a bit higher, and I pushed off the wall to grab the paperwork.

I opened the folded flap and took out the papers, holding them on top of the now empty envelope, and started to flip through the pages until I found the map. The estate was massive, at least the size of four city blocks. The mansion was larger than the entire building I resided in. The grounds surrounding it had stables, several servants quarters, thick wildwoods behind the main structure, and a large river separating the property from the neighboring estate. There was more land on the borders all the way around, but I only saw names of their inhabitants, assuming that their manors were as large.

After a few moments Talos apparently thought that I had been examining the map long enough and spoke to move me along.

"I have a pen for your signature on those other documents. You may keep the map, but I'll take the rest with me." He held out a rather fancy looking pen towards me.

I took it, found the documents that needed my signature, and laid them down on the bar counter and leaned down with my elbows resting on the smooth wood countertop. I skimmed through the confidentiality agreement and it was standard *I will not speak of my assignment to anyone. After the task is completed I will be expected to forget all that I had seen and if I didn't, I would be sued and possibly jailed within the Incubo Courts.* I signed. I knew I wouldn't have any reason not to. I then went through my payment contract and noticed something off.

"This is more than we discussed." I looked to him, my brow ruffled.

"Is that a problem?" His tone wasn't playful now, I'd struck a nerve before and he hadn't recovered yet.

"I'm curious why you think my services are worth almost twice as much as we discussed at our last meeting."

He stood and strolled towards me, setting his glass down near mine and looking down to me. His scent hit me, and I noted a slight hint of mandarin. I stood up straight and lifted my chin to search his eyes but was met with his expression hard and unwavering.

"I knew that you would be an immeasurable asset to me, so I decided to show my gratitude with what we will call a bonus." His eyes dropped to my mouth.

"An asset to *you*? I thought I was hired to protect Lady Althea?" I glanced over to the couch, but realized that she had gotten up from her spot.

I looked around the room, but didn't see Althea anywhere. The door that separated this sitting room and the bedroom was now closed, but I hadn't heard or seen her move or the door shut.

"The Lady was tired, she went to lie down." He inched closer as our eyes met again.

I backed up but hit the wall. His right hand cupped my waist and lightly suggested I move closer, his fingers less than an inch from where my blade was sheathed. I leaned closer, but didn't move my heels from the wall and instinctually raised my right hand to the blade's hilt, my finger ready to undo the clasp holding it in place.

"I should check on her." I tried to move away, but he pinned me to the wall with both hands at my hips, my arm now wedged between my back and the cool, hard surface.

I grabbed his wrist with my free hand, but he only pressed his body against me. I couldn't help but wonder how many encounters with Talos would lead to his body against mine in similar dangerous positions. A flutter of excitement awoke behind my navel, heat starting to fill me from my thighs up to my chest. His eyes lifted and looked darker, a deeper grey than before. His pupils were piercing me, searching deep within mine. Was I even breathing?

One of his hands traveled up my side, grazing over the breast of my jacket, his palm under my ear and his fingers untucking my dark hair from behind my ear. It cascaded over my cheek and brushed against the edge of my jaw. In that moment, I wished I had worn it up. He ran his thumb over my cheek under the curtain of hair and, I parted my lips to take a short forceful breath.

"Your dedication to your assignment is endearing, but she is safe. I, on the other hand, seem to have found myself mere moments from the tip of your blade."

"That seems to be the choice you make often," I breathed, but hardly recognized the spent sound of my own voice.

"It does seem to be hard for me to stay away from you, Isa."

His voice was silk, and the sound of my name slipping over his tongue and teeth sent a chill up my neck. His lips gently brushed across mine as he tilted my head so he could have access to my ear, and his lips spoke against my lobe.

"I can't help envisioning your body draped over that sofa wearing nothing but that belt."

If he hadn't pinned me against the wall, I may have slipped to the floor. A sharp intake of air was all I was able to do before his mouth found mine. He kissed me deeply, pulling me closer at both my hip and neck. The tense heat flooded my stomach, my arm finally free from behind my back and my fingers finding his soft hair. He wrapped an arm around my waist and lifted me into his chest. Before I could comprehend where we were in the room, I was being laid back onto the couch, his chest hovering above mine. My hands found a mind of their own and began to unbutton his shirt, then moved to his belted slacks to pull the shirt loose from where it had been tucked into the waistband of his slacks.

I went for his belt buckle next and made quick work of the button and zipper. He sat up to his knees to take the shirt off completely, and I looked up at his torso and chest. He was fit and lean, but his broad shoulders gave him a strong build. He watched me as I took in the sight of him and the rather impressive bulge pressed against his undershorts peeking through the gap of his open pants. His mouth swept back down onto mine, and placed his arms on either side of my head on the narrow cushion. My legs wrapped around his waist and he drove his hips into mine, driving me further down into the sofa and causing friction between my thighs. He reached down to the waistband of my jeans and searched for the clasp, but became impatient and popped the button clean off.

I gasped and he sat up again, bringing me sitting up with him and pushing my jacket off my shoulders. I threw it to the ground and went for the belt at my waist, but he stopped my hand and lifted my blouse over my head exposing my lace bra. I kicked my shoes off then wiggled out of my pants and underwear. He stood briefly, his slacks falling to his ankles, and looped his thumbs into the top of his undershorts. My eyes fell to his waist, waiting for him to push them down, but he paused. I looked up to his hungry expression and he raised a brow. His chin made a subtle dip to tell me he was waiting for me to take off my remaining clothing. I reached behind my back and unclasped my bra, tossing it to the side, then lay back with my arms across my chest, hands cupped over my breasts.

He pulled his undershorts down, letting himself loose. He was fully excited and my mouth fell open, suddenly becoming as wet as the area between my thighs. He looked down at me and sank to his knees, kneeling before the couch, scooping his arms under my rear, grabbing onto my hips, and pulling me down towards him. The cool leather strap around my waist scooted up onto my stomach, the blade moving to my side. He lowered his head between my thighs and, as if commanded, I opened them wider to him. Lips glided down the inner sensitive skin before his mouth opened and his tongue flicked over my throbbing bundle of nerves. Once. Twice. He looked up. I lifted my head to meet his eyes and he slowly lowered his chin, but didn't break eye contact as he flattened his tongue against me, making slow sweeps up before gently sucking, causing me to inhale small breaths at each stroke, but only hushed moans escaped me.

His fingers dug into my hips feeling achingly eager. My head fell back and my eyes closed, opening the rest of my senses to him. I could feel every nerve in my body vying for his attention, my breasts peaking against my palms. He began consuming me, and as my hips rocked against his mouth, he let loose a deep, pleasurable groan that sent a quake through me, provoking me to crash to pieces moments later. I cursed as I filled and then released, my legs tensing as the wave of it washed over me. I watched him as his tongue lapped over me one last time.

He pulled away to settle his hips between my legs, and I

flinched as his arms moved the both of us up to the other end of the seat. The fabric of the cushion rough down my back as the leather belt made its way back down to my hips. His knees now planted on the couch, his hips readied. He pushed himself against my wet entrance, begging me for entry, but waiting. He gazed down over my body, mouth still damp from my release. Breathing heavily, his eyes darker than I'd ever seen them, almost completely black—his pupils hardly visible. The room around us faded from my vision, the air thick. I knew he was waiting for permission, and a small voice in my mind screamed for me to allow him. I released my breasts, my hands moving to his shoulders. I nodded to him frantically, begging for him as he lowered to his forearms, and in one deep thrust, he entered and sent a gasp from deep inside of me.

My reaction seemed to encourage him as he drove himself deeper than I thought I could handle, but each and every inch of him found space within me. His deep rumbling voice in the crook of my neck with each movement, hot breath against me. I could feel another wave of pressure building and it overtook me. Shattering me again, I moaned in his ear as he started to shudder and thrust faster, harder. I didn't know where one wave ended and another began as he gave several more deep motions, the last deeper than before. He held me there and I could feel every bit of his body pulsate, from deep inside of me to the muscles in his arms under my shoulders.

We both lay there trying to catch our breath. A shiver ran up my body as the aftershocks from between my legs sent tiny jolts to the tips of my fingers and the ends of my toes. He stood a few moments later and turned away from me, lifting his arms over his head to stretch. He lowered them and shook his head and shoulders, his now sweat-damp hair moving in clumps. I sat up and dragged my clothing up into my arms and set the bundle down next to me on the couch. I ran my fingers through my hair and took a deep breath with a little hope that the foggy bliss would dissipate before he turned back around.

I didn't bother putting my bra back on, but slipped my blouse back on over my head. I unbuckled my blade belt to adjust the sheath and put my underwear back on. I headed to the bathroom to clean myself up without saying a word. He was slipping his undershorts back up when I got a full view of his firm backside and the strength of his thighs. They had been hidden beneath his black slacks. I ducked inside the small restroom but caught the profile of his face before closing the door—his expression was utterly satisfied.

# CHAPTER SIX

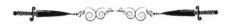

I looked at myself in the small round mirror over the sink. The gold frame matched the accents to the room outside the door where Talos was probably dressed and waiting. My hair was mussed, my eye makeup smudged, my cheeks pink and warm. I turned the hot tap on and cupped my hands under the water, waiting for it to warm, watching it fill and overflow into the sink. I leaned down low and lifted a handful over my face, then another. I grabbed a folded towel on the small shelf over the toilet and held it against my face and took a deep breath.

Exhaling, I took another look at my reflection and wiped the leftover eye makeup away. Green eyes were such a contrast to Talos and Althea's shadowy, smoke-filled ones. Then remembering how his eyes had changed so drastically—there was a drop of my stomach. A shallow well in my gut, maybe hunger or the liquor on an empty stomach.

I finished cleaning myself up. The button of my jeans was long gone so I used the leather sheath belt to hold my pants together. I gave myself a last once over before opening the door and saw that Talos was dressed and casually sitting where we'd shared each other. A strange digging pang of awkwardness hit me as if there should be some sort of indication that we had just been using the sofa for more than sitting and reading the newspaper. I glanced at the bedroom door and wondered if Althea had heard us, heard me. My cheeks flushed and I decided against checking in on her. I moved farther into the sitting area, noticing that he had closed the drapes to the outer windows.

Talos didn't look up from the paper he looked so invested in. Did I imagine what had happened?

I felt a tug at my navel and my stomach tumbled. I needed air and to be away from what was sure to be an awkward conversation or silence. I grabbed my bag and headed for the cabin door, but before I reached the handle I heard his voice low behind me.

"The dining car is closed until dinner, and I have already arranged for meals to be delivered to the cabin."

I didn't look back to him, but paused with my arm outstretched. Looking at the cabin door, trying to make up any excuse to leave, I came up with nothing. We had no indication that anyone who wanted to harm Althea was on the train, his men hadn't even checked in yet. We had only been moving for a half hour, which left us alone with hours left to the trip.

"I should probably do a sweep, check the other cars for anything off."

"I'd rather you stay." I heard a page turn.

I looked to him, but he didn't break his attention away from his paper. I sighed and walked over to the bar. I opened a small bottle of whiskey and drained it in a large gulp. It filled my belly, warm and soothing. I grabbed another and that caught his attention. He folded the paper over and set it on the couch beside him then stood to join me at the bar. He also forwent his glass, opening a clear liquor bottle and gulping it down. He took a couple more with him and returned to the couch, coyly patting the spot next to him. I rolled my eyes and took one more small bottle over to his silent invitation. I sat where he had indicated and wondered when I became so subservient to a being I hardly knew. He watched me as I sat, crossed his ankle at his knee, and folded his hands in his lap, a pose I was becoming familiar with.

"Now that we've gotten that out of the way," his smoke eyes scanned me, a satisfied grin tugging at his lips, "I expect you have more questions, and I'm willing to answer as long as you keep it interesting."

My jaw clenched and my brows knitted together. A dumbfounded look must have been plastered on my face. But he continued.

"To answer your earlier questions, there are older Incubo that don't see Althea's union as a prosperous one. They'd prefer her to remain in Cinder and wait for her to find a more suitable husband. But she has made her choice and in our world that is often unacceptable. Her father, even though disappointed, has approved of the marriage and has requested that she be protected until everything is final."

My mouth went dry. It was sad to think she would normally be unable to choose who she wanted to marry and subsequently breed with, but I knew that was a possibility.

"Typically, her father would have chosen her husband when the time had come, but Lady Althea has a fierce heart and rebels against traditions." He sighed and glanced towards her room with a proud grin creeping across his mouth, before turning his attention back to me it disappeared as if never there.

"Why keep royalty secret? Incubo are already powerful enough to rule over Fata and Mortals. It seems odd that this has been kept secret and only recognized among yourselves."

"Not long enough ago, Incubo came to an agreement with Mortals and Fata to live separately. With that agreement, no one was to pass down that information to their offspring. The Incubo hold land and power that our royal status would not change and would only cause this land more harm than it's worth."

That sounded oddly noble for a breed that often *lost* their Mortal playthings. I thought carefully about my next question and wasn't sure I wanted to know the answer or bring it up, but I asked anyway.

"Your eyes. They changed when we... when we were-" My face became hot and my throat was dry and rough.

He dipped his chin towards his chest and fully smiled for the first time. When he looked back to me, his eyes were almost black again and it caught my breath.

"Not many experience what you just did; it's another little secret of my kind." It must only happen with certain emotions. I imagined not all were as pleasant as I had experienced.

His smile turned to a sly grin and his eyes returned to smoke again. His irises were a whispered outline that focused on my mouth. I resisted the urge to bite my lower lip and took a sip from my whiskey. He shifted, angling his torso towards me and laying one arm across the back of the sofa, one of his fingers brushing against the middle of my back, making a soft circular motion. Goosebumps erupted from that spot and traveled down my back, over my shoulders and chest, and down my arms. There was a small demand to move closer to him, but I ignored it.

"Is it true that Incubo have special abilities that Fata don't? And what can kill an Incubo?" I asked and hoped that the fire stoking in my chest was the whiskey. I took another sip to be sure.

"You are very bold to ask such things." He wasn't scolding, but seemed intrigued that I would indeed ask such personal questions.

"I figure after what is now our third indecent encounter, I may not come back from this assignment alive. May as well be curious," I said, surprising myself. The thought hit me only after it tripped off my tongue.

"Now, why would you doubt your own skills? I sought your

services because I was told you were the best." He looked me over, puzzled.

"I have no doubt that I'll be able to keep Althea living until she isn't under my care anymore, but I know the stories of Incubo taking Mortal lovers. Briefly. They don't usually fare much longer afterwards." I finished my drink and waited.

The corner of his mouth slowly rose, his eyes becoming cloudy again. My chest tightened and I became very aware of his finger tracing against my back, feeling every ridge of his fingertips with each small stroke.

His eyes narrowed and he leaned in a little closer to me. He inhaled slowly, then breathed, "You are positively intoxicating. Not one hint of fear on you; it's exhilarating."

"You didn't answer my question." My attempt to hide how unsettling his statement was.

"Are you suggesting that I'm taking you as a lover?" he teased.

"Are you going to answer all my questions with questions?" I pulled away from his hand at my back.

He reclined his head a bit to the side and considered me for a moment, looking as though he were either trying to decide to answer or continue his game.

"I can't deny that since the moment you came into my presence I've wanted to be entangled between your legs." He paused and took in my expression and finished his statement at almost a whisper, "and I was not disappointed."

My stomach jumped, my body feeling hot again.

"When Incubo find such pleasures, we tend to take as much as we possibly can. Unfortunately, that sometimes has dire consequences when the individual is weak," he said with a challenging tone, daring me to prove I could withstand him.

"So, you have used other Mortals as toys and thrown them away after using them up completely?" The fire in my chest now giving rise to anger at his arrogance.

"None of them seemed to complain. It seems to be hard to decline what an Incubo can offer."

"And what is that?" I crossed my arms at my chest, my brows furrowed.

"I'd be honored to show you exactly what I'm capable of when not holding myself back." His eyes dropped to my inner thighs.

If he had been holding back before, I wasn't sure I wanted to know what he was able to do. I'd had many men in my bed for the night and none of them had the earth moving beneath me the way he had. Instinctually, I squeezed my knees together.

"That causes you fear? Interesting." He ran a hand through his hair and fixated on me again, waiting for my reaction.

"You can sense me?" I was admitting it, but I doubted I would be able to lie to him now.

"In a way. I am observant and I suppose the easiest way to explain it is that I can feel your temperature elevate or drop. I can taste a shift in your essence when you're anxious, angry, or aroused. In a way, I can anticipate what your body is screaming to have from me."

I suddenly felt more than naked or exposed, I was stripped away from every last defense I had. I reacted on pure adrenaline, reaching behind my back, grabbing the blade's hilt, and pinning him to the back of the couch with my arm. The blade to his throat and quicker than I could even see, he had me on my back on the ground. He had one of his legs between my knees, his chest hovering over me, holding himself up by one arm, the other on my wrist holding my knife. Blade still pressed against his neck, a small sliver of skin nicked and a thin line of blood began a trail.

His face wasn't shocked, wasn't angry. He smiled wickedly and hardened against me, his breath heavier, but steady. My body full of mixed reactions, heart pounding, the nerves between my thighs started to ache once more.

"Would you like me to decide which emotion you should give into? I'm partial to the one between your legs, but I haven't had a good sparring match in ages." He sounded excited and rogue.

Before I could answer, the door to Althea's room flung open. She stood looking over us, staring down, and spoke for the first time, "Oh, I'm so sorry. I—"

"Lady Althea," Talos spoke sweetly to her and lifted himself up and stood in front of her.

He straightened and then extended his hand down to me. Which I took and he brought me up to my feet with little effort. The blood on his neck looked dry and had already begun flaking. The small cut completely healed without leaving so much as an irritation of where my blade had bit.

"Is everything alright, dear?" He spoke sweetly to her, moving to stand in front of her.

"Can I get you anything?" I asked, and she looked as if she wanted to ask me a question but still didn't answer.

I looked to Talos, but he was focused on her with what looked like a mix of concern and maybe guilt.

"I'll go get you some water." I didn't wait for either of them to respond; I turned and left the cabin.

I shut the door quickly behind me. I leaned back against it for a moment to breathe and compose myself. The door directly across the walkway flung open, and a tall and ruggedly handsome man stood in the doorway. His eyes unmistakably Incubo, he was part of the team Talos had brought with us. He looked me over then glanced to the door I had come out of. He stayed silent but didn't return to his cabin.

I knew I had no reason to explain myself. Talos was very specific about who I was to answer to and didn't seem to think it was important to introduce me to the rest of his security team. I looked him over before turning to walk to the dining car. He cleared his throat, and, without fully turning to face him, I glanced back.

"I'm going to get some water." My tone dry and slightly annoyed.

He looked back into his own cabin and spoke to someone who must have been with him. "I'll be right back."

"That isn't necessary," I said.

He had already closed the door behind him and stepped closer to me.

"My orders are to keep an eye on the well-being of anyone in that cabin." His voice was pleasant but bored.

"Then you should probably stay near the cabin," I snarked and began walking again.

His hand gripped my shoulder and in one breath I spun, grabbed his wrist, crossed his arm in front of his chest. and pinned him up against the wall. My blade out once again and pressed to another Incubo's throat.

The look of surprise on his face faded quickly into amusement. "Forgive me, I was merely—"

"I suggest you go back to your cabin before she paints the floor with your blood, Amil." came Talos' voice, and my eyes shot to where he leaned against the doorway that he had silently come out of.

"Yes, sir." Amil's eyes did not leave my face as he answered Talos and raised his brows as if to ask me to let him go.

I released him and backed up enough for him to take a few steps away, holding my blade lax to my side as I watched him. He stopped in front of his door and turned to Talos. "Can I get you anything?"

"No, thank you. Isa seems to be able to handle it." Talos grinned and turned his face to me again.

Amil nodded, glanced back to me, then entered his cabin. I didn't say anything before walking away, needing more than ever to gain some space and air. I heard Talos close the door and

59

glanced back to see the walkway empty and quickly started walking. I passed through several other cars that had private cabins, and then general seating, before getting to the dining car.

The red velvet-covered booth seats were all empty, the tables set for the next meal, and the smell of coffee came from a long cart at the back of the car. The sun was setting outside as we passed sprawling green hills bathed in the golden-hour light and gleaming off of a large lake out in the distance. I wondered what sleepy town we were passing. I'd never spent much time in the countryside. But there was something soothing about watching it grow and recede past the train car window.

A young waiter came out from the kitchen and filled several small carafes with water. He looked to be Mortal, tall and thin with copper hair. He turned and looked at me with slight confusion "Can I help you? Dinner doesn't start for about another hour, but I'd be happy to take your order."

"No, I'm fine. Just looking for some water." I pointed to the cart of water next to him and he picked a jug up and brought it to me.

"Do you need any clean glasses? Someone should be coming around to refill supplies and glasses soon," he said as he looked past me to the window in the entrance door that I'd come through.

"This will be fine, thank you," I said. He nodded to me and remained quiet.

He didn't turn away, but gave a light bounce on the balls of his feet, and I assumed he was waiting for me to leave again. I took that as a sign that I shouldn't linger, so I turned back around and begrudgingly headed back to the cabin—nowhere else to occupy my time. The waitstaff must have known what type of beings were on the train. They would be understandably curious and nervous.

When I got back to the door of the cabin I glanced at the

door across from it and wondered how many other men were in with Amil. How many other Incubo roamed the train? I shook my head and opened the door to see Lady Althea back on the sofa with her feet tucked under her and a book in her hands. Talos was nowhere to be seen. Unsure if I was relieved or not, I went to the bar and set down the water.

"He said he'd be right back. He's checking with the other men at the back of the train," Althea said over her book but not looking up from it.

Her voice was soft and sweet and matched her fair features. I guessed she was in her mid-twenties by her appearance, but I wasn't going to ask. She had her long blonde hair up in a pretty braided bun which completed her comfortably simple ivory sweater and slacks. The black belt around her waist cinched her thin figure and was accented with an elegant decorative buckle. She had kicked her black, high-heeled shoes haphazardly on the floor in front of her. Her style was classy, but her body language gave me the impression that she favored comfort over fashion.

"I brought some water, I think the waitstaff will be around shortly to deliver our meals." I poured myself a glass of water and drank it quickly.

"I'm fine, thank you." Her eyes still busy, scanning her pages.

The door opened and I reached for my blade before I realized it was Talos. He flashed a slanted smile and shut the door behind him before walking over to the sofa beside Althea.

"I hope your walk was pleasant," he said as he crossed an ankle at his knee and rested one of his arms across the back of the couch.

"Likewise." I crossed my arms over my chest and shifted my weight to one hip.

"Nothing to report," he paused and glanced over to Althea who continued to ignore us. "It will be a rather uneventful evening, wouldn't you agree, Isa?"

He swiveled his head towards me, his eyes darker again, and

a shiver shot up my spine. Looking back to Althea he spoke gently, father-like.

"My dear, can I turn the light on for you?"

She looked to him and smiled warmly at him. "I'm going to go back to the bedroom now. Call for me when dinner has come."

Without acknowledging me, she walked into the small room and shut the door. Talos looked to me and I couldn't help but roll my eyes and sigh. Letting loose my arms and swinging them in annoyance, I went to the closet to retrieve my laptop. I could feel him looking up my backside and, when I turned back around to walk over to the couch, his eyes followed my every move.

"Alone once again, Isa," he purred and looked absolutely satisfied with himself.

"Would you like me to find another place to sit? I suppose I could share a cabin with your men across the hall. Amil seemed to be a great conversationalist." I raised a brow at him.

"Oh, they would probably enjoy your company, but I would miss you terribly." His lips curled into a tantalizing smile.

Looking away from him, the corner of my mouth tugged upward and I huffed a laugh. I opened up my laptop and began going through emails, aware that he was still watching me.

"May I ask you something?" He lowered his arm from the headrest and laced his fingers together, laying them in his lap.

"I suppose you can; I may not answer though."

He smiled at my reply.

"The night I approached you, why did you come with me into that room?"

My eyes shot to his, confusion weighing down my brows. He had to know why I did. I was in disguise and had just fulfilled a contract. But did he want a more complicated reason?

"As a Temptress, I had to obey. I didn't know who you were

and had to keep up appearances in case Jaara had been discovered."

"Perhaps I should have requested your services as a Temptress before revealing my true intentions." His sly smile widened at his own wit.

"It seems you didn't need to do so." I glanced down at the couch, then back to him.

"That was rather satisfying, but to have you entangled in such a way would have been very interesting." He bit his bottom lip and a flicker of something confusing rippled through my stomach.

"Do you often get enjoyment from manipulating situations?" I pursed my lips and narrowed my gaze.

He gave a low throaty laugh and turned his eyes down to his lap. "I get enjoyment out of many things, but I don't believe they would have offended you as much as I have just done."

"I'm offended by the insinuation that you would feel you missed out on an opportunity to take advantage of my situation more than you did."

"You're right. I will not need to take advantage of a vulnerability for you to submit to me completely."

I blushed and swallowed hard. I had nothing to say to that, no come back or witty response to that assumption. I couldn't very well argue that he couldn't have me at any time or anywhere as I was fighting my own gut to resist doing somersaults. I didn't have any reason to believe that I would have resisted him the night we met if he hadn't revealed who he was and what he wanted. I could feel a pull to him even now, even after we'd already been together, the hunger rising inside me again.

"You're enjoying my reactions, aren't you?" I took a shaky breath, coming to a realization that he'd been holding something back.

"What gave me away?" He met my eyes, storms brewing in his.

He could influence me. That's why I felt so drawn to him; why every fiber in my body screamed for his touch before.

"It doesn't seem fair, but in my defense I can't always control it. Especially, when I'm so drawn to someone myself." Heat crept up my neck to my cheeks.

"So these feelings. They're not real?" I started to question trust in myself.

"Catching feelings for me already?" He paused and looked me over, "Those urges are your own. They're suggestively amplified by my own greedy desires."

I was breathless and a little queasy and wondered which was a response to his words or his emotions being reflected onto me. My head felt heavy and full, but so many rumors I'd heard about Incubo started to make sense. Other Mortals who'd found themselves enthralled with their kind always ended up seeming off, hollow of their normal selves. They must have given themselves completely over to their lovers until nothing was left.

"Do others know this about Incubo? Do Fata respond as Mortals do to your influence?" I shut my laptop to give him my full attention.

"Fata have their own natural defenses but are still affected minorly. Mortals who become involved in a relationship with an Incubo often realize, but by the time they do, they've become dependent. They are able to leave when they choose but would often rather die than walk away." He knowingly shrugged.

I had never felt something that deep for anyone. I could hardly imagine being so deeply invested in a relationship that I would rather end my life than be without someone. It was almost poetic, and almost impossible to comprehend.

"I will do my best to restrain myself when I am around you. I don't need you distracted." He glanced at the bedroom door.

"You truly care for her, don't you? And not just as her head of security." It was a statement, an observation from our inter-actions so far.

"I don't believe I will be able to explain the affection I have for Althea in a way you as a Mortal would understand. But she is as much a part of me as the blood running through my veins. I'd kill anyone who merely looked at her disrespectfully." He looked back to me. "Which is why I have entrusted you with her care."

I wasn't sure whether I should feel honored that he had charged me with someone so important to him or worried for my own life if something did happen to her while under my watchful eye. I had no idea that Incubo felt love or protection so deeply. Admittedly, I'd always gotten the impression that they didn't care much about anyone but themselves, and more importantly, their power. An oddly misplaced feeling of affec-tion bloomed in my chest; it was as if their kind having such emotions was a goal finally accomplished.

"You never answered my other question. What kills an Incubo?" I needed to know. He should have told me during our first official meeting, but reluctance now etched his face.

"Alexandrite," his shoulders tightened, knuckles turning white as he spoke, "that is the only substance that can kill one of my kind. And that information never leaves this cabin."

I nodded, mind full of questions, but did not ask anything more. He looked me over one more time, all traces of lust or interest leaving his eyes. We sat silently sharing space for a while. Eventually he pulled out his newspaper and I opened my laptop again to return some emails and move money around my various accounts.

Keeping money separated out into multiple accounts ensured protection of assets and suspicion if anyone came snooping around my private estates. Money, real estate, stocks, and investment knowledge was part of my training with the Banners. A Black Banner who gets desperate for cash can put us all at risk for taking jobs to keep afloat and getting involved with the wrong clients.

Some time later, a soft knock came from the door. Talos checked his wristwatch before answering it. The sun had set outside the train completely, so I expected it to be someone from the meal service to take our order or deliver appetizers, but before I could look, the lights in the cabin went out. I heard a scream from behind me in Lady Althea's room, then another from outside the cabin. There was a scuffling noise and then Talos cried out with a thick voice, as if he were being restrained or muffled.

"ALTHEA! GO!" he yelled, and I drew my blade and shot for the door.

Althea was huddled in the top corner of the bed when I opened the door, emergency lights at the bottom of the wall dimly illuminating the small room. I shut and locked the door behind me and pulled her off the bed, silently instructing her to get low on the ground behind me. I stood facing the door, waiting, blade in hand, and heard more yelling, more grunting, and more commotion on the other side of the door. Looking around there was a small window that was completely sealed shut, meant only for sightseeing during the voyages, but the train had slowed to an emergency stop and if I needed to, it could be easily broken and Althea and I could escape out of it.

I heard what sounded like Amil's voice and two others entering the room, but they weren't yelling; they seemed calm. Then came Talos' voice, rough, but no longer distressed. I waited and looked back at Althea who held her knees to her chest as tightly as she could, tears streaming down her terrified face.

"Althea, I think it's all right. Wait here." She shook her head and closed her dark, cloudy eyes.

"No. No, please. Don't leave me here alone." Her shaky voice came through her knees, hardly above a whisper.

"I'm not going to leave you, I'm going to take a peek out the door." I cracked the door, ready to strike if rushed.

I could hardly see anything. The emergency lights at the foot of the walls were blocked by furniture and large heaps resembling bodies. I spotted three men standing in the middle of the room speaking low amongst themselves. I shut the door again softly and locked it again. Turning back to Althea, her eyes were wide on me.

"It's over. Whatever it was, it's over, but let's stay here until the main lights come back on and the train starts moving again." I turned back to the door, weapon still in hand.

About thirty minutes passed before we heard the train begin to rumble under our feet. The lights hadn't come back on, but we had started moving slowly. Talos' voice came through the door before he gave a soft knock.

"My Lady. It is safe to come out now." His tone was gentle and soothing.

I put my knife away in time for Althea to rush past me and slam herself into the door, unlocking it frantically, opening it and throwing herself into Talos' arms. Shock hung from my face. I stood staring at them for a moment before realizing Amil and the two other men were still waiting in the cabin, but the debris was cleared from the room and the furniture returned to its natural state. The lights around the room did not fill the space, but without obstructions there was enough remaining light to get a full view of the cabin and the beings within it.

One of the men looked me up and down, then gave Amil a nod before leaving. The other crossed the room to the couch and sat down. Amil's eyes met mine when I looked back at Althea and Talos still embracing. His eyes were distinctly Incubo in feature but had a liquid or oil quality to them, reminding me of a single candle flame flickering low in a windowless room. He dipped his chin, as if acknowledging me as another protector. He moved towards me, and I stepped around Talos and Althea into the sitting area to meet him. Not one of them looked at all mussed from the altercation, even Talos who had been in a physical confrontation when he demanded I go to Althea. Their shirts looked almost freshly pressed and not a single hair out of place.

"She seems a little shook up, but I'm sure she'll be fine. What happened out here?" I asked as I looked around the floor as if there were still bodies piled up.

"Two of our men were incapacitated at the rear of the train and two Fata boarded the train in an attempt to either kidnap or kill Lady Althea. They're no longer a worry," Amil answered quietly so only I could hear him.

"Fata?" I looked over my shoulder to Talos who had finally been released and was now encouraging Althea to sit with the other security guard on the couch.

"We are under the impression that they were hired by an Incubo," Amil said, drawing my attention back to his roughly stumbled face.

"You think Fata would risk the wrath of a group of Incubo for money?"

This was so hard for me to believe because for the most part, Fata were docile, typically working in the arts, academia, services, and factories. They each had certain abilities and many had features that set them apart from Mortals, but they stayed out of the way of Incubo dealings as much as possible. There had been plenty of rumors of Incubo having Fata as flunkies but then killing them all if they pissed their bosses off. There weren't many laws that Incubo couldn't skirt around, and often murder was one of them. Incubo rarely got their hands dirty; they were very skilled at covering their tracks and vouching for one another when authorities came asking questions about missing lesser beings.

"We didn't have much time to chat about their concerns." Amil smirked and glanced to the other Incubo men in the room.

"Isa," Talos approached us and cupped the back of my arm, "I am going to go with Amil to check on the other men. I will give you a full report when I return. Yamir will stay here with you and Lady Althea until I get back."

He nodded to Yamir on the couch who raised two fingers to his dark brow and gave a solute of agreement. He and Amil left the cabin and I locked the door behind them. There was no reason to believe there weren't more attackers lying in wait for our guards to be down. It seemed so easy for the Incubo to defuse the situation; they were laden with immortal strength and agility. Even without any weapons, they dispatched our would-be attackers within moments. Something wasn't adding up, my gut screaming that something was wrong. But Talos gave me a direct order and I had to follow it.

I stood in front of the door for a few moments and the overhead lights flickered and then ignited. Althea sighed with relief from where she sat on the couch, catching my attention, then the sudden thought of what the time was and how long we had been delayed hit me. I searched the room for a clock but realized there wasn't one inside the cabin.

"We have been delayed but should still be in Arta by midnight," Yamir stated as if reading my mind.

"Thank you," I replied and sat next to Althea who was now sitting very still with her hands folded in her lap and looking at a spot on the rug.

I followed her line of sight and saw a small pool of dark, damp substance, blood. I went to the bathroom and retrieved a towel to lay over the spot and sat back down. She sat back, drawing her knees up to her chest, and wrapped her arms around them. I debated trying to comfort her, but decided against it. She didn't know me. I wouldn't be comforting. I looked to Yamir and wondered if he was more familiar to her, but his bored expression told me he wasn't.

He was also handsome. It seemed that all Incubo I had

encountered were almost unnecessarily attractive: tall, muscular, sharp jaws, and the smoldering essence of a challenge. Yamir's dusky complexion against his thick dark hair and brows gave focus to his misty grey eyes. Flecks of gold seemed to drift across his vision as if dancing. He wore all black and hadn't removed his suit jacket. In contrast to Talos and Amil, his face was smooth and hair teased to one side, perfectly manicured. The suit he wore was tailored to fit his shoulders and slim waist. The jacket, buttons undone to reveal a black silk skirt that clung tightly to his abdomen, left little to the imagination of the physique underneath.

I must have been staring at him for too long because he shifted awkwardly and cleared his throat. I looked to the door and waited.

"You must be Isa." His low voice smooth as our eyes met.

"Eh, yes." I didn't know what he knew of my employment and didn't care to share that information so freely.

"Amil was impressed with you earlier. I told him that my money was on you if he crossed your path again." He laughed and spread his arms across the back of the couch.

"Amil should learn to keep his hands to himself," I quipped back.

"Most women wouldn't agree. He has quite the reputation for being popular with his companions." His eyes trailed from my face down to my hips then back up.

"I would imagine many say that about all Incubo?" He laughed at this.

"Do you not know from experience then?" His lips parted in an amused smile, one brow lifted.

"I don't often interact with your kind."

"Perhaps that will change." The gold flecks glistened in his eyes as they flickered wickedly, and my stomach sank.

I straightened my spine and looked away from him, clearing my throat. He gave a soft chuckle and turned his attention to the shadowed scenery out the window. We all sat in silence for a long while before normal sounds of passengers and the rattle of dining carts returned to the hallway outside. When Talos and Amil returned, they brought trays of food and beverages. Yamir and Amil returned to their own cabin to dine and monitor the hall.

Talos told me that the two men that had been the first point of contact were recovering after being blindsided. There were no other concerns on the train and our train car would be completely locked down until the end of our journey. We had several hours left, but he assured Lady Althea they would be uneventful, and he wasn't wrong.

# CHAPTER SEVEN

The rest of the journey was almost painfully boring. Aside from eating our meals, there was near silence. Althea could not rest but resided to read in the corner of the couch. Talos ended up falling asleep in the other room, and I tried to find things to keep me lucid. I ended up clearing out my email inbox, reorganizing my carry-on bag, and mostly pacing from one side of the cabin to the other. When we finally arrived at the Arta train station, we waited for Yamir and Amil to escort us to the waiting cars.

Althea's soon to be husband was not waiting to greet us, but his valet assured us that Lord Welp was awaiting his dear Lady's arrival. It was well past midnight by the time we arrived at the estate. The long driveway was flanked by tall, box-shaped shrubs that created a wall effect which shielded the view of the property, opening up to the circular driveway of the white stone-washed manor. The four visible floors paneled with large windows, separated by white stone pillars. Balconies dotted each floor by way of distinguishing the large rooms on each level.

The short stairway at the center of the house led up to a

double, dark oak door. The Lord and four others were waiting just inside of the vaulted foyer. The inside of the manor was as grand and proper with a sweeping stairway to the second level. Dark hardwood floors met white walls and stairwells. Every inch of it was spotless and seemed to shine against the high chandelier.

Lord Welp was standing right inside the door and reached to shake Talos' hand, who was leading the rest of us up the stairs. I came up behind Talos and stepped aside for Lady Althea to leap into Cornelius' embrace. I gave a nod of greeting to the others standing in front of our incoming group. Yamir and Amil brought up our bags and set them down before retrieving their own from the vehicle. The rest of Talos' men were already prowling the grounds as instructed, finding any weak spots in security or entrances to the manor.

A slightly older looking man approached Talos and extended his hand in greeting, then took a step back for a lavish looking woman to offer her hand to Talos. He graciously dipped his head and smoothed his lips over her fingers. The man turned to me and dipped his chin before taking a few steps closer. He was wearing a light blue, short-sleeve collared shirt and tan slacks, looking as though he had tried to dress casually so late at night.

"You must be Lady Althea's companion. I am Stavros, and this is my wife, Camilla. We welcome you to our home. If there is anything you need please do not hesitate to ask. Hariss will escort you and Lady Althea to your quarters. Is this all your luggage?" He gave a broad wave to my bags and several other black and gold accented bags that I assumed were Althea's.

"Thank you, it's nice to meet you. I'm—" Talos caught my eye and interjected, clapping his hand on Stavros' shoulder.

"Stavros, you are too formal. Isabella here is a lovely girl who will ensure this union stays pure." He winked to me and I inclined my head attempting to hide being caught off guard.

"Come ladies, I will follow you up and help you settle in." Talos continued and grabbed one of his own bags.

Yamir and Amil were directed down the hall from us on the third floor, the visitors' wing of the massive manor. I watched as Amil walked down several doors past ours. He paused with his hand on the door knob and looked to me; I could see that small flame that made my stomach flip and quickly looked away into the suite that Lady Althea and I would be sharing.

The double, heavy white doors opened up into a large sitting room and floor-to-ceiling windows that opened up onto a balcony seen from outside. A set of three white, plush sofas sat in the middle of the room with a low table in the middle of the arrangement. On either side of the room were large doors that led to our bedrooms. Lady Althea was taken into the door to our left by Hariss, and I was directed to the right by Talos. The bedroom was as grand as the entry room with a sizable canopy bed, the white head and footboard were embellished with gold-leaf flowers carved into them. The whole bed was covered with a white gauzy drape that was parted and tied to the bed posts. The lush ivory linens were adorned with gold embroidery. A mountain of pillows piled up at the head of the bed looked so comfortable. I wasn't sure I would be able to resist them long enough to dress for bed.

Talos entered the room as I was setting one of my bags on a chair near a large dresser that looked to be the match to the bed furniture. He stood looking around the room with his hands on his hips.

"Does Althea need help with her things?" I asked, wondering why he was standing there so quietly.

"Lord and Lady Welp have extravagant taste, don't they?"

"I suppose they do." I stood up straight and looked to him fully. "Did you come in here to point out the interior design?"

"I came to discuss a few things with you before we all retire for the remainder of the night."

74

"Has it to do with my new name? Isabella, right?" I gave him an incredulous look.

"I am sorry about that. It is strategic, but I didn't make that choice until we arrived at the train station and Cornelius wasn't there to greet us. He was acting particularly standoffish and I had a foul feeling about it."

I nodded. "I can understand that. You want me to watch over Althea and Cornelius closely?"

"Very good." The side of his mouth tugged upwards. "You are intuitive. That makes my job a little easier."

He walked over to the bed and sat on the large ornate footboard, watching me. He crossed his arms at his chest and didn't speak.

"Is there anything else that you need to tell me now that can't wait until morning?"

"It would be a great favor to me if you stayed away from Amil and Yamir. They don't need to be distracted."

My jaw dropped. Surprise must have flooded my expression because he cocked his head to the side and his eyes started to cloud in a new way that felt more like danger than arousal.

"I saw the way Amil looked at you in the hall. He is very good at his job when he isn't distracted by wickedly gorgeous women."

Scorching heat filling my cheeks, my brow furrowing, I said, "I'm here to do a job, not sleep with every Incubo I come in contact with, and I do not appreciate you assuming I can't keep focus."

"I didn't mean to offend, I am merely requesting you show them mercy. I don't think you quite understand how difficult it is for my kind to resist our urges."

"Sounds like the personal problem of men who should hear the word no more often." I began taking my weapons out of my bags and securing a few of them in the dresser beside me.

He scoffed and looked to the floor. "That we are. Not many of us have been denied before."

I certainly hadn't told Talos 'no' yet, and even through my anger and revulsion from the audacity, my body felt a pull to his. I shook a flash vision of him bending me over that footboard from my mind as I crossed in front of him to the bedside table. I opened the small drawer and placed three throwing knives and a small handgun inside and shut it. I trailed back to my luggage, but he caught my hand as I passed him. I looked down at his hand around my wrist then followed his arm up to the hunger on his face and his eyes starting to turn once again to a more familiar smolder.

"I also have a very hard time sharing. Not to imply you belong to me, but..." He shrugged and gave me a crooked smile.

Hot anger rose to my cheeks again, and I snapped my arm back from his grip. "It's a good thing you aren't implying that you somehow own me because that would be extremely unprofessional."

I knew I had no room to talk with what had happened on the train, but I was lacking in words to describe how I was truly feeling: angered at my own lack of control, this unbearable draw to him, the slight shame of each occasion I had been left alone with him, and how childish I felt trying to pretend that I was still somehow being professional by ignoring these mixed feelings.

"We couldn't have that now, could we? And we are in agreement that any type of relations while on assignment would be distasteful?"

His fox-like grin did not reflect his words and wasn't at all convincing, but I nodded in agreement anyway. I went back to unpacking, and he silently left my room. I heard him bid Althea good night and the door of the suite shut behind him.

After I showered and dried off with possibly the fluffiest towels I had ever used, I got dressed and went to lie down in bed, but found a black, matte box lying where Talos had been sitting earlier. I didn't recall it being there before I took a shower. I looked around the room for any sign that someone else had been here, but only saw the door still locked.

I ran my fingers across the top of the smooth surface, no note or writing on the rectangular lid. I lifted and shimmied the top off. Inside, sitting on a satin puff, was a dagger with an Alexandrite blade. The carved violet and indigo gem gleamed in the dim room light. Breathlessly, I picked it up and turned it over, the black leather hilt in my hands, admiring the razored edge. I'd never seen anything like it and probably for good reason. I replaced the dagger in its pillowed box and placed it carefully in the side table drawer.

Unsure whether this gift was planned or another last minute adjustment to his plans, the thought of Talos sneaking it into my room filled my head as I pulled back the linens of the bed. I heard a small knock on the door and for a brief moment thought I knew who it would be. I grabbed the heavy robe that was provided for me in the bathroom and wrapped it around my bed clothes to answer.

To my surprise, Althea was standing outside the door, the two rooms behind her dark. She was also in her night clothes, a pretty silk nightgown and a robe that matched my own. Her expression distressed and her voice hushed, "I'm sorry to bother you."

"You're not at all, what's wrong?" I answered, opening the door wider and stepping to the side to get a better view around the shared sitting room and through to her door, but not seeing anything concerning.

"Um. This is silly, but," she looked behind her then back to me, "Talos said if I needed anything to come to you."

"Of course, do you want me to check your room?" My mind shot to the weapons in the drawers.

"No, Talos did before he left, but I'm just uncomfortable alone. Could I—" She looked down and blushed.

"Come on in, this bed is too big anyway." I smiled warmly trying to mask my slight amusement.

She smiled back at me and walked right over to the bed, pulled back the linens, and nestled in. I shut and locked the door, walked back to the bed, and got in on what was now my side. She rolled over to face me and said with her eyes closed, "Thank you."

"You're welcome." I turned the light on the side table off, darkening the room, and lay down to sleep.

# CHAPTER EIGHT

S everal hours later, I was awoken by another knock on the door. I sat up and grabbed one of my knives from the nightstand. I looked over to where Lady Althea was still sleeping, undisturbed. Streams of muted, blue morning light were coming from the breaks in the window drapes, and I cursed how low the sun was still on the horizon. Grabbing my robe once again to answer the door, I suspected that I knew who it was. And this time I was right.

"She's fine Talos," I said quietly as I opened the door, "she needed a safe space."

He was already dressed in a fine, dark blue suit with white shirt. Rising slightly, he looked over my head to the bed and relief smoothed his face. Behind him, her door was wide open. He had gone to her first.

"May I speak to you?" He took a few steps back. I looked behind me to Althea and walked with him, shutting the door behind me softly. He looked concerned again.

"What's happened?"

"The Welps' security found a man roaming the grounds about an hour ago, I've just come from questioning him myself."

He slipped his hands into his slacks pockets and looked to the door, and I could feel rage fueled heat coming from his body.

"I thought you said that she would be safe once here?" I asked, crossing my arms to pull the robe tighter around me.

"I said once the marriage was finalized, I believed she would be safe. But I'm not so sure about that now. I'll have a breakfast service sent up while Yamir and Amil stand watch outside the room. Discreetly arm yourself and be prepared to depart at any moment. I am to go speak with our gracious hosts about the intrusion and dismiss their security team. More of my men will be arriving this afternoon. If all goes well, then our original plan will be carried out without another issue."

"Was he another Fata?" But he didn't answer, he turned before I could even finish my questions and shut the door behind him.

I looked out the large windows over the grounds laid in front of the manor. The sun was starting to graze the tops of the trees lining the property, and a dreamy mist hovered above the lawn. It was only six in the morning, but I didn't think I'd be able to go back to sleep. I went back to my room and Lady Althea was still sleeping soundly so I grabbed under clothes, a pair of dark jeans, a black blouse, and shoes. I carried the bundle in my arms to the bathroom to dress and ready for the day. I put on some light eye makeup and tossed my hair up in a loose bun. When I came back out, Althea was gone.

I walked out to the sitting room and found her in a cozy spot at the center couch with a tea and coffee service laid out in front of her on the low table. She hadn't dressed yet, but was wearing her robe and lounging with her legs across the seat reading a paper. When she noticed I had entered the room, she looked over the paper to me and smiled. She seemed so kind towards me when alone but ignored me completely during our journey here.

"Good morning," she said. "Hariss will be bringing up some

pastries and sausage in a few minutes. I didn't know how you took your coffee, but there is cream and sugar here." She looked back to her paper.

"That'll be fine, thanks. Did you sleep well?"

"Oh yes, thank you." She was awfully cheery this early in the morning. "I've summoned the dress designer, kitchen manager, wedding planner, and groundskeeper. We have a lot to do before the wedding!"

I blinked at her, utter confusion across my face. I would definitely need coffee if I was to be playing her personal assistant for the day.

"Neil and Talos will be joining us for lunch here in the suite. Amil and Yamir are outside already."

"Sounds like a busy day you have planned." I sat on the couch nearest my room door and started to make myself a cup of coffee.

"Well, I think Talos is going to suggest that we move up the wedding date and why wait, you know?" She sounded giddy and a little clueless to the danger she was in. I wondered if someone had told her about the intruder this morning.

She sipped from a delicate tea cup and read through her paper while I sat back on my couch and drank my coffee in a slightly larger, matching chinaware cup. Glancing towards the double doors of the suite, I felt like I should check with Amil and Yamir on anything new that has happened or if they knew of all the upcoming appointments, but remembered the conversation I had with Talos last night. A small rebellion flickered in me, but I didn't give in to it. Talos may have been obnoxious, but he was still my employer and I had to respect the terms of our agreement.

After Althea was done with her tea, she went to her room to get ready for the day ahead. Breakfast had been delivered to me by Hariss; he was Fata with sunshine hair and pale, clean skin that reminded me of the white linens and walls of the manor.

He didn't linger and didn't speak to me aside from bidding me farewell. Althea came back out over an hour later in a sleek, moss colored dress that hugged her curves but still looked comfortable. Even though we weren't leaving, she wore strapped high-heeled shoes and she'd done her hair in a high ponytail with a full face of makeup. She really was stunningly beautiful and regal.

Not long after she emerged, her first appointment arrived and was escorted in by Amil, who stayed inside the door. The plump Fata woman was from the kitchen. She came in with a clipboard and menu options to go over for the big event knowing that the day may be changed, but prepared to order more food if needed. She had a kind voice, but I could tell she ran a tight ship in the kitchen. She was able to keep Althea on topic and to the point so she could get back to work. She had brought up samples of cake, soup, and hors d'oeuvres. All delicious and luxurious. I was glad I didn't have to choose between them.

After she left, Amil stayed in the room and Yamir allowed the groundskeeper to come in. He was also Fata with a slight green tinge to his golden sun-tanned skin. It wasn't uncommon for Fata' skin to change to blend in with their surroundings or take color from plants or animals they were in contact with on a regular basis. His hands looked completely stained deep green as if he never wore gloves. He assured Althea that the grounds would be proper for her outdoor ceremony and that he had ordered the many flowers she had sent him from the florist.

The wedding planner was the next and longest of all the meetings. She was a local Incubo who lived in the nearby town. Her eyes were a very light smoke color and her irises were actually more blue than grey. She was very beautiful, her outfit a smart and flowing cream-colored pantsuit with a crimson blouse underneath the low cut jacket. Her blonde hair trailed down her back and looked impossibly soft, like strands of silk. I caught Amil staring at her several times. A small part of me felt offended, but I attributed that to the Incubo lure to Mortals and made a note to myself to ask if the influence works on their own kind.

It seemed to be hours of going back and forth between seating arrangements, event timing, photographs, dancing lessons, updates on attendees, and so much more that my head was swimming with boredom. I lost count of how many times I had yawned and Althea offered me coffee. By the end of the meeting, I'd had three full cups.

Talos was first to show for the lunch date and sat next to me after greeting the wedding planner. He gently suggested that she should be on her way, and I was so grateful for him at that moment. He seemed less tense than I had seen him this morning and hadn't stormed in to retrieve us, so I assumed the conversation with the Welps had gone well.

"How many more meetings do you have today, My Lady?" he asked as he poured some hot water over his tea bag.

"Just a couple more, but I may need a lie down after lunch." She arched her back and lifted her arms up over her head in a stretch.

"And Isa, how have you been faring?" He flicked a quick glance to me before sipping his tea.

"Oh, Isa has been wonderful! She even helped me pick out the soup for the wedding: potato and leek with truffle oil," Althea answered for me, and I gave a laxed smile in agreement.

"That is very kind of you." One side of his mouth tugged upward in a private tease which I returned with a narrowed look.

"The dress designer is due soon. He'll be bringing my dress for alterations, but he has a surprise for you, Isa." Althea lifted one hand to her lips doing little to hide her full smile.

I couldn't help but smile back to her. "I can't wait."

Cornelius arrived bringing with him the kitchen manager

with a cart full of food. She had decided to do a full test run of the wedding meal for our luncheon. A four-course meal with soup and salad, appetizers, a fish dish, and small squares of the cakes she had prepared earlier for testing.

At every new course, Althea turned to Cornelius to ask him what his opinions were on the food. He was rather handsome but more plain than the other Incubo I had met so far. He had sandy blond hair, a thin, smooth face, and was as tall as Talos but slimmer framed. His clothing dripped of finery and was tailored to fit his lanky body. He looked very bored by all the wedding discussion but nodded along in agreement with everything Althea said like a seemingly good soon-to-be husband would.

Talos to my left had inched his way closer to me and our knees kept lightly brushing against each other every so often. He leaned back on the couch and rested his arm across the back of it, his hand lazily hung down close to my shoulder. Purposely, I sat close to the edge of the seat to avoid contact. I could tell he was still wary of Cornelius and often noticed his knee tense up when they spoke to one another.

When Cornelius was summoned away for a meeting of his own, he promised to come back for dinner. Amil showed him out and shut the door behind them. Althea looked after him and her expression was almost heartbroken. Talos assured her that he would ensure Cornelius was available for dinner and would escort him. She nodded in response and announced she would be in her room taking a nap and asked to be woken up when the dress designer arrived.

"If you would also like to lie down for a bit, you are welcome to. I will have Amil or Yamir wake you both when the next meeting begins." Talos stood and buttoned his jacket.

"I might just do that. It's been quite the day." But I stayed sitting as he took a few steps to the door and turned to face me.

"Would you like company? Althea seems to have found

comfort in her own room." His cunning smile caused my breath to catch, but I returned it with a sly smile.

"Are you offering or would it be Amil? Or perhaps Yamir? Come to think of it, Hariss looked spry." I leaned back on the couch and crossed my legs.

"You are rather cheeky, but I'd be incredibly jealous if you chose Hariss over me." His voice rumbled with an amused laugh.

"I'll be fine on my own." I returned an amused smile and stood to walk towards my room, but he quickly and silently caught the back of my arm, his body flat to my back.

His warm breath at the top of my head, his chin pressed to the side of my head. He slid a hand down my back, stopping at my hip, and stilled. My whole body felt a pull, and a tug behind my navel ached. I flattened my hand against his thigh behind me and could feel him reacting as the front of his slacks became tight.

I took a deep breath and pulled away a step. "Talos."

"Isa," the sound of my own name zipping down my spine as I closed my eyes, "I'd like to thank you for your service to Althea today."

He slipped his hand from my hip, up my blouse, and over my bare stomach. My skin seemed to ignite, and I could hardly feel the air in my lungs. I leaned back against him as his hand found my breast and held it firmly. I could feel the soft tissue begging for my bra to disappear to reveal its tender peak. Lifting my chin and pressing my head against his chest, I tried one last time to get a hold of my senses before I let him have me completely, but he dragged his lips down my cheek and stopped right below my ear.

A knock at the door sounded before it opened, and he withdrew his hands and turned around, stepping a bit over to shield me from who had entered. It was Yamir.

"I'm sorry, sir. But Stavros is requesting your presence in his study. Our men have arrived and he isn't pleased." I turned around after collecting my thoughts and saw both their jaws tight.

"Why am I not surprised by his bull-headed reaction. Thank you, Yamir. You will come with me. I'll need you to give direction to the new men." He turned to me, looking me up and down, and gave a ragged sigh.

"Until later?" He winked and made his way out of the suite with Yamir at his back, shutting the door behind them.

I turned and opened my door, walking straight into the bathroom to splash cool water on my face. My whole body felt like it was about to erupt, my face hot and flushed in the mirror. I ran my hands over my eyes and smoothed under them with a cloth, trying to straighten up my running makeup. The ache between my thighs calming and the tug in my stomach loosening as I took in several deep cleansing breaths.

# CHAPTER NINE

I didn't sleep, but I did rest awhile before the dress designer arrived. Another gorgeous Incubo with thick, black hair that he wore in a tight bun at the top of his head walked in. His bright-blue silk shirt was tucked into the waistband of his fitted black slacks. He bustled in with his arms full of large, white garment bags and laid them down neatly on the third couch.

"Lady Althea, I have outdone myself this time!" he cheerfully cooed as he unzipped the largest bag and revealed the most stunning dress I had ever seen.

Althea squealed, holding her hands over her mouth and nose and bouncing on the balls of her feet in joy. She hurried towards him and ran her hands over the layers of tulle skirt and lace bodice.

"Can I put it on?" She looked to him, and the smokey glaze across her eyes became a haze, her irises almost looking Mortal.

He nodded enthusiastically, and in response she rushed to her room, dress in hand. I smiled after her and waited on the couch.

"She will be a lovely bride," the designer started to unzip the next bag, "and you will make a beautiful bridesmaid."

My eyes shot to him and the long-sleeved dress he was taking out. There wasn't any tulle, but it was covered in lace in a pale shade of lilac, a sheer layer under the lace a creamy beige, almost exactly matching my skin tone. He held it out to me beaming with pride and waited for me to react.

"Oh! Wow, it's pretty." I smiled trying to hide how uncomfortable I'd become at the thought of so much of my body being on display to hundreds of strangers.

"I will have to pin it a bit. It looks like Talos had known the correct size but was a bit unsure about your height." I took the dress and held it up to look it over.

"Go on!" He waved both his hands towards my room, still smiling from ear to ear.

I pushed the awkward thought of Talos being some kind of savant when it came to guessing women's dress sizes and went to change. By the time I came out in the revealing dress, Althea was on a stool in front of a large mirror on the wall. She indeed looked lovely, her arms out and shifting from side to side to look at herself from different angles. She caught sight of me in the mirror and turned.

"You look perfect!" I didn't think her rosy cheeks could take any more excitement.

"So do you, absolutely beautiful." She took a handful of her dress and stepped down from the stool to meet me in the middle of the room.

Pushing me up onto the stool and turning me to the mirror, she gazed into it with me. Her shoulders relaxed as she admired us, pleased with the color combo and the dresses' accenting lace, and she turned to the designer and waved him forward,

"I'd like her dress to be mid-calf. Maybe an inch or so higher." She took a section of my dress hem and folded it up as the designer pinned.

A knock on the door came before the voice of Amil,

announcing that dinner would arrive shortly. He stood in the doorway, looking me over.

"I better go get changed for dinner. Can't have Neil seeing me in my dress before the wedding." Althea rushed off to her room and the designer finished pinning.

"You are all set. Please slowly turn so I can check the fit in the chest," he said, standing with his hands to his waist.

"Seems to fit fine, at least from what I can see from here." Amil's voice was deep and not at all hiding his teasing tone.

"Yes, well. You would say that," The designer scoffed and rolled his eyes, not amused by Amil's critic.

I smirked and subtly shook my head, but Amil did not look away. He watched as the designer lifted the dress fabric under my arms, adjusting the crease between the sleeves and bodice, then the low neckline. I could feel Amil's eyes on me and saw the small flicker reflecting in the mirror before me. The designer pinned and pulled, and I tried not to squirm.

"Move it, Incubo brut!" Came a gruff female voice from behind Amil as he was practically pushed out of the way by a food cart.

Behind the cart was the kitchen manager bringing in the evening meal followed by another kitchen staffer wearing a white chef jacket and white slacks. He was younger than the manager, but taller and thin. He was carrying a tray of wine glasses in one hand and two bottles of wine between the fingers of his other. The meal cart was set against the far wall near the windows and balcony door. Amil had retreated back to his post outside the suite as the kitchen staff left together.

"Alright. That should do, darling. I'll have this dress hemmed, taken in, and delivered by tomorrow evening." The designer began putting away all of his tools and pins as I stepped off the stool.

I smiled and nodded before going to change out of the now dangerously sharp dress. When I came back out, Talos and

Cornelius were back and Althea was hanging on the arm of her betrothed. The love she held on her face for this man was both heartwarming and depressing. If that type of love put her in the crosshairs by her own kind and possibly the Fata, I wasn't sure it was worth it.

"Ah, Isabella. Lady Althea was just telling us all about how lovely you looked in your bridesmaid dress." Talos eyed me up and down as I handed over the dress to the designer.

"She was breathtaking!" Althea beamed at me then looked back to Cornelius.

We all bid the dress designer a good evening, poured glasses of wine, and filled our plates before rounding the small table and sofas to settle down for our meal. Talos did not sit with me. He chose to sit on the couch opposite me, the soon-to-be newlyweds cozied up on the couch between us. Althea went into every detail about the afternoon, then dove back into invitation replies, seating arrangements, flower deliveries, refreshment plans, and much more that could not hold my attention. I'd filled my glass once, but Talos had not filled his own at all. He'd hardly touched the glass that had been poured and only seemed to pick at his plate.

After exhausting Cornelius with wedding plans, Althea and Cornelius decided to take some time together out on the balcony. They left the large doors open and the fresh evening breeze flowed through the sitting room, occupying the room like an old friend I didn't realize I had missed.

"Should I go out there with them?" I asked without turning my face from the opening.

"That won't be necessary. I have two men posted beneath the balcony; they are safe for now."

"You seem worried." I glanced at him quickly, unsure if he was paying attention.

"I am distracted." He swirled his now warm glass of wine and stood up to face the balcony doors as well.

I kept quiet, it wasn't my place to inquire. If his distractions had anything to do with my ability to keep Althea safe, he would have told me by now. He owed me nothing, and I had no obligation to care what was weighing so heavily on his mind. I took another sip from my wine glass and admired the beautiful gold leaf pattern on the rim. As I turned to set it down on the table, Talos appeared next to me with a bottle of wine. He tipped it slightly, a silent request to fill my glass. I nodded and held the glass up to him. He set the bottle down and then sat down next to me, but nestled into the corner of the couch, his back lying back in the crevice, a plush, white accent pillow cushioning his spine. I gazed at him as he let loose a thick breath and gravely hum.

"That bad?" I took a long drink, draining about half my glass at once.

He huffed out a short laugh and let his head fall then shift from side to side to relieve tension. I couldn't tell if he actually wanted to talk or if he was staying to watch over Althea, or more so Cornelius.

"It's flattering that you pretend to care for my tensity," he said, bringing his head back up and meeting my confused, blinking eyes. "Forgive me. It has been a long and frustrating day. Many disappointments and interruptions," he continued when I kept quiet.

I drained the rest of my glass and set it on the low table near my empty dinner plate, sitting back on the couch and looking back out the doors. The sun had set not long ago and the last bits of gold and purple were quickly giving way to inky black.

"Yamir will be posted outside the suite tonight." His voice sounded tired.

"If you think that's necessary," I sighed. My mind was sluggish, but I also felt restless with little movement through the day.

"I don't think it's too prudent to provide a first line of defense."

"Understood."

"Do you think you'll have a bedmate tonight?" he teased.

"If that's where she is comfortable, I have no objections. It's not as if I have any reason to turn her away." I wasn't sure if my cheek would be appreciated.

"I suppose you don't." It wasn't.

He stood and began to walk to the door, but stopped half way without turning around. Apprehension in his stance as if he were conflicted on what to say or do, but I wasn't sure why. I looked from him, around the room, then back to the terrace half expecting to hear the door shut.

"Earlier, after lunch," He paused as I looked up at him as he turned to face me, his hands sliding into his slacks pockets, "I-..."

He stood waiting for me to speak, but was met with continued silence. He'd taken off his suit jacket earlier and rolled up the sleeves of his shirt, the top two buttons undone. The feeling of need started to bubble up in my chest at the sight of his bare skin and tattoo, an unexpected want heating and cooling me as my eyes roamed over his muscular body. An overwhelming sensation began to creep through me and settled between my thighs. I opened my mouth, but before anything could come out he was crouching over me, hands on the edges of the couch, holding himself above me. His mouth lingering a breath away from mine, his scent sweeping over and through me as I took a shallow gasp. I could feel my skin through my clothes begging for his touch, but I pushed my hands further into the seat cushion to stabilize myself.

His eyes black and cloudy were searching my face and pausing on my lips, parting his own, waiting for me to make the choice. My shoulders quaked as ragged breaths left my rigid lungs.

"Is everything alright?" Came Althea's voice from the balcony doorway, shaking us from our entanglement.

"Of course, My Lady." Talos straightened and looked towards her and Cornelius who were standing together with stunned expressions.

"Um. Well, Neil has invited us to accompany him and his father to the city tomorrow afternoon. I have a bit of shopping to do and they have meetings with the township leaders." She was shifting her gaze between Talos and me waiting for one of us to speak.

"That sounds lovely, but..." I looked to Talos.

"I will inform Amil to be ready to leave when you are ready. One of our men will drive you and Isabella." He looked to me, then back to Althea who looked crushed but didn't want to reveal it.

"It's settled then. My dearest, I have to finish up some work before turning in. I will see you and Ms. Isabella tomorrow morning for breakfast, then we will set out on our adventure," Cornelius squeezed Althea's hand at the crook of his arm then continued, "Goodnight, everyone."

He smiled at all of us before walking out of the suite doors. Talos watched after him as he passed. Looking back to Althea, he bid her goodnight, but only gave me a nod, not fully lifting his eyes to mine and leaving quickly.

"What was that all about?" Althea crossed her arms and watched Talos shut the door behind him.

"I should shower and get ready for bed." I rose and began walking to my room.

"Isa, would it be okay if I slept in your room again tonight?" I smiled at her and nodded my head, the casualness in her voice sounded as though we were friends having a sleepover.

She returned the warm smile and went to her room to clean up and change. Not long after I had bathed and dressed for bed, Althea came in and nestled down beside me in bed with a book, a pad of paper, and a very expensive looking pen. She scribbled notes and lists for a while, then read until after I had fallen asleep. I wasn't sure when she had finally gone to sleep herself, but her side table light was still on when I heard a knock on the door in the morning to alert us that breakfast was to arrive soon.

# CHAPTER TEN

T he morning was filled with a quick breakfast, Cornelius
giving us the schedule of the afternoon, getting dressed,
and trying to hide as many weapons on my body without it
being too obvious. Cornelius and his father thought I was just a
close friend, Isabella, who was along to help with wedding planning. And as Talos had questioned their intentions, I was to
keep my true identity hidden as long as possible, which
included concealing the seven throwing knives and Alexandrite
dagger.

When Amil knocked on the door to tell us it was time to
leave, I gave myself one last once over in the mirror and
couldn't see any outlines against my clothing. The body-
forming weapon guard under my clothing was perfect for
discrete assignments. Over the guard I wore more lax fitting
clothing, including a black blouse that I tucked into a flowing
knee-length peach skirt that sat right above my navel. The skirt
masked the dagger's sheath strapped to my thigh. A trained eye
may have been able to catch it, but I wasn't worried about the
Welps taking notice.

Amil looked me up and down in the hallway, one corner of his lips turning up into a smirk. "Five."

"What?"

"I count five weapons on you right now." He adjusted his cufflinks.

"A very close guess." I winked and his smirk turned to a wide grin, running his bottom lip between his perfect teeth.

I immediately regretted engaging with him, even if it was harmless banter. Talos had requested that I not distract Amil or Yamir, but hadn't explicitly told me not to speak to them. In fact, how was I supposed to effectively work with his team if I wasn't supposed to talk to them without fear of distracting them? A feeling of annoyance and disdain started to burrow into my stomach. The previous insinuation that I was a hindrance and disgust for these men who couldn't put their positions before their hormones or whatever was driving their kind to become disturbed in the first place was maddening.

Althea joined me in the hallway moments later and we, along with Amil, made our way down to the first floor entryway to meet with Cornelius and his father, Stavros. They both looked very handsome and slightly overdressed for a simple meeting with the township leaders of their cities. They both wore black slacks and black jackets with silver butterflies and green vines embroidered midway up the sleeves. Two cars were waiting for us out in the drive just outside the door.

Althea kissed Cornelius on the cheek before bounding into the car that Amil would be driving for the two of us. Amil opened the back passenger side door for her, then rounded the back of the vehicle alongside me and opened my door. He stepped back and gave me a mocking dip of his chin as I rolled my eyes and slid into the seat behind his.

We were to meet with the Welps right after lunch. Althea had her pad of paper and as we pulled away from the manor and down the long driveway, she started going through the plans she had for the three of us before our rendezvous. I looked to the front windshield and caught sight of the rear view mirror and Amil's eyes darting away from mine. I tried to give all my attention to Althea's lengthy shopping list in order to avoid any wandering glances from our driver.

Our first several stops were luxury clothing stores, two different cosmetic stores, a lingerie store, then finally a shoe store where we spent a good portion of our time matching shoes to outfits that Althea had bought previously. Amil had no chance to be brazen with his arms laden with bags and boxes. I held three bags of some essentials, if anything to look less suspicious for anyone who might be keeping tabs on my behavior or the whereabouts of our group. It was better to look blended in.

After loading the car up, we started towards the restaurant to which the Welps had made a reservation for us. The small cafe had cleared out a whole corner of the indoor seating area for us even though we only took up one little table. They insisted that the Lords had paid them handsomely to give us a private meal, but it also helped Amil and I keep an eye on who was passing in and out of the front door. We were treated to a full tasting menu of the chef's choice. Many dishes had meats and vegetables that were grown locally, the spices exotic and fragrant. Every side dish was full of bursts of color. I couldn't remember the last time I had eaten at a restaurant outside of Cinder City that had been so enjoyable.

The owners came to check in and brought out the chef. It seemed they were all Fata from the same family. They all shared a very distinct, sharp facial structure and their ears looked to be pinned to the sides of their heads. Without those features, I would've thought they were Mortals. The chef explained how he came up with our meal's menu, modeling it after all that the surrounding areas had to offer: the local farmers who only sold to local restaurants, butchers who only raised enough animals that their land could support ethically, and every detail of how the honey was a cooperation between the two. I didn't leave one morsel on my plate and appreciated every effort in the experience the cafe was providing. I made a mental note to find a place like this in Cinder.

When we were done and had thanked the proprietors several times for their hospitality and warmth, we got back in the car to meet with the Lords at their offices several blocks away. They had a large, high-rise building at the heart of the city of Arta. Pure black stone studded the building along with large glossy windows. It was beautiful, but daunting compared to the many pale colored buildings covered in ivy on either side of it.

Cornelius met us in the lobby to escort us to the top floor conference room. Several men silently sat around a large, polished oak table. The hairs on the back of my neck and the sudden wrenching of my stomach were telling me to run. My instincts were rarely wrong, but I was having a hard time trying to come up with a diversion. Althea held Cornelius' hand as he led her to a chair near what I assumed was the head of the table, next to his father. He stood behind her chair for a moment before pulling the chair next to hers out, indicating for me to sit. I glanced up at Amil who was stone-faced, his whole body poised, which didn't make my unsettled feelings calm.

"I'm fine standing, thank you." I tried to sound sweet.

"Nonsense, I'm sure my darling has had you both traipsing around the whole city to shop. You must be tired." He tipped his hand to the chair, more insistent this time.

I nodded and moved towards the chair, but caught Amil's hand and squeezed gently, hoping to alert him that I was also wary about our current situation. He gave me a light tug in response and sat in the chair closest to the door.

A few seats down from me Stavros was stoic, two fingers to his temple as he waited for his son to sit down for the meeting to continue. One of the unfamiliar men cleared his voice and looked to the Welps before he started to speak of cattle lands, trade with surrounding lordships, his constituents' issues with how high their taxes were, and about a dozen other grievances. He was dressed smartly in a three-piece, light grey suit. He seemed older than the rest of the men at the table and was either a well blending Fata or Mortal. I couldn't tell from where I sat, but since he addressed the men we were with as "Lord", it was safe to say that he was either a very high profile Mortal or inner circle Fata.

After he was done with his rant, he turned to his right to a younger Fata gentleman who introduced himself as Lawrence. He was dressed in a deep blue jacket with silver stars embroidered around his sleeve cuffs. He had white, blond hair slicked to the side and brushed against the tips of his extended pointed ears, the edges of which were pierced with silver hoops. I'd never seen a Fata like him before, but there were many Fata I hadn't seen outside of Cinder. He straightened his lapels as he spoke of his farmers' crops, their livelihood being threatened by new trade deals with Cinder City.

My city.

He glanced to me, gave me a quick once over, and turned his attention back to Stavros. I looked to Amil who had watched the whole silent exchange very closely. I was becoming more curious as to why I was even permitted into this room, why Althea was being invited so close to the wedding date.

But then it hit me, she would be merging the two lordships. Hers and Cornelius' union would make these men's issues her own. She would have to sort out whatever underground dealings were being done behind the backs of Mortals like myself. How all of this was being conducted without Mortals having any idea was baffling. We voted in our government officials every five years. Very rarely had our leaders been Incubo, and I'd always thought they preferred staying out of Mortal lives and government. Having little interest in our foreign policies and never once being an ally in wars or disagreements amongst ourselves, I hadn't considered that they were pulling the strings behind the curtains, or that they had any interest in the beings they lived amongst.

This concern didn't seem to bother Althea, she was too busy writing on her notepad, probably more notes about the wedding. It wasn't until the last man, an older Incubo gentleman, stood up to speak that Stavros straightened in his seat to hear what the man had to say.

"My Lords, we have done all we can to support this agreement, but the unrest from our citizens is becoming too loud to ignore. I strongly suggest you agree to our demands or we will be forced to terminate our ties." He did not sit, his fingertips pressed into the table as he crouched over its polished edge.

Stavros exhaled and shook his head then faced his son who was gazing at the man standing with his mouth slighting agape. Stunned, they were both lost for words and that was causing the other men around the table to shift in their seats. Unrest was mounting in their lands and in this room, the tension becoming palpable. I shot a look to Amil. He was sitting on the edge of his seat, elbows on his knees, hands laced below his chin. He was primed to pounce if needed.

"Damon, the demands you have are difficult to navigate at this time. Perhaps after the wedding," Stavros gave a gliding wave of his hand in Cornelius and Althea's direction, "we could discuss next steps of the merger and land acquisitions."

Damon slammed his fist onto the table, and my hand darted for the weapon at my thigh beneath my skirt. From the look on her face, Althea was also taken aback. She grabbed Cornelius' hand on the table and every being in the room was waiting for the next move.

"You speak as if we haven't given you this throne, that you didn't give promises you knew you were not going to retain in order to keep your family's hold on these lands." His voice was deadly cold.

In a flash, he pulled a gun from his waistband and pointed it at Stavros. I unsheathed the dagger and waited. My heart pounding in my chest, I quickly glanced to Amil for his reaction, but he hadn't moved. He sat waiting, the smoke in his eyes turning black, but far more vicious than I had seen it.

"Put it down, Damon." Came the casual voice of Lawrence in the star-studded blue suit. "We don't need their blood on our hands."

Damon lowered his weapon, but did not holster it. Lawrence straightened, weaved his fingers together, and set his forearms on the table. He looked up at Damon, then to Stavros and parted his lips in a smug smile.

"What Damon is trying to convey so heatedly is that our situations are dire. If we do not come to some sort of new and improved agreement, you will be dealing with our forced replacements and our heads will be at your pretty doorstep. Literally." Cunning venom dripped from his words. He was not going to let what he was inferring to happen, but it was a threat he was not unprepared to handle.

He wouldn't let Stavros be the end of him without a fight or revenge already in play. I'd been the tool in those games dozens of times and each paid well enough that I never bothered to ask questions. I wouldn't be surprised if he already had an assassin, possibly even a Banner, in mind for the task if this meeting went south, which it clearly was. I needed to get Althea out of this room before the bloodshed started. The warmth of my blade's hilt was growing to a burn in anticipation of the next man who decided to become brave.

Cornelius got to his feet, Althea clinging to his hand still. He was attempting to stare down both of the men, but neither of them were showing any indication of worry. He opened his mouth to speak, but an ear splitting bang rang through the room. Althea's scream was all I heard as I dove under the table, blade in my hand, landing almost on top of Althea as I pulled her underneath the table with me. The feet of men around us began to rush towards one another while another gun sounded off. I drug Althea by the arm towards the door we had come in, but we were blocked by someone in a pair of black slacks. I slashed at their ankle and they jumped aside howling in pain. I pushed Althea ahead of me, but told her to keep low, sheathing the dagger as we leapt out from under the table.

She reached the door and frantically tried to turn the handle, but it was either locked or she was too distressed by the scuffle around us. I turned around to look for Amil. He was holding one of the men in a headlock and using him as a shield as Stavros and Cornelius had crouched behind him trying to make it to the door. I spotted Damon aiming for Amil and reacted: throwing a blade from my chest into his upper arm. He shrieked in pain and dropped the gun, but another weapon had appeared in one of the other men's hands before I reached to try the doorknob.

I pulled my blouse up and unstrapped two more throwing knives. I aimed for the man's hand and thigh. The impact on his thigh landed before he could jump out of the way, and he went down at Lawrence's feet who was backed against a wall, his eyes on me and his expression a mixture of intrigue and being pleasantly surprised. I grabbed a fourth blade and threw it, pinning him by his jacket to the wall behind him, not allowing him to attempt to join in on the scuffle. If he had any fear, he didn't show it.

Amil, having enough time to reach the door and break through it, pushed Althea through the splintered doorway then pulled me through behind him. Stavros and Cornelius appeared next to me to lead us to the emergency stairs, the fire alarm going off as we opened the door. It was then, standing on the landing, that I realized that Althea was hurt. She had blood staining her clothing, but I couldn't tell where the source was. Amil saw where my line of sight was focused and moved to gather her up in his arms before carefully descending the stairs. Security met us about halfway down. A few kept running towards the top floor while two others stayed with us to escort us completely out of the building.

Once outside, police had arrived and were roping off the entrance. Stavros turned to Amil. "Take the ladies back to the manor; we will deal with this."

# CHAPTER ELEVEN

"What were you thinking? You could have gotten Althea killed!" Talos paced the floor of the suite after we returned. He had already heard what had happened and was furious but taking it out on me.

"I was keeping to this ridiculous story you've weaved about me being her friend and not her last line of defense from these wolves who are trying to rip her throat out." I took a heavy breath, trying to steady my anger.

"You don't seem to have an issue with seducing then executing your marks. How is it so difficult to fulfill this expectation?" He stopped but still didn't meet my eye.

I clenched my jaw. He wasn't wrong, but it was much easier to cut someone's throat and leave them to bleed out on a hotel bed than to convince a room full of businessmen not to shoot and kill two young women when their power is on the line.

Althea had been seen by the Welps' doctor who found only a flesh wound on her side. After a couple stitches, she went to her room and was in tears worried sick about Cornelius. She refused dinner and all of her bags and boxes from shopping were piled up in the sitting room next to one of the couches.

"I shouldn't have allowed her to go. I should have known better than to trust this to someone like you."

"You hired me, remember? I did not seek out a deadly babysitting position." I stood near my closed bedroom door with my arms crossed at my chest. He had come in so fast that I hadn't had a chance to put my weapons or shopping bags away.

"I did hire you. I was told that you were discrete and could get the job done better than anyone else." His anger started to reach his voice heavier now.

"My assignments don't normally involve me keeping others around me alive. I'm trained to kill anyone who is in my way which makes diplomatic meetings more difficult when I'm posing as a timid companion."

He began pacing again, hands clasped behind his back. I stood with my arms wrapped around myself waiting for his next outburst. Amil stood at the door of the suite, silently inspecting his shoes. Talos hadn't rounded on him yet, but surely would soon.

"She is the future of my kind. The future that affects not only Incubo, but the rest of this country. And you almost let some filthy traitor shoot her in the head." He had found his second wind of anger and his voice boomed across the room.

"I hired you to protect her, to use your training to sense danger and predict what these men have coming next! I was unaware that you were only skilled at killing men with their pants around their ankles as you posed as a Temptress!" He picked up a vase from the low table and threw it against the wall only feet from me, glass bursting into hundreds of shards spilling over the wooden floor.

Out of the corner of my eye, Amil had taken a step forward to put himself between us if necessary. I took a deep breath and didn't give any emotion away. The attacks on my profession and character were out of fear, I knew, but biting my tongue was more telling of my strength than arguing with him.

"The wound was from the broken door as we escaped. Damon or any other being in that room would not have been able to put pressure on a trigger if I thought they would turn the gun on her. He was aiming for Stavros." This was the truth. I had been ready if Damon had looked to Althea with any malicious intent.

He strode over to the sofa that faced the door to my room, that faced me. Sitting and propping his arms up on his knees, head in his hands. I briefly looked to Amil, his eyes meeting mine, his expression anguished. He'd also failed Talos today. Neither of us had a good feeling about that meeting from the moment we entered the conference room, but had no way of knowing how badly it would go so quickly.

"I know how important this union is, how important she is —" I began, but he cut me off.

"She is more vital to me than the air in my lungs, than the blood in my heart and veins," he said unnaturally calmly, raising his eyes to meet mine, the pain on his face almost unbearable.

My anger melted away as something inside of me wanted to desperately comfort him, soothe his mind and worry. I blinked away those thoughts and looked away from him to the window and pressed the top of my fist to my lips.

A small tap came at the door, and we all turned our attention towards it. Amil opened it a crack, nodded to the person on the other side, then shut it again.

"The Welps have returned, sir."

Talos looked to him, then back to me before standing and turning to leave. "Stay with them until I return. No one enters this room, no one leaves. Yamir will be on night watch." And he was gone.

Amil locked the door behind him and crossed the room to stand in front of me. He looked down to me, only a couple feet between us, and slid his hands into his pockets.

"Are you hurt?" He looked me over and met my eyes again.

"I'm fine. Just need to change." I fingered a small rip on my blouse near my stomach.

He slowly raised one of his hands and smoothed a finger over a small cut on my cheek. He moved a half step closer to me, but I took a small step back, only inches from my door.

"I'm sorry. I should have gotten you and Althea out of there sooner." His voice was remorseful and disappointed in his own failure.

"Don't. We both knew, but we weren't given a choice until it was too late. She will be fine and we won't make that mistake again. If we both aren't fired after today." I tried to laugh, but it only sounded like an audible sigh.

He half smiled. "Well, I doubt I will be fired until we return to Cinder. Talos didn't bring enough of his own trusted men to replace me so easily."

"He does have a hard time trusting others, doesn't he?"

"When it comes to Lady Althea, no one is good enough to protect her. Not even him." The solemn look he gave me brought back the pang of helplessness I had felt as Talos spoke of Althea.

"Why is he so attached to her?" The question had come to me so many times, but I hadn't wanted to ask Talos himself, and even now Amil looked to be struggling to decide whether to tell me or not.

"Her mother, Alessandra, and Talos were lovers once. Alessandra's father didn't approve and betrothed her to Althea's father, Pytr. By cruelty, Talos was hired as the family's head of security after the union. Alessandra died in childbirth, and if you were to ask me, I believe Talos took it as a personal betrayal that her husband didn't do more to save her life. He has never left Althea's side; he has been there for every milestone, every heartbreak. She is as close to family as he has and it is by hierarchy bullshit that she is not his own daughter."

My mouth went dry, and my body began to tremble. My

chest started to feel uncomfortably sharp as I looked to Althea's closed door. Talos had lost so much, it was no wonder that he spoke so severely about the young woman he was sworn to protect. Painful realizations about the encounters Talos and I had shared started to come to the front of my mind. He had been so concerned with me being a distraction to Amil and Yamir, but it was him who had been using me as an escape and it almost resulted in Althea's death.

"Isa?" Amil's voice shook the thoughts from my eyes.

I met his gaze, the small flame-like reflection starting to cloud his dark, stormy eyes, a pulling sensation awakening in my stomach. He took a step closer, taking my hands in his and pressing me back against the door. Our fingers interlaced and our brows gently pressed together. His hips pressed to mine, and his steady deep breaths began falling onto my chest. The familiar tug in my stomach was becoming tighter as each one of his exhales cascaded down my lips and jaw. He smelled of woods, bergamot, and notes of persimmon. Closing my eyes, I let my chin lift, taking in his scent. He tightened his grip on my hands, willing me to inch closer, but with nowhere to move, he pressed his soft lips to mine.

He hummed as he exhaled and sounded relieved, letting go of my hands and trailing up my sides to cradle my face with both of his hands, fingers lingering in my hair. I slid my hands up his lower back, curling my fingers around his shirt.

The kiss was soft and sweet, but only lasted a few seconds before he pulled away, looking down at me and searching my face. The flame in his eyes was brighter than before. A breathless ache pulled on me, desperately wanting to feel his skin on mine. I opened my mouth to speak, but nothing came out.

"I should try to clean up this glass." He completely pulled out of our embrace and I felt as though my heart were trying to rip through my ribcage to follow him.

He turned and walked towards a small closet near the front door, apparently a cleaning cupboard. Without speaking, I turned into my room and shut the door behind me, leaning against it for support while I caught my breath and reeled in my senses.

# CHAPTER TWELVE

S everal hours later I sat in bed, reading over a police report that Talos had given me during his brief return to check on Althea and relieve Amil. I hadn't seen either Incubo leave. I hadn't even left my room since the argument and the kiss that followed. I had no deep attachment to either man when they weren't in the same room with me, and their attraction to me was as confusing as the emotions I felt when they were around. That first moment I had been alone in that elevator with Talos, I'd felt as if he were reaching out for me. Some sort of imme-diate spark between us. But he had known who and what I was then, had been looking for someone like me for an assignment. I doubt his actions were some sort of love at first sight reaction and, as he said, Incubo have urges they have a hard time controlling when they see someone or something they even remotely like.

Amil, on the other hand, was surprised by me on the train. He had seen me as an ally and fellow employee to flirt with in passing. Then he saw me called into action, and we worked together to save Althea. I could only think that the reason he stopped our encounter earlier was out of respect for Talos. I had no idea if they'd had a conversation about me together, if Talos had warned him to stay away from me in any other aspects besides protecting Althea. It wouldn't have been overstepping or out of his reach as our employer.

I had been reading the same paragraph about a dozen times when I heard a knock on my door.

"Come in." I tried to make my voice sound warm and not as confused or frustrated as I really was.

I'd expected to see Althea walk through the door, but it was Talos. I furrowed my brows and irritation hung on my face.

"Althea is sleeping in her own room tonight."

Had he been in her room this whole time?

He was still in the same slacks he was wearing earlier, but his jacket was gone. The sleeves of his shirt were rolled up, his tie hanging loosely around his shoulders. Looking to the floor, he slid his hands into his pockets and only took a few steps into the room.

"I wanted to speak with you about our discussion earlier. I let my temper get the best of me and I wanted to apologize." He looked up to me and I nodded as a sign of understanding, but didn't speak.

He took a few more steps to the foot of the bed and leaned against the bedpost. Letting loose a sigh, his shoulders dropped as he looked me over. I wasn't sure what to say, his emotions during our last conversation were heated, but I hadn't taken it personally. His apologies weren't needed or an obligation, so him being in my room was unexpected unless he wanted something more. Something I was willing to do not long ago with Amil.

"It's pretty late, I should probably go to sleep. Have to be alert for any more high stake business meetings. Unless you are no longer in need of my services, then I can go back to catching pantless men off guard." I crossed my arms over my abdomen.

"Unfortunately for them, I will still be in need of your skills a while longer." He gave me a crooked smirk.

"If you didn't trust the Welps today, why allow us to leave with them?" The question had been bothering me all evening and I was starting to feel annoyed at how easily he was shifting the tension in the room from remorse to playful.

"I actually thought today would be a good day for me to let go a little bit. To try to put trust in Cornelius, to the men Althea would be depending on from now on, but—"

"That went awry." I rolled my eyes, but smiled. "If it's worth anything, Cornelius did put Althea first when hell broke loose."

"She told me." He took another step closer to where I sat up on the bed. "She also said she owes you her life."

"That's sweet of her, but not necessary." I felt a warmth for Althea, but also a guilt that she had been in danger at all.

He nodded, then sat by my side, propping his arms on his knees and looking to the ground between his feet. I wanted badly to caress his arm, that feeling of need to comfort him digging at my chest again. He looked over to me, his eyes cloudy and focused instantly on mine. A tumbling flutter started in my stomach and ended between my thighs, his pull starting to take hold of me. I should've told him to leave, told him what had happened between Amil and I after he had left this afternoon, but I couldn't. All I could do was watch as his eyes went from thin ash-smoke to a color resembling a cloudy night sky.

He reached up and tucked a lock of my hair behind my ear then let his hand fall gently to my lap, his eyes tracing to my mouth. I don't know who moved first, or if I even had control of my own body at that moment, but within a breath our lips met. His hand gripped my thigh, slightly tugging to invite me closer. My hands found his chest as I pulled at the buttons on his shirt. I sat up on my knees, getting closer to him. His shirt came off and he went for my camisole next. He stood up and pulled the blanket back, and took his belt off as I shimmied off my sleep pants and sat back to watch him.

His pants and undershorts fell to the floor as he removed the rest of his clothes. Placing one knee then the other between my legs, he separated them. Dropping his mouth down to mine, he kissed me deeply causing an eruption of butterflies in my gut. Propping himself up on one arm, he ran the other hand up my body and cupped my breast, squeezing gently and running a finger over its rigid peak. A small moan escaped me, which he returned with a grave exhale. His mouth replaced his thumb, hot, wet breath tumbling over my chest as his tongue flicked over and around my breast. I moved my hips against him, breathing in sharply and arching my back—wanting him to consume every inch of me.

He slid his arm underneath my lower back and moved to the side, taking me with him so that I was now straddling him with my hands on his chest. His hardness pressed against me and his hands found my hips and gripped me, moving me roughly over him. Throbbing bloomed between my thighs as I rocked my hips along with his motion, feeling intense pressure gripping inside of me.

My fingertips dug into his skin, causing him to moan. He lifted my hips slightly and pulled me back down onto him, sending a rush of pleasure up through me. One of my hands found stability on the headboard as each to and fro of my hips pushed me closer and closer to the edge. He cursed under his breath as he spoke my name and pushed his hips up, plunging himself deeper inside of me. Both my hands now on the headboard, tension finding the breaking point and tossing me over the edge, jolts radiated through my core down through my thighs and toes. Moaning loudly, he pulled me harder onto him, his face pleased at my reaction.

Settling his hips down then lifting one of my legs to bring

himself out from under me, he moved behind me on his knees. He ran his hands up my sides, under my breasts, then wrapped his arms around my middle. I let one of my hands fall to his on my waist, but he forced it back to the headboard

"Don't you dare move" His voice rough and breathy in my ear.

The command made me whirl and obey. He held me close and entered me from behind. He pushed slowly and released, again and again, so slowly I thought my body would catch fire from deep inside. He paused, pulsation finding me again as he let go of my waist and his hands found my hips again. Palms and fingers gripped me and he began thrusting deeply, then rapidly, then deeply again, pushing me over the edge without stopping. I held on to the headboard as hard as I could as my body clenched around him. He slowed again, allowing me to catch my breath only for a moment before thrusting harder and deeper than before.

His husky exhales caused me to beg for more. But he stopped, leaning into my back and finding my ear.

"Tell me that you are mine." His voice thick and low, waiting for me to answer him. He eased further into me, agonizingly slow.

"I'm yours, Talos." My voice breathless, I'd never wanted anything more than for him to take me in anyway he chose.

"Again," he demanded, repeating the motion and waiting for me to obey.

"I'm yours!" I begged. "Please!"

He burst into rapid deep thrusting, and I hardly had a chance to take in a sharp breath. I spilled over again, my whole body becoming weak and collapsing onto the bed. Without missing a moment, he pushed me down into the bed, continuing his motions as I lay on my stomach. Gripping one of my shoulders as he moved, continuing to send me into pleasure again, I moaned into the pillow, holding on to it and curling my toes. My whole body began to feel wrecked, fire still pooling within me as he pulled out of me.

He bent low to me and kissed my shoulder. I lifted my head and arched my back, feeling his teeth glide over my skin, then light pressure at the nape of my neck, his teeth holding rather than biting. A low guttural sigh came from him and reverberated through me. I pushed up an arm against the mattress, bringing my shoulder closer to his body, and rolled over onto my back.

I pulled my knees up to his sides and over his chest. He kissed the inside of my calf then my inner thighs, spreading them as he settled between my legs. His mouth dipped and his tongue found my overly sensitive nerves with small circular motions. His hands eased under my rear and lifted me closer to his mouth. Throbbing tension jutted through me with every pass and suction of his lips. Another moan crept up my throat, I tried to stop it with my hand.

"I want to hear you scream," he spoke into me between strokes.

A curse and moan ripped out of me, my fingers combing through and grasping his hair. My hips rolled against his mouth which sent me over the edge once again, my legs clenching around him. He gave an amused huff and looked up. With my chest rising and falling rapidly, I tried to focus on his gaze, but he slid two fingers inside of me and dipped his mouth again, not breaking eye contact, causing me to immediately gasp but the air not fully reaching my lungs. With every sensitive part of me being teased, I called out his name with a curse. He withdrew his fingers and sat up on his knees, looking down on me, his lips coated in a wet sheen. He brought his fingers to his mouth and tasted me again before burying himself deep inside of me and bringing his body close to mine, our chests meeting.

I flung my arms around his neck and held him tightly as he thrusted deeper and faster. His breath in my ear became more and more gruff as he came closer to climax. Throbbing hard heat flooded me inside and out as he spilled over inside of me. Every pulse of his pleasure caressed me as his body became lax on top of me.

# CHAPTER THIRTEEN

When morning light started to stream through the curtains of my room, I rolled over to hide my eyes a little longer and found Talos lying next to me. Both of us naked and wrapped up in the sheets together. His chest rose and fell soothingly as he slept. A different kind of ache between my thighs reminded me of what had happened hours ago.

We'd fallen asleep in the afterglow euphoria. He looked as if he'd barely moved from where he collapsed next to me before I had rolled over to sleep. Still naked, and as quietly as I could manage, I padded to the bathroom to wash up. I started the shower to warm it up and turned around to look into the mirror. I could see some light fingertip-shaped bruises on the top of my shoulders, my hips, and legs. The feel of my fingers brushing against them sent a chill through me, and flashes of his skin on mine crossed my mind. He'd awakened something inside of me that no one before had. I'd never had someone like him, someone so determined to bring me to climax so many times before reaching it himself. By his reactions, I wasn't sure if it was more for my benefit or his own.

The steam from the shower started to fog the glass and fill

the air. It was almost a shame to wash off the last bit of his scent from my body, but I got in anyway. The warm water trailed down my body and between my thighs causing a small sting of satisfaction. I stood under the water for a while before washing myself to enjoy the calm escape, not knowing what Talos would do or say once he woke up. But then I heard the door open and close softly, and he stepped into the shower with me, his expression sleepy, but blissful.

"Good morning." He kissed me gently. "I hope you don't mind. I have a meeting in a few minutes and wouldn't want to miss my last opportunity to see you naked before I leave."

His smile was playful and caused my cheeks to flush as I moved aside for him to get under the shower. He turned his back to the water and ran both of his hands through his hair, his muscles perking and flexing with each movement. He gave a heavy sigh and ran wet hands over his face. I couldn't help but stare, letting my eyes feast upon his slender but muscular body, his brassy skin glistening under the water. Before I could stop myself, my hand was moving over his chest, then his stomach and lower still. He looked down at me, hungry again. He became hard in my hand as I stroked him gently.

He began to breathe heavier. He pressed one hand to the shower wall to balance and the other to my side, pulling me closer, the tip of him pressing into my stomach as I moved my hand up and down. I got down on my knees, taking him into my mouth and feeling him fill it as I moved my tongue to take in as much as I could. His hand gripped my damp hair, guiding me at the speed he craved. A low grumble from his throat, a curse under his breath, encouraged me to keep going. He held me still for a moment, deep in my mouth, as a gush of need filled my stomach. Letting go and letting me pull away to take a deep inhale, he pulled me to my feet and turned me around to the wall. I braced myself and lifted my leg up to the side of the tub as he pulled my hips closer to him, entering me sharply.

He cupped my breast and thrusted deep inside of me over and over again, this time not stopping as I spilled over the edge. He shuttered in his release from behind me while throbbing deep within me. He laid his head on my wet shoulder and pulled his hips away from me. I pushed off the wall and turned into his embrace, but he broke it abruptly.

"I'm going to be late, but not for lack of a good reason." He tilted my chin up and kissed me before getting out of the shower.

He wrapped a towel around his waist and left. A feeling of emptiness squeezed my chest, as if him leaving took something inside of me with him. The crushing sensation started to take hold of me and forced me to sit on the floor of the tub, water falling over me, taking in as much air as I could pull into my lungs. There was an ebbing, the tight grip starting to release, and a soothing calm washed over me. My head was full of lead and the pit in my stomach started to slowly close.

# CHAPTER FOURTEEN

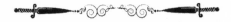

After dressing, I went out into the sitting room where coffee and breakfast pastries had been brought up. Althea was sitting on a couch sipping her tea and reading the paper. She looked up to me and smiled warmly before returning to the article.

"How are you feeling this morning?" I grabbed a muffin and took a bite as I sat down.

"Oh, I'm good as new." She lifted her shirt without looking to me and not a scratch remained where she was injured yesterday.

Shocked, I stared at her until she looked up to me when I hadn't given her a verbal response.

"It's a perk to being an Incubo. We are rapid healers, but it can take a very long rest depending on how wounded we are. Did you get much sleep last night?" The sip she took was telling.

"I slept fine. Thanks." I poured myself a cup of coffee, trying to avoid her gaze.

She smirked and went back to reading. We sat together for a while before she began filling me in on all the appointments she had set up for us to take in our suite. Apparently, there was a mishap with the decorations not matching with flowers so the gardener and the decorator were coming for a joint meeting, and the wedding planner was coming back with samples of linens for the tables and napkins. If the events in the boardroom upset her, she wasn't showing it.

Cornelius was to join us for lunch, but his father and Talos would be in meetings of their own all day. There was a spark in her eye as she searched my face for a response to not seeing Talos for the rest of the day, but I didn't have to pretend to not be interested in seeing him. The feeling I had when he left earlier still had me reeling, and I wasn't sure I wanted to experience that again, no matter how good the sex was. I needed time to myself to sort out what my feelings were and what were amplified feelings being projected onto me during heated moments.

I sipped my coffee and Althea began picking apart a pastry, eating small pieces at a time, likely not wanting to smudge her ruby red lipstick. I decided it was as good a time as any to ask her a few questions about herself, her kind, and Talos.

"Althea, do you... umm, do you feel things?" She looked up to me over her paper, one brow raised. "From me?"

She folded up the paper and set it down on the low table, scooted over to the edge of the sofa, and scrunched her nose at me. She looked me over, then curiously reached out her hand and placed it on my knee before closing her eyes.

"Well?" I cocked my head, waiting for her verdict.

"You are confused... and hungry." She giggled and sat up straight again, removing her hand from my knee.

"Very funny." I shook my head. "I just mean, Talos has said—
"

"He said that they can feel when you're flustered, or angry? Yes, male Incubo can feel many things from Mortals and Fata. It's completely sexist, but that's how it is. I'm sure it has something to do with mating, but they rarely care to tap into those skills when it comes to female Incubo." She sighed and tossed her arms in the air, exasperated.

"So they can control it?"

"Not always. They've had years of practice holding back emotions from other Incubo, so when they are around Fata or Mortals, it can get a little intoxicating to them and in turn the objects of their desire."

"The feelings I have around them are not mine then?" I was starting to feel silly asking her these questions that I should know about myself.

"I can't really answer that, Isa. I can only imagine the incertitude you must be feeling from the both of them. Sometimes it's an intensification or amplification of feelings you could be having, or it could be them projecting and implanting their feelings onto you. Then it could be a mixture of each. The exchange of emotions between species can be toxic. These things aren't studied or certain and could be different for every being." She shrugged and truly looked sorry that she couldn't clear up any of my concerns.

"And you have special abilities. Is telekinesis a skill all Incubo women have?" I asked as she picked up her teacup without use of her hands.

"Actually, I'm not sure. I've not encountered many Incubo at all who have my gift. And it's not well developed. It's taken years of lessons and practice and concentration to manipulate flatware." She sounded disheartened.

I'd only seen her gift twice and wondered what abilities other Incubo possessed. I didn't ask any further questions, but nodded in understanding and was further frustrated by both Talos and Amil's attention.

"Isa, Talos is a good man, but I wouldn't be a good friend if I didn't warn you to be careful around him. He has never taken to anyone for long." With that she picked her paper back up and began reading again, likely hiding after practically betraying her oldest friend for her newest.

We sat in silence until the wedding planner arrived for the meeting with Althea. The planner arrived loudly and began a lengthy conversation about the guest list which I decided would be a good time for me to check emails and assets. With the first notification, I saw an email from Zaida:


*Isa,*

  *Argo has gone dark. We need to speak. Call me.*
  *-Z*


It felt like a large rock was sitting in my stomach. Argo hadn't been seen or heard from in the few days before I had started this assignment, and that either meant he hadn't been checking in or hadn't finished his assignment. He was either dead or going to be very soon. Only half a year younger than me, Argo was always what I thought having a kid brother might be like. Strong-willed, thick-headed, he was too good at his skills, but not cautious enough. This isn't the first time I'd gotten a message similar to this, and I was the one who had to go after him and save him from being skinned alive by a mark. But I wouldn't be able to leave Althea, not after the attack yesterday.

I went to the door and opened it. Amil was standing outside on duty for the afternoon. He gave me a quick glance, but didn't speak. Standing with his hands clasped in front of him, he looked down the hall away from me to avoid me further.

"I need to make a call. Can you sit with Althea?" He nodded, but still didn't meet my eyes as he passed me in the doorway, closing it quickly behind him.

I'd have to talk to him later...or not. I didn't know what to say to him after what had happened with Talos last night and this morning. If Amil saw Talos leave earlier, he would already know that Talos had been with me all night. Unsure if that was the source of his cold shoulder, I walked down the hall to find a room that I could duck into.

When I found an empty study full of old books and one lonely hardwood desk sitting in the middle of it, I pulled the door shut and locked it. I found the furthest corner of the room and faced the wall to muffle my voice. Pulling out my secure line cell phone, I dialed Zaida's number which I knew by heart. I knew all the Black Banner secure lines. If something were to ever go wrong I had several numbers to call. The other line only rang once before she answered.

"We do not shy away from the dark," she answered.

"For we are the shadows," I recited our code to assure her I was alone.

"Argo hasn't been seen in over two weeks, I've sent Talia and Deric, but neither could find him. He was supposed to be done with his assignment three days ago."

"What was his assignment?"

"He said it was a reconnaissance job on a senator from Amples. His employer wanted dirt for a campaign to run against them next session." Her voice wasn't worried, but a little annoyed.

We typically weren't hired for such menial tasks, our skills far too advanced and expensive for common spy work, but Argo liked to take odd jobs to keep himself busy. Amples was south of Cinder by three hundred miles, but it was a major city that was the largest producer of emerging technologies in the country. Several of the companies based there provide work for half the country alone, making it the richest city and the largest in the lower lands. Which would make tracking Argo down much harder than I expected; I wasn't surprised Talia and Deric couldn't find him.

"What can I do? My assignment isn't over yet."

"Reach out to his lines. After the last time you saved his ass, he owes you. If he's still alive." I didn't want to think about the alternative.

The twelve of us all had our strengths and weaknesses, but we always had each other's backs when assignments or life became rough. We didn't always get along, but the respect was ingrained into us from the moment we met. We were all we had. But Argo could be crass at times and not return messages if he didn't feel they were important. I hoped this was one of those moments.

"I'll call him now and let you know by email. I can't talk long."

"Be careful, I've been hearing the Incubo have been meeting more often than usual here in Cinder. Fata have been whispering that there is supposed to be a shift in power within the Incubo's ranks." The union I was protecting was the reason for that, but I couldn't tell her.

"Stay vigilant." And with that I heard the click of her line ending.

I dialed Argo's number. My heart pounded against my ribs as the first and second rings went unanswered. The third brought me more dread and panic, but I wouldn't leave my post to go after him. If he were dead, his body would have been delivered by now. But if he were still on assignment, he was breaking protocol by not checking in. If he had finished the mission and still had not reported back, he was going to have to contend with Zaida, Talia, Deric, and then me when I was done here with Althea. On the fourth ring, the line was answered, but the other end was silent.

"We do not have fear." I waited, my stomach turning.

"For we are terror..." His voice sounded rough, cracked, broken.

"Where are you?" Anger started to rise in my throat.

"Amples," he whispered "Isa." His voice faded with distance.

"Are you safe?"

"No." Came a male voice I didn't recognize on the other end.

I swallowed hard, fighting the fear growing in my chest and the stinging in my eyes. Argo was in trouble and I couldn't reach him.

"What do you want?"

"We will be in touch, Isa." And the line went dead.

I clapped my hand over my mouth as hot tears began to fall. I had to tell Zaida and the others. Talia and Deric may still be in the city. I called Talia first. Her line went straight to voicemail. I called Deric.

"Isa?" His answer so frantic, he didn't bother using our code.

"Deric, are you safe?"

"Yes, but Talia is hurt. We are on our way to the hospital now. Argo's—"

"I know. What's happened to Talia?"

"She'll be fine, but I need to get her to the hospital. I'll send word after. Keep watchful until you hear from me. I have to go." A click then nothing.

Next I called Zaida, but her phone went to voicemail. I assumed she was now on her way to the nearest trainway to get to Amples, to Talia. To our family. And here I was in the middle of an assignment hundreds of miles away.

After a few moments to pull myself together, I headed back to the suite and Amil was standing outside the door again. He looked down at my puffy eyes and raised a brow in question, but I ignored him. I started to open the door, but found it locked. My eyes shot to his.

"Talos needed to speak to Althea and Cornelius. He said it was private."

I looked somberly to the door, wondering if I should knock or wait, not sure of what Talos' reaction would be to find that I had left the suite with Althea alone with Amil and the wedding planner. A little late to worry about it then.

"Is everything alright?" I met his gaze, concern in his voice.

"Just some family issues." Not fully lying.

I turned and walked to the wall on the opposite side of the hallway, leaning against it and crossing my arms. The worry still filled my chest, tightening around my lungs and making it hard to breathe or think of anything other than the unknown man's voice who had Argo. Him being alive was a relief, but also detrimental. He answered with our code, that information now available to whomever else was in the room with him.

"Isa?" Amil took a few steps closer to me.

"My... brother. He's in trouble and I can't help him. It's the downside to jobs like ours. My other siblings are on it but—" Another step closer to me, his eyes searching my face.

The door to the suite opened then and Talos stood in the doorway. He looked the both of us over, then spoke to Amil.

"I'll be back in two days. You and Yamir will be trading off shifts as you have. Althea doesn't leave the grounds." I looked from Talos to Amil, both giving a nod of understanding before Talos turned to me.

"Do not leave her side again. Whatever the issue is, it will have to wait until I get back." I nodded, already knowing this.

He turned and started down the hall. Amil and I looked at each other then watched after him as he turned to descend the stairs to the lower levels.

"What was that about?"

"A meeting has been set with Althea's father and Stavros. Talos is traveling back to Cinder to escort Pytr here." He looked back to me, and I didn't bother to respond.

It was a slight relief to hear that Talos would be gone for a few days, but that also made any chance of me going to find Argo more impossible. I moved past Amil into the suite and found Cornelius and Althea out on the balcony in a close embrace. I sat at the sofas and wrote a short email to Zaida, asking for an update on Talia as soon as possible. I began an email to Deric but decided against it. He would contact me when he had a moment. I put my laptop away as lunch was being brought in, but I couldn't eat with all the knots in my stomach. Argo's short words still filled my head. Deric's haste to get Talia medical help plagued me. And here I was, picking at a plate of roasted duck in a citrus reduction.

# CHAPTER FIFTEEN

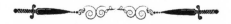

The rest of the day was a blur of wedding plans and checking my email for updates. Before I retreated to my room for the evening, Deric finally updated me on Talia. They had been in an area where they had heard Argo was staying, but the informant was compromised and had sold them all out. They had been cornered by Fata who worked for the would-be opposing senator in the hotel Argo had been staying. They escaped, but only barely. Talia was shot in the shoulder, but no major arteries or organs were hit. She had been in surgery for hours, but was resting and would be transferred to Cinder in the next few days if there was no sign of infection. I replied with the very skint information I had from my call to Argo earlier and waited for Deric or Zaida to respond, but fell asleep with the computer open next to me in bed.

The next morning I hadn't heard anything from anyone. Not my fellow Banners or the kidnappers who were holding Argo. I came out to the shared sitting room to find Althea and Cornelius sharing breakfast and snuggling on the middle sofa. Since Talos had left, Cornelius had only left long enough to sleep in his own room. It was customary for the bride and groom to sleep apart until their union, and with Yamir at our suite door all night, I was sure they were upholding that tradition.

I joined them in the center of the room and poured myself some coffee. As I sat down they both looked at me, Althea giggling. I hadn't dressed for the day yet and felt exhausted. But the couple cooed and giggled amongst themselves, letting me wallow a bit longer.

They wanted to spend the day together on the grounds. Cornelius had planned a picnic lunch, a horseback ride, and lounging in the large flower garden for himself and his bride. Feeling like an awkward third wheel, I waited for Cornelius to leave and check in with his father to remind Althea that I was to stay by her side at all times.

"It might be a little strange if I'm accompanying you on your romantic day alone."

"Oh Isa, don't be silly! Talos left the other grounds guards, Amil, and Yamir. You don't have to come with us. Take the day for yourself." She began bouncing off to her room before I stopped her.

"Althea, Talos explicitly told me not to leave your side while he was gone." I crossed my arms.

She sighed and her shoulders slumped. She turned to me and hugged herself, her expression not angry or rebellious, but disappointed.

"I only wanted to pretend we weren't in constant danger for one afternoon." I really did feel for her, both of them.

"Amil and I will keep our distance, but any sign of danger, and you will have to take my direction only," I bargained, her face lighting up with glee again.

"Thank you, Isa!"

She continued her bouncing to her room to get ready, and I checked my email one last time. Nothing. I walked to the suite door and opened it. Amil was standing guard as instructed, dressed in a light blue-grey suit and a white under shirt that complimented his deep complexion. He turned his attention to me in the doorway, waiting for me to speak.

"Hope you're ready for an outing." He raised an eyebrow to me in response.

I shut the door and went to get ready. Since we were staying within the grounds, I decided to dress comfortably. My abilities weren't a secret anymore, but my true purpose here still was. I didn't bother hiding my knives or the dagger strapped to my thigh under my dress as discreetly as before.

A while later, Amil and I walked together several yards away from Althea and Cornelius as they strolled through the blooming garden, trying to give them space but also trying to keep all areas around them in view. The two other guards that Talos had hired to keep watch over the grounds were walking the perimeter of the large, sprawling garden beds. They had already done a sweep and felt confident that it was secure, giving us the okay to wander while they became the first line of defense.

"How is your brother?" Amil's voice brought me back from looking over the west side of the garden.

"I'm not sure. I haven't heard from him yet." I wasn't sure if I was glad for this or not.

He turned and completely faced me, the sun shining into his deep brown hair revealing strands of gold peeking throughout. His eyes were dark, more grey in the bright light, the irises more visible than indoors. He almost looked Mortal. The concern on his face was kinder than I expected as he looked me over.

"I know you don't have a blood related brother, Isa." Shock stopped me in my tracks. "I know you're a Banner and he's your Bannermate."

It wasn't unknown in the right circles that The Black Banners were a connected web and team. But our upbringing

131

and connections weren't so public. It was also unknown that we were all orphans who didn't know of our blood relatives. Our origins were kept secret from everyone, even those who relied on our services the most. But as far as I knew, Talos hadn't told him that I was a Black Banner. Who else here knew?

"I can help you. Help him—if you ask."

I couldn't ask him though. We took care of our own. We never went outside our own ranks for any services, even if our lives depended on it. We only relied on each other, our network, our Bannermates. I didn't know what to say. I was desperate for Argo to be safe, but asking for Amil's help would compromise the rest of my organization. Not just my Banner House, but every Black Banner.

"I know you can't trust me. But if you let me, I can make a call."

"How long have you known what I was?" I looked around us, avoiding his eyes.

"Since you almost slit my throat on the train. I've only met one other Banner and she too almost took my head off in a similar manner." He chuckled and gave me a relaxed grin.

"Talos didn't tell you?"

"No, he has only told us that you are the last line of defense when it comes to Althea. He likes to keep information close to the vest." That was a small relief.

"I can't ask for help. I wouldn't even know where to send help if I did ask." The pang of helplessness sank in again.

We continued walking to shorten the distance between us and the fawning couple who had settled under a tree outside the garden. We stopped at a low wall about twenty yards away, and I sat down. Amil looked around, spotted one of the grounds guards and gave him a nod of command. The guard nodded in agreement and began to make a wide half-circle around the tree and stopped several yards south to keep watch. Amil then turned his back to me as he scanned for any potential disturbances in the outer tree line of the forest that backed the property.

"I'm sorry." I looked to the back of his head, but he didn't turn to me.

"For what?"

"For kissing you." He slid his hands in his slacks pockets and continued, "It's hard for my kind to shut out Mortal emotions and I may have misread yours."

I blinked at him, not finding words to respond with. The pull I felt around him and Talos often made me feel things that I wasn't sure I would feel if they weren't Incubos. I wasn't sure if he was apologizing for his influence or misreading my emotions due to his influence. Either way, the sun was starting to get very warm, contributing to an oncoming headache.

"Can you feel my emotions now?" I was sick of not being in control of my own emotions or understanding these Incubo.

"I can feel pain. A deeper pain than I have felt myself."

"I don't need your pity. We take care of ourselves and our own. Just like your kind would." I looked back towards Althea and Cornelius who were now lying on a blanket and feeding each other finger food.

"I also feel your confusion. And I don't think it's all to do with your family situation." He turned around and looked down to me, his eyes darkening to their normal stormy black.

"That seems to be an average response for Mortals who hang around Incubo for too long. I don't particularly like not being in control of my own feelings."

"You're not wrong and that is understandable." He shrugged, amused.

"Does this apology come with any other explanations?"

He looked away and walked a few paces away before turning to me again. He was silently contemplating, clearly unsure of how to rectify our situation.

"You don't need to apologize; it was one kiss." I pushed on, to end the tension.

"Can I give you some advice?"

I raised my brows and nodded in response.

"You should distance yourself from Talos. You wouldn't be the first casualty of his internal struggles. He has a preference for beautiful Mortals until they become too close. Then he shatters them to pieces and doesn't lose sleep after."

I stared ahead. I didn't know what Amil knew of what Talos and I had done, and I wasn't about to discuss it with him. I didn't doubt what he was saying wasn't true, especially after what Althea had warned me about earlier. The way Talos had left me feeling that morning in the shower, I never wanted to feel that way again. But now more questions were filling my aching brain.

"The pull I feel from you, from him. How do I stop it from affecting me?" His face fell, as if it hurt him to know I didn't want to feel his influence.

"I will do my best to keep myself under control. But for Talos, you have to keep grounded. Focus on others, don't allow him to reach you. Limit your time alone with him."

That sounded a lot easier said than done.

"Does that work on you?" I stood and closed the gap between us.

"Do you want to find out?" There was a tug at the deep knot in my stomach.

His eyes became as deep and endless as night, the familiar flame igniting. A soothing warmth filled my chest, chasing away the tightness of worry I had been holding on to. His hand found my hip, he pulled me gently towards him. I tried to think about anything or anyone else around us. Althea and Cornelius under the tree or the guard in the distance watching over us all. The gardener near the rose bushes. But nothing was severing the tie he had around me. Looking to his slightly parted lips, I became

134

heavily aware of my own lips. My skin pimpled trying to get as close to him as it could. I wanted so badly to give into him, like I had with Talos.

Talos. My mouth tasted of ash and Amil released me physically and emotionally. The mere thought of Talos sent a look of disgust to his face before he turned away from me.

"I'm sorry, " I said, the words coming out obligatorily.

"No, that was my fault. I overstepped."

There was a tone in his voice that I couldn't place. Perhaps he was confused or hurt but also had pity for me. I swallowed and pulled at his shoulder for him to face me again.

"Try again. This time, only let go if I manage to sever the tie."

"Isa, it's more complicated than that." He shook his head and looked to the ground, avoiding my eyes.

"Why?" I crossed my arms.

"Because you have a lot of emotions right now and I can't control my influence when you are so deeply wrapped within them."

"Amil. Please?"

He gave me a weak smile and a subtle shake of his head before answering with a shoulder shrug. He readied himself reluctantly. I knew I was asking a lot of him for only having exchanged so few words, but I was more vulnerable to Incubo right now, being surrounded by them at every corner and with Talos being hot one moment then cold the next. As much of a relief it would be to feel only his emotions writhing through and around me, I needed to learn this skill before I became another victim of Talos' destructive path.

I shook out my arms and shoulders, took a deep breath, and blocked out my concern for Argo and the others. I focused on Althea and met Amil's gaze. He sighed and reached his hand out to my shoulder.

His scent reached me first as he pulled me closer, sliding his hand to the back of my neck with a firm grip. His fingers spread and took full hold of the base of my head, small hairs there waking at his touch. A shiver ran down me and the feeling of soothing warmth found every corner of me. I lifted my chin to him and his eyes dropped to my lips. He started to lean in closer, his cheek brushing against mine as his lips brushed my earlobe.

"Do you want me to kiss you, Isa?" His whisper shot lightning through me, causing me to let out a small gasp.

I nodded my head too eagerly as my eyes closed. His hand pulled away from my neck, and I felt myself fall forward into his chest. He caught me in his arms and we sat down on the low wall together. I started to feel his pull end, and a hollow feeling was left behind instead. It was quickly filled with my own worry and concern for Argo. I'd failed at pushing his influence off me. I pulled away from him and sat up on my own.

"Again." I stood up and stood in front of where he sat.

"I don't think that's a good idea. The more I try when you aren't ready, the easier it will be for you to slip too deeply into my influence. Too far and you will end up like the Mortals you've heard rumors about. Work on centering yourself alone in your room. If you want to try again later tonight after Yamir is on duty, we can."

Frustration and disappointment hit me, but I was sure he was right. What did I really know of the power of Incubo? It had been much easier for his pull to fill me that time. He stood and walked closer towards Althea and Cornelius, alerting the other guards it was time to move on from the picnic.

The rest of the day was uneventful, Althea and Cornelius spent the entire day together with several of us shadowing them through the grounds. They had a candlelit dinner alone in one of the dining rooms, and I took dinner in my room to get some distance from all Incubo and Fata. I still hadn't heard from any Banners or from whoever had Argo, which I took as decent news, so I waited for Amil to get off duty.

# CHAPTER SIXTEEN

When Amil came to knock on my door around seven o'clock, I was feeling more ready. I had been working through my thoughts and strategies to expel his and other Incubo influences by focusing on the blades strapped to my thigh and torso. I'd also decided to wear a necklace that Zaida had given me for my birthday several years ago. A large purple gem pendant on a thin silver chain that was long enough to nestle between my breasts. If I could focus entirely on the pendant, the weight of it, the space it took, the pressure on several points on my chest, then maybe it would be enough to keep me from being sucked into Amil's pull.

He seemed tired as he entered my room, ragged from the day. He pointed to my bathroom door and said he was going to freshen up before we got started. I took my shoes off to better feel the rug under my feet, anything to give me a better advantage. When he came back in, he had his jacket and tie over his arm and set it down on my bed. He joined me near the footboard at the center of the room. I took in a deep breath and so did he.

The sun was starting to dip in the sky outside my window,

the golden light seen between two drawn drapes and at the bottom crest of the pane. The shadows cast to all corners of the room where the light was no longer clinging. Only a dim lamp at my bedside table behind me to cast light on his handsome, etched features.

"Are you sure you're ready?" He rolled his head around his shoulders to release tension.

"Are you too tired?" I narrowed my eyes to him playfully and he smirked.

"For that, I won't take it easy on you." He winked.

"Good." I nodded, and I was ready.

Just like any other training I did, I wanted it to be real practice. I wanted to know that I wasn't going to fail when it really counted. This was no different than learning how to fight or learning how to throw blades. If I was going to learn how to defend myself on a more mental level, it needed to be treated as if I were defending myself physically. He gave me a tilt of his head as if to say *As you wish* and his features started to shift, his eyes starting to darken. I waited for the flash of flame before I started to focus on the rug beneath my feet. The smooth feel of it between my toes and the soft twists moving as I dug the balls of my feet into it.

The familiar warmth started to tug behind my navel as he took a step closer to me. A trembling feeling rose into my chest as his eyes fell to my mouth, then down the front of my body, lingering on my chest, then stomach, and landing on my hips. A feeling of longing bubbled to my chest and my hand extended on its own. He gingerly took it in his fingers and began caressing the top of my knuckles with his thumb. I tried to swallow, but my throat was suddenly dry, the tension starting to swarm me.

He raised a hand to tuck a lock of my hair behind my ear, and I pulled away from his hand slightly. In response he slid his fingers through my hair and took a handful before pulling me towards him. My hands landed on his hips to stop me from completely crashing into him. His hard muscles flexed under my palms. He looked down into my eyes and parted his lips into a thin cocky grin. I started to melt into him, but tried to focus on my necklace. The smooth stone cool against my skin, the weight of it pulling down on the chain around my neck. I tried to envision the color of it in sunlight.

"You look beautiful tonight." His voice soft, and butterflies started to fill me.

Screaming internally to myself, I tried to pull away and managed a half step back, but was met with the strength of his resting hand at the nape of my neck. His thumb smoothed over the sensitive flesh at my clavicle. My skin begged for more so loudly that I was sure he could actually hear it. My heart beat harder against my breast as he dipped low and hovered over my lips.

"Tell me what you want, Isa." My knees weakened at the sound of my name falling through his teeth.

"You," I breathed.

And I did, more than anything I wanted him.

I pushed up onto my toes to meet his lips, gripping his shirt through my fingers to pull him closer to me. He kissed me deeply, parting his lips and exploring with his tongue. I wrapped my arms around his torso, wanting to be as close to him as possible, wishing the few layers of our clothing would fall apart. I could feel him becoming hard against me, the bulge in his slacks pressing into my stomach.

I couldn't stop myself from giving a small sigh of pleasure as his hand trailed down my spine to cup my bottom, lifting me a little farther up into him. I could no longer feel my necklace pendant or the rug underneath my feet. Nothing in the room was grounding me, and I couldn't force myself to tear away from him. I felt an odd thrumming coming from him, seeming to wrap around us, further blocking me from everything that wasn't his scent, the feel of his body, or the tension mounting between my thighs.

Suddenly, he pulled away from me and I barely caught myself from falling to my knees on the floor. An emptiness grabbed hold of me as he turned away from me and hid his face in his hands. I took a deep breath and sat at the edge of my bed, remembering the feel of anything I could to chase the immediate emotional hangover.

"I thought you were ready?" He sounded frustrated, with himself or me I couldn't tell.

"I was." I took another deep breath and took my necklace out of my shirt, feeling the heat of it between my fingers and palm.

"I don't think you fully grasp how impossible it is for me to not respond to you when you are so open to me. You have to try harder to block me out." He turned back to me, almost surprised to be finding me sitting on the bed.

"This is new to me. I'm trying to resist, but—fuck," I shuttered, trying to shake the memory of his hands on me.

"If I wasn't in your room right now. Would you be thinking about me?" He looked as if he were bracing himself.

"I... I don't know. I'd probably be thinking about my family." But I would be thinking about him too; his offer to help me.

His eye caught the pendant between my fingers as I twisted it against each finger's tip. I looked down to it, realizing it was Alexandrite. Realizing now that I possibly wasn't the only Mortal to know of the Incubo's weakness to the stone. He took a small step towards me, raising his sight to mine.

"Isa, what do you know of Incubo? Before Talos hired you, what did you know of us?" He turned and sat in the chair next to my dresser, reclining with his knees apart.

"Not much, only what I had heard from others. You take Mortals or Fata and use them up until you've had your fill then move on. Some don't get seen again. You only marry or breed when an Incubo dies."

"And what did Talos tell you?" I wasn't sure where he was going with this line of questioning.

"That your kind have a weakness to Alexandrite and that some of your lovers would rather die than leave their Incubo. As far as I've heard, many do." I let the pendant fall to the front of my blouse, crossing my arms at my waist.

He nodded but didn't say anything right away. He looked off to the corner of the room, obviously thinking of the next question or comment about my ignorance to his kind. He wouldn't be wrong to do so. I didn't know anything about Incubo or their abilities; the pull or influence they had on Mortals and Fata that I had been under myself, and rapid healing, which I only recently learned fully about from Althea's wound. He and Talos were able to sense my emotions and imprint their own on me, having difficulty restraining themselves when doing so.

"Talos gave you that dagger, didn't he? Did he give you that necklace as well?"

"I assumed he was the one who left the dagger in my room, but no. My sister gave me this necklace years ago. As far as I know, she was unaware of its true value."

He sat quiet for a moment more as his eyes shifted back to their normal smoke grey. Rolling up his sleeves and unbuttoning his shirt to his mid chest, he readied himself for another round.

"Let's try something new. No touching." He sat on the end of the chair, his arms resting on the tops of his thighs.

I nodded and his eyes held mine from across the short distance. The familiar color change of his irises and pupils faded to the storm cloud black then the spark. The tug at my navel was only a twinge, and I took it as a cue to focus on something else. I reached to my necklace, holding the pendant between my thumb and forefinger, rubbing the smooth surface. The tightening released feather light, then was gone completely. He smiled and sat back again and waited for me to relish my accomplishment. I had done it.

"We'll have to start slowly. I know that's hard for you, but you have been around too many of us to resist my heavy-handed influence." His shoulders slumped and I wondered if he was a little disappointed.

"Why is it so hard for me to be around you or Talos alone, but I don't feel the same way around any other Incubo here?" The question tumbled out of me faster than I expected and he looked to me again.

"Isn't it obvious?" His devilish grin reached his eyes, and he raised a brow coyly.

"Because you find me attractive?" It sounded foolish and smug, but I wasn't wrong. He nodded.

"I'm sure we are not the only ones, and I can not speak for Talos, but I can't seem to control my urges as easily around you. Something about you makes me want to reach out to you." He looked me over as if there would be an arrow pointing to something obvious.

"Because I'm a Black Banner." It wasn't a question. I was Mortal, but a mystery in some aspects to other beings.

"Perhaps. I feel drawn to you nonetheless and wanting to taste you becomes unbearable to the point that I can't hold back." The pull flickered with the small spark in his eyes, and I resisted again with a scolding glance.

"And Talos? He just wants someone to play with, someone he may not break as easily?" I wasn't so much asking as I was realizing this for myself.

"That would be one way of looking at it." He blinked back his urges.

"And what would be another way?" I crossed my legs and propped myself up onto the bed with my arms.

"That he wants to see how long it would take to break you."

# CHAPTER SEVENTEEN

W hat Amil had said about Talos hummed through my
mind in the hours that I tossed and turned in bed after
he had left for the night. We planned to meet up again the next
evening to further develop my repelling and resisting skills. I
wasn't expecting him to be as invested as he was, but it was a
quality I didn't know Incubo possessed. It seemed I had a lot to
learn about their kind and it seemed that Amil was willing to
teach me.

I'd checked my emails and voicemails several times before
finally giving in to my soft mattress and attempting sleep. It felt
as if I'd finally closed my eyes when I was awoken by a soft
tapping at my door, the morning sun streaming through the
fabric of my curtains. It must have been later than I normally
awoke because Althea, fully dressed and made up, opened the
door a crack and peeked inside to see if I was awake, or perhaps
to check if I was alone. I waved her in as I sat up in bed, and she
sat at my feet and started to rattle off the plans for the day.

She had another fitting for our dresses scheduled since the
delivery for mine had been canceled due to the estate being
locked down after the attack in the city. Table settings had to be

finalized, the wedding planner was coming to assist her with the gift registry, and about a half dozen other tasks that I had to sit in with her on. It would not be another day of lounging around on the grounds, but at least we wouldn't be on high alert outside of the suite. She informed me that breakfast was waiting for me out in the sitting room and that she would be waiting for me to be ready for the day.

She shut the door behind her as she cheerfully left me to dress and prepare, I got out of bed reluctantly—my muscles and mind protesting from lack of sleep and my neck stiff from worry. I dressed comfortably again before grabbing my laptop and heading out to the shared space. Althea was sipping her tea and reading the paper, how I often found her in the morning. Unfamiliarity struck when I found Amil standing on the inside of the door. I cast a questioning glance to him and he winked in response.

"I hope you don't mind. One of the grounds guards is sick so the balcony is locked and the other guard is stationed outside the door." Althea pointed her chin to Amil but spoke to me.

"Hopefully the sickness is brief." I smirked at Amil then sat in my usual spot on the nearest sofa as a knock came from the door behind him.

It was the Fata groundskeeper, holding an armful of beautiful soft pink peonies and silver green rods of eucalyptus. Suddenly the room smelled of the flowers but also fresh soil and rain. I realized as the Fata sat down across from me that it was his natural scent. In Cinder, I rarely met Fata that didn't work in office buildings, shops, or kitchens and they didn't have such aromas. Or possibly they did, but I took it for the city odors. Another note to myself to find out when I got back home. He and Althea were busy discussing the amount of flowers needed per table, the arrangement design, the weight of each flower, and what filler plants she wanted to help fill in the bare spots.

I poured myself some coffee before I grabbed some bacon

and fruit and watched them interact for a while. Althea was completely in her natural element; she had pure joy on her face with each decorator or party planner. She would make a wonderful Duchess, or whatever the Incubo equivalent was. I'd have to ask about that too. After I had my fill of listening to the both of them banter about plants and guests, who would likely hate anything they decided on, I pulled my laptop onto my lap and proceeded to check emails and saw I'd gotten one each from Talia and Zaida.

*Isa,*

*Sorry to worry you. I'm fine and healing back in Cinder. Deric is searching for Argo. We will find him, I promise you.*

*-Talia*

Deric would let me know if he found anything, I knew, but part of me wasn't sure it would be enough. He was one of the best target trackers, and he'd often worked for high risk bounty hunters in foreign countries. He'd collected countless rewards for most wanted criminals who had evaded law enforcement. He was also very skilled in internet and security hacking. If he could find a way to pinpoint the signal of Argo's phone, he could at least narrow down a search area. That's what I would have done if I weren't here watching flower arrangements being decided on for what felt like the hundredth hour.

*My Sorella,*

*I made it to Amples and have brought Markus with me. We'll be meeting up with Deric in a few hours; he may have found something. Let me know if you hear anything. I'll update soon.*

*Stay vigilant.*

Knowing Markus was also there with Zaida and Deric lifted a small bit of weight off my chest. Markus was another Bannermate from our house we grew up in. He and I weren't the closest, but he was the one most of us called for backup if we needed it. He was brute force, solid muscles, and over six feet tall. His specialty was usually intimidation or making a hit look like a mugging gone too far. He rarely needed weapons other than his own fists on his assignments. But he was as viscous as he was protective of his fellow Banners. I'd called on him a few times when an employer had gotten too rough with me after a job had been taking longer than they had expected. Zaida rarely needed back up, but if I was busy, she'd call Markus next.

As much as I wanted to hear from my Bannermates, their emails only made the pit of worry in my chest deeper. In fact, in a way it made it worse than not knowing anything at all. They had also not heard from whoever had Argo and were no closer than I was in finding him. I contemplated calling his phone again but didn't want to risk accelerating the kidnapper's plans or spooking them into hurting Argo. So, I gave a heavy sigh and closed my laptop and set it down next to me on the couch.

After several more hours of meetings with decorators, wedding planners, kitchen staff, and so on, it was time for the dress designer to show us the alterations. Althea went first and squealed when she saw herself in her dress and veil. She was absolutely giddy and I couldn't help but smile with her. The excitement she exuded was so pure that I almost forgot that her union was putting her and so many others in danger.

When I was dressed in my bridesmaid dress, I came out and Amil's face caught my attention first. His jaw dropped and he stood, mouth agape, staring at every inch of me. I bit the inside of my cheek to stop myself from smiling, but the heat creeping across my face was hard to hide. I looked away from him to

Althea who had both of her hands over her nose and mouth trying to muffle her excitement. I smiled and rolled my eyes. I didn't bother to stand on the stool, but instead did a quick twirl for effect.

"It fits beautifully, thank you," I said to the designer then turned towards my bedroom door.

"Wait a moment! Is that a spot?" He bent low to look closer.

I turned my head and craned my neck to see what he was pointing at, but was unable to see any discoloration of the lace.

"It is, oh no! It looks like dirt. I think we can get it off." Althea rushed over and started pawing at the spot she saw near my rear end.

I looked up to find Amil silently laughing into the palm of his hand at the sight of two beings swatting and looking attentively at my bottom. I scowled at him and shook my head subtly before huffing, "Let me take it off and we can see if we can get it out."

I pulled the dress away from their hands and quickly went to change. When I returned, the designer was packing up Althea's dress and whirled to take mine before examining it further. He hummed to himself and nodded, agreeing with his own internal assessment of the issue before wordlessly bustling out of the suite, apparently late to another appointment and needing to get back through the estate's security measures quickly.

Cornelius didn't join us for lunch. He had meetings with his father that were taking place in the city, but he had promised Althea a gift and dinner alone later. Talos would be returning the next morning with Althea's father, and it was likely she and Cornelius would have even less time alone together until their union, which was quickly approaching. She had been practically counting down the days to their wedding and repeated it with every new appointment, only three more weeks and she would be Lady Welp.

The rest of the afternoon passed agonizingly slow. Once

Cornelius and his father had returned, he flitted into the suite to present Althea with her gift: a gorgeous diamond necklace with stones the size of peas separated by a small length of white gold chain and a ruby pendant the size of a quail egg surrounded by more pea sized diamonds. She gasped as he laid it over her chest and clasped it for her behind her back. He had to leave quickly after to check on their dinner plans and freshen up, but she mooned after him.

"I can't wait to be his wife." Her voice dreamy as the smoke of her eyes lightened to a sea haze.

"You both seem very happy together." I was leaning against the doorframe of my room with my arms crossed at my chest.

She turned to me and her smile was bright. "I never thought I would marry someone I truly loved. It's a true miracle."

Talos had explained that an Incubo in her position would normally arrange to be married by their families to ensure future power and lands. Their choice to go against that tradition, causing the threat on their lives, seemed silly when seeing their love in front of me. I couldn't imagine anyone who would rather they separate for wealth or land gains.

"How long have you been together?" I hadn't asked before, it didn't seem to matter.

"Don't laugh," she paused for me to agree with a nod, "we've known each other for years, but we've only decided to marry so that we could actually be together. We have never really been together longer than a few hours at a time. But we've kept in touch over the years and our feelings for each other were undeniable."

They never had a courtship, but they loved each other deeply despite their families' opinions. The short time they spent together during this trip was the start of a formal relationship and preparation of their union.

"That's wonderful. I'm happy for you. The both of you." I smiled.

"Thank you. There aren't many others who are. I'm always prepared to hear how we are a disappointment to our kind, but once our union is complete, it won't matter anymore. Incubo don't break their unions."

I didn't know this, and now I understood why so many were willing to hurt or even kill Althea to stop their union. Once it was final, there was no going back. They would be bound together until they were parted by death, which would be a very long time for Incubo. They could easily outlive several generations of Mortals.

"Will you live here when you're married?"

She ran her fingers through her hair, primping it to behave. "Neil wants to travel for a year while our new home is prepared for us. It's not as grand as this one, but it's still here in Arta. My father is still bound to Cinder until he relinquishes control to me. It was an easy choice to stay here and away from Cinder for now."

"It won't be hard for you to be away from your family?"

"You'll understand better once you meet my father. He's not the kindest of Incubo. He can be cruel and stubborn." Her smile faded for a moment. "Thankfully, Neil is his obverse."

There was a knock at the door and Amil opened it a crack before closing it again. He turned to us and spoke to Althea, "Cornelius is ready for you, Hariss is here to escort you to the dining room."

I instinctually jerked to follow her which she caught. "Don't worry. I'm only down the hall and Yamir will not leave the doorway, I already asked."

She winked with a smile as she bounced to the door and waved goodbye to me. Hariss and Yamir followed her out and headed to the dining room. Amil tilted his head and dipped his chin to me. A greeting, as if we hadn't been in the same room all day together. He strode over to the sofas and sat down facing me. A smile tugged at the corner of my mouth as I kicked off the wall to sit at my usual seat. There was another knock at the door and a cart was being pushed through the doorway a moment later.

"Care to join me for dinner?" I crossed my legs and leaned against the back of the sofa.

"I haven't had a better offer." He grinned and gave me a playful shrug.

Dinner was brought in by the young, tall kitchen Fata. He had prepared the meal himself and was beaming as he served us before leaving. Dinner was flawless: roasted chicken breast with garlic and herb potatoes and glazed pear salad with blue cheese. The young Fata was very skilled at every small detail. Once we were finished, we piled our empty plates on the cart and I wheeled it out to the hall to be retrieved.

Turning to where Amil sat, he had his arms raised above his head in a deep stretch, his ash-black jacket with silver embroidery details at the cuffs undone and the shirt underneath stretching over his taut stomach. He yawned and I started to feel guilty for keeping him another night after his shift was over.

"If you're too tired, we can skip tonight's lesson." I strode over to my sofa but didn't sit.

"Where else do I have to be?" The corner of his mouth crinkled his cheek at my offer.

"Start out slow. Let me ease into it." I sat at the edge of my seat and leaned forward, resting against my thighs, hands clasped in front of me waiting for him to engage.

He stood and moved to the edge of his couch closer to me, unbuttoning two silver buttons on his shirt. Mimicking my pose, his rugged features both softened and sharpened, concentrating on the contours of my face. Moving from my eyes to my lips then down to my neck, then lower. His gaze seared my skin, the flame dancing in his darkened eyes. The tight pull of need behind my navel spread up to where his eyes were fixed, begging to be touched. I could feel myself start to inch closer to him as the air in the room thickened, my breathing shallow against the tense air around us, each inhale not fully filling my lungs.

I swallowed hard and realized I had forgotten my necklace. Instead I looked to his jacket and the cufflinks gleaming from the chandelier's light. I focused on the color, the tiny floral design melded into them. I imagined their cool feel in my hand, thought about them against my skin if he ran his fingers through my hair before his lips would press against mine. *No!*

I shook my head and pulled myself back. Sitting up straight and taking a deep breath. An amused grin bloomed across his face as he leaned back and clasped his hands behind his head. He was having fun with me tonight.

"That was good, I thought I almost had you."

"You almost did." I smoothed my hands over the tops of my thighs, wiping away moisture from my palms.

I shook out my hands at the wrist and brought my attention to him again. "Can I have one of your cufflinks to hold?"

He looked a little surprised by my request, but handed it over to me without question. He took his jacket off, shrugging the shoulders down and folding it on the back of his sofa, rolling up his sleeves and leaning forward once again. He waited until I nodded for him to start.

This time the feel of him circled me, his scent becoming more noticeable. Even though he was a few feet away, it felt as if I were pressed up against his chest and breathing him in. I closed my eyes and started to finger the small cufflink keeping hold of my senses for the moment. When I opened my eyes again, a playfully smug look hung on his face, challenging me to make a move, egging me on in a game I was trying my best not to play. I wanted to give in; I wanted to best him, but I had to resist.

"Are you ready for me, Isa?" His voice was husky but calm, and I felt aflutter.

"I can handle it," I gulped, lying.

He gave a gruff chuckle, a sensation like warm honey filling my mouth and throat. Sweet and thick, it was making it harder for me to focus on anything but his pillowy lips.

"We'll soon find out exactly what you can handle," he quipped.

I pressed the nub of the cufflink into my palm to center myself, but it wasn't until I felt a sharp pain in my hand that I was able to shake his hold over me. I'd held the cufflink so hard that I pierced the skin. Cursing, I dropped it on the floor and held my thumb to the small puncture mark, stopping the bleeding. He leaned toward me, taking my fingers in his hand, as concern filled his face.

"Are you alright?"

"I'm fine," the bleeding had stopped. "It was more startling than painful."

He looked up to me and I met his eyes. The flame had not completely extinguished in the lingering darkness. I realized how close he was, my fingers curled and laced through his. He edged closer to me and tilted his face. He wasn't trying to ensnare me. I didn't feel the rush of him around me or the pull surge in my stomach and chest. I only felt him. I didn't know if it was the looming feelings of want still clouding my judgement, but I leaned in and met his lips.

One of his hands found my cheek, pulling me into him closer. I let myself follow his lead, and before I could give it a second thought I glided into his lap, straddling his hips. His other arm wrapped around my hips and held me down tight as our kiss grew deeper. I could feel him hardening between my thighs, the heat coming from us both.

He pulled away from me, his voice heavy and horse. "Isa, I—"

"Don't stop," I cut him off with another deep kiss.

I didn't want him to stop touching me or kissing me. I wasn't feeling the desperate need like I had with Talos, it wasn't all consuming. The pressure in my chest felt like it was coming from me, not from him. The frustrated worry from the day melted away at each pass of his lips against mine.

With more ease than I thought was possible, he stood up with my legs wrapped around his waist as he headed to my bedroom. The room was already dark as the sun had been setting and the curtains were drawn closed. When we got to the side of my bed, he set me down and looked down to me as he unbuttoned his shirt—eyes not leaving mine—shrugged it off and let it fall to the floor before making quick work of his belt, slacks, and shoes. He stood before me in only his undershorts, his hands clenched at his sides as if not wanting to touch me without permission.

I lifted my shirt up over my head and stood to pull my own slacks down, standing in only my undergarments and stilettos. I raised my hand to his chest and traced a thick scar above his heart. I watched my fingers as they smoothed down over his muscular torso, then to his shoulder, down his arm, and then opening his hand against mine.

He lifted my chin and his eyes seemed to be trying to memorize my face, seeing deep inside of me and trying to devour me. Wrapping his arms around my back, he scooped me up and gently laid me back on the bed, lifting me and pulling me up to the top of the bed with him. His body was sculpted by hard, constant defense training, but his strength was due to what he was. He settled one of his legs between mine, spreading them apart and gently opening me up to him. An audible sigh rumbled through me as he kissed me again causing a damp heat to start to pool between my thighs.

I reached up and ran my fingers through his thick, dark hair, taking it in my hand and pulling him away from me. He gave me a cheeky grin and began slinking down my body. His hot breath against my skin caught my breath. He tugged my remaining underwear off, his lips only briefly leaving my skin with each movement. He hoisted my legs over his shoulders as he lay down between my thighs watching my eyes on him. The smooth material of my shoes gliding over his skin and the heels pressed into the bed linen. One of his arms looped around the back of my leg to rest on top of my stomach, the other hand on my inner thigh gliding down to my very center. His fingers worked my tight nerves in agonizingly slow circles. When I tried to arch my back, he wrapped an arm around my waist to hold me down and still.

He wore his wicked smile as he continued to tease at me. Without warning, he slid two fingers inside of me and his tongue began working to replace his fingers. My hand sank into his hair once again as he quickened his pace both in and outside of me. Tension began coiling deep inside of me, and I could feel my body start to move along with his rhythm. I let out a low moan and he responded with a throaty, pleased sound that rippled up through me and filled me, finally pushing me over the edge. A sweeping ecstasy from my toes to the tips of my fingers burst inside me as he moved up my body to hover over me again. In my bliss, I hadn't even noticed that he'd taken off his undershorts.

The hard length of him slid over my pulsing core, the friction causing my hips to beg for him. I wanted every thick inch of him to be inside of me. With the pounding in my chest and between my thighs becoming too much to stand, I reached for his rear end and pulled him closer against me. His mouth met mine, his hips now rocking against mine in long, slow motions. The curve of his lips over mine in a boastful grin, he was enjoying this so much. I pulled my chin to the side to curse him, but only choked out the first syllable before he dove deep inside of me.

His teeth caught my lip for a moment as I gasped and closed

my eyes tight, feeling the jolt radiate. He pulled away slowly, but thrusted back in only a heartbeat later. Another heavy breath escaped me and he grinned, pleased at the response. I moved my hands up his back and held on to the blades of his shoulders as he thrusted once again before a short burst of quicker paced strokes. I started to feel the pressure inside of me mounting again, but he quickly moved out of me and flipped me over onto my stomach in a fluid motion. Sliding his arm under me to get a better grip on my hips, he filled me again, harder than before.

He paused for a moment as I caught my breath, and ran his hand up my back and neck, grabbing a hold of my nape before thrusting deep inside of me over and over again. One of my hands found my mouth, trying to muffle the moan quickly turning into a ragged scream as I crashed to pieces again around him. He half pulled me up to my forearms and leaned down. His husky deep voice in my ear threatened to send me over the edge again.

"If you think you can simply cover your mouth as I fuck you, you are greatly mistaken. I will tie your hands to this bed. I want everyone to hear you enjoying me, understood?" He waited for me to eagerly nod in agreement. "Good, now scream for me."

He released my neck and held my hips with both hands as he began thrusting deep inside of me. And I gave him what he wanted: I screamed his name, I cursed, I shouted commands, I filled and spilled again.

I pulled away, and sat up on my knees, pulling one of his arms to silently instruct him to lie down, his eager eyes not leaving mine as I straddled him. He cupped my breast as I slid onto him, breathing in short, stuttered breaths as I sank down, taking him in completely to hilt. It was my turn to tease and take control of his pleasure. I started by lifting my hips then settling down again slowly, whirling my hips on the way down. He kicked his head back and cursed on the third ascent.

I started to roll my hips against his, holding onto the headboard, more pressure building as his hands found my waist and tried to keep up. His fingers pressed in on me and his hips raised off the mattress, slightly deepening himself. He pulled me down as I moved faster. My name escaped his lips in darted breaths and I felt his climax mounting inside of me, the sensation instantly sending me over the edge again. Spilling over into each other, I collapsed onto his chest and his arms wrapped around my back holding me there as if he were afraid I'd regain my senses and leap away. I wouldn't have. Something other than his hold was keeping me there, and I didn't want to part with him.

His breathing slowed, the thin sheen of sweat cooled our skin. I yawned before rolling off to his side in the crook of his arm. With his fingers gliding in circles on my hip, his eyes closed and a look of peace settled on his face. Surprising myself with the instinct, I kissed him softly before pulling away from him to clean myself up. The bathroom light stung my eyes as I closed the door and turned the tap on to heat. I washed my face and put my hair up in a messy bun, there was no saving it from the mess it had become without showering.

I washed up and pulled on the robe from the back of the bathroom door, half expecting Amil to be gone when I opened the door. But he was sitting up in the bed, his undershorts on. He got up and walked towards me, hands cupping my face and a kiss on my forehead as he passed me to get into the bathroom.

I turned on the side table light and checked out the sitting room, but it was dark, Althea's bedroom door shut. I thought about walking the distance to check on her, but heard Amil open the bathroom door.

"Everything alright?" He came up from behind me silently and swiftly.

I turned into him, shutting the door and leaning against it.

"Yeah, I was just wondering if Althea had come in yet." I tugged the robe around me tighter.

"If she hadn't, we would know by now." He winked and leaned down to kiss me.

"Do you want me to go?" He sounded sincere, but there was a small hint of wanting in his question.

"Should you go? Probably. But no. I don't want you to go." I bit my lower lip out of nerves.

"Does that scare you?" He took a step back and turned back to the bed, pausing only a moment before walking over and sliding down between the linens.

"Why would you ask that?" He wasn't far off, I was a little worried about this conflicted feeling I was having about him leaving.

"Because I know how the Banners are. Lone wolves. Never take lovers longer than a night unless they're on assignment or if it's essential to finishing the job." Shock, utter shock hung on my face. How could he possibly know that?

"I've heard some rumors. And by the look of it, they aren't false." He gave a cocky grin.

"What else have you heard?" I went to the bed and sat at the edge of it out of his reach.

He stretched and linked his hands together before resting them on the top of his head, shrugging as he sighed. "Not much else really. Your organization does a good job of cleaning up loose ends."

"And the Banner you met before me? What did she tell you?" I needed her name if she did tell him anything, if she betrayed us.

"I only met her momentarily and she didn't tell me anything. She was hired to kill Pytr a few years back by a rival Lord. One you've met." He wiggled his brow as my jaw clenched.

"You're not serious. Stavros hired a Banner to kill Althea's father?"

"Not Stavros." He lowered his arms and rested them comfortably on his bare stomach.

"Cornelius? Why? Does Althea know?" Questions began to fall out of me before he could answer the previous one. "The Banner, what happened to her?"

"Isa." He leaned forward and pulled me towards him, bumping our knees up against each other. "The workings of Incubo Royalty are complicated. I do not know if Althea is privy to all the details of her future husband, but I would assume she doesn't if he had planned on killing his future father in law." He paused as I digested his words.

When he began again, his tone was more somber, as if comforting someone who lost a family member they cared deeply about. And possibly to his knowledge, she was someone I cared deeply for as a fellow Banner.

"The Banner I met did not succeed, and she was executed after questioning. She was posing as a Temptress at one of the King's parties in Amples. I encountered her long enough for a private altercation and then heard of the failed attempt on Pytr's life days later, making the connection."

There is an Incubo King, and he has parties in the same city that Argo is being kept in; that didn't feel like a coincidence. I'd have to ask my Bannermates if they'd heard of this assignment. Heard of this Banner who had failed to kill an Incubo Lord. A Banner who had been hired much like myself by the Incubo that I was currently residing with. Who had a scuffle with the one I had just been entangled with, whose name I had been screaming. A Banner hired to kill the father of the Incubo I have been hired to keep breathing. My head was swimming, and my chest filled with these stones of truth.

"Talos must know this. Why would he hire me?"

"Because she got very close to completing her assignment. But she was missing one bit of information that you have."

"The Alexandrite dagger." He nodded at my realization.

"After hearing about what she was and what had happened after my run in with her, I asked around about The Black

Banners. I didn't get much information, nothing I could confirm."

"I can't tell you anything."

"I didn't ask you to, Isa." He leaned back, resting his head against the headboard.

He lounged half naked, and not at all wanting anything but to be in this space with me. I couldn't recall the last time I'd spent time with anyone who knew my name, or who wasn't an assignment, and especially never with someone who knew what I was. Being lonely wasn't something I felt often, but in this moment I felt it deeply. I'd felt more since meeting Talos than I had since I was a child. The sadness of that must have been apparent because Amil fluidly pulled me into his lap and encircled me into his chest.

"I can't stay all night, but can I lie with you for a while longer?" I nodded against the cool dampness of his bare skin.

He didn't ask for himself, he had felt my pain and for reasons I could not grasp, didn't want to leave me alone inside of my own sadness. We lay curled up together in silence, only the sound of our steadied breaths to lull us. I wasn't sure when we fell asleep or what time it was when he kissed my brow gently to tell me he was going back to his room.

# CHAPTER EIGHTEEN

I woke up naked and wrapped in sheets several hours later, alone. The sun outside streamed in through the cracks of the curtains. After I showered and dressed, I met Althea in the sitting room. I realized I hadn't heard her come in last night, but was sure she had heard Amil and me. Part of me didn't want to face her, but I didn't have that luxury. She was already eating breakfast and reading the paper, but she didn't seem to be her usual bubbly self. Something about the way she was sitting stiffly or the blank look on her face brought back the image of the train ride here. I sat down and poured myself some coffee like any other morning and waited for her to speak, to run through the long list of appointments she had planned today, but she stayed silent.

"Althea?" She looked up to me, but her expression only looked a shorter distance away than before she heard my voice. "Is everything alright?"

Her shoulders rose then dropped heavily as she folded her paper in her lap. She stared at her hands for a moment before speaking, "My father will be here today."

"Are you not a little happy to see him?" I already knew the

answer, after everything Amil told me last night Pytr must be as horrible as the Incubo I'd heard rumors about.

"I wasn't expecting to see him until the wedding day. We still have so much to prepare for and I worry he will do everything in his power to make each item as difficult as possible."

I moved to sit next to her and placed a hand on hers. In our short time together, I started to care for her as a friend and not just a hired hand. Seeing the amount of love she held for Cornelius, and the effort she had put into making her life her own made me feel a sense of fondness. I wanted her to have the wedding of her dreams to the man she chose for herself. I wanted them to enjoy each other every moment of every day. They didn't ask for all that was expected of them or to offer up their futures to be decided by their families. I could see the worry in her cloudy eyes, that everything she had imagined was going to fall apart at any moment. That one slight complication could change her entire life.

"I will do anything I can to ensure your wedding day happens the way you want it to." I didn't know how I was going to keep this promise, but I truly felt it.

She smiled and nodded in gratitude, one tear threatening to fall onto her cheek. She excused herself to get ready for her father's arrival, and I didn't doubt that she wanted to stay hidden in her room until the wedding day.

I took the time to check my emails and voicemails because I hadn't heard anything new on Argo or my fellow Banners out looking for him. Zaida sent an email letting me know they were tracking down a lead, but nothing had come of it yet. I was starting to think that the man holding Argo was lying when he said he would be in touch. I couldn't think of any reason why they would be holding him so long without contact. Why they would be keeping him alive this long if he didn't have something they wanted or wanted from another Black Banner member. It was pretty rare for one of us to get caught or captured while on a mission, and even rarer still to live longer than a day if it did occur.

There was a knock on the door and Amil stuck his head in. He looked around for Althea and entered when he didn't see her, closing the door behind him. He only took a few steps into the room before stopping and sliding his hands into his pockets. He looked fresh, rested, and just as handsome as any other day. Not at all like we had been up fairly late together in my bed.

"Talos called. He and Pytr will be arriving any minute. Is Lady Althea prepared?" He looked me over without giving away any sentiment.

"I think she'll be fine; she's resting for now." I crossed my legs and rested my arms on my knees.

"About last night," he started, but trailed off.

"Yes?"

"I..." He looked to be searching very hard for what to say next. "Talos, um."

"I don't see last night being any of his business, if that's where you're failing to take this conversation." His sudden lack of backbone wasn't appealing.

"It's not that." He took his hands out of his pockets and sat at the sofa facing me.

He ran his hands through his hair, and I furrowed my brows. "He's going to sense what happened, isn't he?"

He nodded and it became clear. He wasn't worried about me telling Talos that we had slept together, he was warning me that Talos would know when he got back. Something about this realization dug deep in my stomach. Talos had told me to stay away from Yamir and Amil, not to distract them. Not to mention Talos felt he had full access to me when he felt so inclined. It would be an interesting conversation, but I had no obligations to anyone or anything except to keep Althea alive until her union.

"I'll be right outside if things get inimical." He stood and started to walk to the suite doors.

"He's going to see you first." He stopped and looked over his shoulder to me but didn't say anything before leaving. He didn't want to say it, but he was more worried about my safety than his own. He was Incubo after all, he could handle an altercation with one of his kind much better than I could.

I knocked on Althea's door and let her know that her father would be arriving soon, but she only gave a brief reply through the door. I went to the balcony door and saw the large black vehicles coming down the long drive. I had the urge to leave, a common sensation when I was cornered. A mix between instincts and years of training to survive. The interactions between Incubo men and I had gotten more complicated with each passing day on this assignment. More complicated since the night I met Talos in that elevator. That seemed so long ago.

The cars reached the outer limits of what I could see past the balcony; they'd be approaching the manor. I couldn't move, didn't know where to really go or what to do with myself. Part of me wanted to go into my room and wait as Althea was doing, but it was expected of me to be present. So I waited awkwardly for a long while before I heard voices in the hall beyond the door before it opened. I had hardly enough time to knock on Althea's bedroom door to alert her to come to the sitting room.

Pytr entered the suite first, followed by Talos and two other tall Incubo I hadn't seen before. The new security took a post on either side of the suite entrance, standing sentinel. Althea's father was about the same height as Talos, handsome in his own right with salt and pepper hair that didn't age him. He seemed to be a little older than Talos, but I had no idea how the Incubo aged, I realized. He lifted both arms and spoke to Althea, who was standing sheeplike next to me with her head down and hands clasped in front of her.

"My darling, how are you?" He reached her, but didn't

embrace her, merely laying his hands on her shoulders and planting a kiss on the top of her head.

She didn't say anything, reminding me of when I first met her in Cinder. I looked from her to him then to Talos, who was standing before the low table between the sofas with his hands clenched into fists. He was focused on Pytr, who released his daughter and turned to him.

"All seems fine here, Talos. You worry for nothing." Pytr's voice was teasingly dismissive.

Talos looked around him to Althea, then finally to me. His gaze piercing, almost feeling his fury on my face, I looked away to Althea. She hadn't moved and was giving no sign of being aware of who else was in the room. Her distance tore into me, leaving me wishing I could send Pytr away again.

"The Lords are waiting for you in the study," Talos spoke deep and deadly.

"Let us not keep them waiting." Pytr turned to me, smiled, but it didn't reach his eyes, then began walking out of the suite.

"I'll be there in a few moments; I need to update my staff." Pytr nodded to him in response.

Talos didn't move or take his eyes off me. He waited for the sound of the two guards and Pytr to shut the door behind them before speaking again.

"Althea, will you give Isa and me the room? I will be in to speak with you after." She silently retreated to the solitude of her room.

He waved a hand to the sofa and waited for me to take a seat. Approaching him, there was a fire starting to spark to life in my gut, preparing for what was surely coming next. I crossed my legs and leaned back against the sofa, my hands in my lap, waiting, annoyance not easy to hide on my face as he started to pace the space in front of the low table, looking to the ground. I waited still, I wasn't going to be the first to speak.

"I have no words," he spoke finally without stopping his pacing.

"Then this will be a short conversation." My tone came off more mockingly than I intended.

"Save your cheek. You disobeyed a direct order to stay away from my men."

"We were both off duty, and neither of us have lost focus in our mission here." I had nothing to apologize for, and I wasn't going to.

He stopped and turned around to face me, the fury stoked his expression and eyes again. A swift movement and he was hovering over me with his hands on the crest of the sofa on either side of my head. Our faces only a few inches away, I could feel anger thrumming through him, almost pulsing on my exposed skin. I didn't look away as his eyes became darker than I had seen them. Living black masses, daring me to move.

He lowered his lashes, and I couldn't tell if his gaze landed on my lips or throat, but either seemed dangerous at this point. I was starting to feel his pull trying to envelop me, the air in the room feeling thicker. I felt for anything to focus on and found the seam of the cushion and held it between two of my fingers, feeling the threads and smooth texture. Air pushed into my lungs and the pull released. Realization, anger, and awe mingled together in his expression as he sensed the lost connection. Standing up fully again before me, he stared, his eyes beginning to lighten.

"I see Amil has taught you a new trick. Interesting." He looked to the door as if to see Amil standing guard outside.

"Disappointed?" I crossed my arms at my chest.

"Why would I be? No one likes an easy chase." He looked back to me then strode over to the couch across from me to sit.

He crossed his ankle over his knee, reclined, and rested an arm across the back. His typical regal stance. He scanned me, his sights snagging on parts of my body he'd found captivating before. I took in another deep breath and relaxed my shoulders a bit, an ache coming to the surface from either being too tight or from last night. An amused smile flashed across Talos' face, a challenge looming in his eyes for a brief moment. He looked to the balcony doors and spoke.

"Before I was called away, you were having an issue. Did you get it resolved or did Amil assist you with that as well?"

"A fellow Banner is wrapped up in a complication, but others are seeing to him." I was ignoring his brazen attempt to provoke me.

He took in the information, but I wasn't sure what he would be doing with it. I hadn't left to pursue finding Argo, and I didn't intend to. I didn't expect him to offer his help the way Amil had. He looked to me and I tried to keep my face neutral. If I was going to attempt to keep my promise to Althea, I needed to be here. He considered me for a moment then got up and stood looking down to me before turning to Althea's door.

"Let's get through this evening and I will decide what to do with you." And with that he strode into her room, not waiting for me to respond.

# CHAPTER NINETEEN

Not long after Talos left, without saying anything more to me, Althea came to the sitting room. Her demeanor was less rigid, but she still seemed upset. She sat on the middle sofa and let out a sigh of relief.

"Talos is going to speak with my father and Neil's father to let them know that I don't need any more stress about the wedding."

"I'm sure they will understand." I waited for her to continue, but she looked conflicted on whether to believe me.

"Perhaps. Talos is my father's most trusted friend, but he has never been swayed by other input. Especially when it comes to my desires."

"Does your father get along well with your soon-to-be family?" I felt like I knew the answer but wasn't sure how comfortable she felt sharing that information with me.

"They have had their fair share of disputes over the years. I'm not sure why he's come except to show some good faith for the union." She looked sad, as if disappointed that he was not truly here to see to her safety and wellbeing.

"I'm sure the meeting will go well."

"Talos is going to report back to me the moment they're through." She nodded to herself before grabbing her notebook and pen to jot down notes and questions to bring up to the wedding planner.

All appointments for the day had been canceled, but Cornelius arrived with the lunch cart a few hours later and Althea's mood was only slightly lifted when she saw him. He, on the other hand, had a look of gloom on his face. He had been sitting in with both of their fathers and Talos for the whole morning and there didn't seem to be an end in sight to their negotiations. They had been discussing lands, estates, farmers' protections, and several other things that Cornelius was expected to take over once his father stepped down. He stayed for lunch, but had to go back to the meeting quickly after finishing his meal. They embraced deeply and I felt for their situation. Neither of them wanted to contend with Pytr, and Stavros was taking the brunt of the trauma.

I wanted to ask him about the Banner he had hired, how he'd heard of our organization and if he knew that I was a Black Banner. And why he had hired her in the first place. But if he somehow didn't realize what I was, I didn't want to draw attention to it and didn't want to betray Amil's confidence.

A few hours later, a note was delivered to the suite for Althea and myself. We were expected to attend dinner in the main dining room with the Lords, Lady Welp, Pytr, and Talos. Althea was not pleased and grumbled the entire rest of the day before going to freshen up. I didn't know what to expect but imagined some agreements had been made through the day for a large friendly dinner to be taking place.

Hariss came to call upon us when dinner was about to begin. Yamir was outside the door waiting for us, but I had expected Amil. Confusion must have been plain as day on my face because he said without prompting, "Early shift change."

That did not clear any questions I had, in fact, it gave me

images of Talos firing Amil and sending him back to Cinder. What had happened between Talos and me earlier was first to cross my mind. Then I had the thought that possibly worse things were happening to Amil because of me. He had said that Talos was a dangerous being. I didn't want to have to wonder where he was, or what might happen to me next if Talos was that furious. I tried to push the thoughts out of my mind as we walked down the hall to the stairs.

The dining room was on the second floor and was large enough to fit at least two dozen beings, the long wooden table set in the middle of it. Tall windows overlooking the gardens behind the manor made up the entire far wall. Talos, the Lords, and Lady all sat around the table waiting, talking amongst themselves. We were escorted to our respective seats. Althea was brought to a chair between Cornelius and her father. Stavros sat at the head of the table with his wife to his left, and I was seated next to Talos who had taken the seat next to Lady Welp.

I looked over the elegant tablescape, with satin ivory table-cloth, dark blue table runner, and fine bone china at each setting. The low hum of voices across the table and through the rest of the party were general greetings—asking how the other was doing. Althea gave a weak smile to Cornelius, but was silent when her father greeted her. I glanced up the table to Lady Welp who was chatting with Pytr and her son. She seemed to be playing hostess— asking about Pytr's trip and if he had any plans to tour the closest city while visiting.

Talos spoke for Pytr, drawing my attention to him. "I will be escorting Pytr back to Cinder tomorrow."

I raised a brow at this. I didn't expect either of them to be leaving again so soon. But I could tell Althea's ears perked up when she heard her father would be on his way back home. She gave her father a confirming look and he nodded.

"Yes, I will be heading back. I have many important details to work out on my end for this union to take place smoothly. But I will be back before the wedding day, don't you worry, dear." He winked at his daughter and a tiny shutter ran through her.

The first course was brought out a moment later: a hors d'oeuvre of snapper crudo with chiles and sesame were placed in front of us. Only several minutes later, a small strawberry summer salad was presented. Then on to the soup course of creamy wild mushroom and shaved truffles, each more decadent than the last. Between each of these courses, one of the kitchen staff would come and announce the dish and give a brief history of the produce and meat being used.

For our main course, a large cart was wheeled out with a huge beef tenderloin roast. It was carved up in front of us before being served with roasted root vegetables and a rich wine reduction. The beef had been raised only thirty minutes away from the manor, the vegetables on a farm only an hour away and delivered weekly to surrounding communities. The Welps seemed to be trying to show Pytr that their lands were worth his daughter's union, or that their pride for their lands was deeper than issues with the Incubo of Cinder. He nodded politely and ate every morsel on his plate.

For dessert we were presented with a fruit and wine compote under a thick gelato, all from a winery in the foothills between Arta and Patras to the south. The wine we had with our meal was also delivered from this winery. The staff described the rainfall and altitude contributed to the undernotes of each grape varietal. I almost wished I knew more about wine to follow along, but they complimented each dish well.

Our last small course was a mignardise of custard tartlet with a dollop of dark chocolate and raspberry compote. The chocolate was the only item not grown in the region, but the cacao beans were imported then processed at a chocolatier in Arta that specialized in roasting the beans to perfection before grinding and only adding the highest quality of local ingredients to highlight the luxurious chocolate.

After our meal, we were served another glass of wine to aid us in conversation. Little was spoken during the meal and now that everyone had their fill of lovely food and drink, topics were broached lightly. Althea had opened up a little more after a second glass of wine, but only spoke when directly spoken to. Talos was still and quiet, his focus on Pytr most of the evening which I didn't mind. I was asked a few questions about where I was from and if I had been enjoying my time at the manor. I didn't have to lie much. I answered that I was from Cinder City and that my time with Althea had been enjoyable. I quickly shifted the discussion to Cornelius and Althea about whether they had heard back from the wedding planner.

That sent the rest of the guests, aside from Talos and me, into discussions of flowers, guests, and seating arrangements. A suggestion that the local chocolatiers come to do a whole dessert table was submitted by Pytr as it had been his favorite course of the whole meal. The evening was coming to an end, several yawns had made their way around the table when Pytr stood and began to excuse himself.

"I thank you again, Stavros, for your hospitality to myself and my Althea. I have a very early train to catch, but will be back very soon." Another wink and peck on the cheek to his daughter before he left the table and dining room.

Althea looked after him as he went, then turned to Cornelius, placing a hand on his arm. Possibly the first physical touch she had given him since we were seated, he put his hand on hers and smiled at her. They both seemed instantly more relaxed and content as if realizing they were a little more alone than before. Stavros and Camilla were the next to excuse themselves, but before Stavros left he spoke to his son.

"We will need to discuss matters with the Arta leaders

tomorrow morning, get some rest." And he offered his wife his arm, then politely bid Talos and me goodnight.

I looked to Althea who was now much more wrapped up in Cornelius' arm, their smiles loving and warm to each other.

"I will escort you and Althea to your suite before I turn in. I will be accompanying Pytr back to Cinder tomorrow morning and Amil will be coming with me." I didn't react as he spoke more to the room than directly to me.

I wasn't fully surprised, but I was a bit relieved to hear Amil was possibly not dead somewhere in the manor for disobeying orders. I didn't have true proof of that, but I chose to believe it. I waited for the cue to head back to the suite.

"You're not going to say anything?" He asked and I looked up to his confused face.

"What would you want me to say?" I took a sip of the last bit of my wine.

"Does it not upset you that Amil will not be here? I'd think you had grown attached to him considering how intimate your friendship has become in my absence." His tone was irritated and low.

I looked to Althea and Cornelius who hadn't heard a word of what Talos and I were discussing. I was thankful for that. Althea wasn't nosy and frankly too wrapped up in her own world to really care about what was going on in mine at the moment.

"He is your employee, as am I. We go where you send us."

"But neither fully followed my orders."

"If you'd like to have this conversation, I'd be happy to do so in the suite, but I will not do so here." The kitchen staff was still buzzing about clearing unused table settings and I didn't know how much longer Althea and Cornelius would ignore us.

"Fine." In a swift smooth motion, he stood. "Lady Althea, it is time to retire for the evening."

She nodded to him and gave Cornelius a kiss on the cheek before they both stood and walked to the doors. They walked behind us up the stairs and down the hall. Cornelius wished Althea a goodnight and proceeded to his own quarters. Yamir was standing outside the doors of the suite and gave a nod of acknowledgement to Talos as he passed. His eyes landed on me momentarily and something in them felt smug as if he were accusing me of something scandalous.

Once inside the suite, Althea, obviously sensing the tension between Talos and me, went to her room without bidding either of us a good night. I began walking to my usual spot on the sofa, but he spoke before I reached the low table.

"So, who was the better lover?" Stunned, I turned to face his challenging smirk.

"You can't seriously be asking me that." My stomach sank and began filling with viscous liquid fire.

"It's a fair question. You've had us both. You would be the best judge, would you not?"

"It is not a fair or appropriate question. I don't belong to either of you just because I've slept with you." I crossed my arms, my spine stiff.

"Is that right? How would Amil feel about that?" He slid his hands into his pockets, his expression cool and unreadable.

"I suppose you can ask him yourself. I haven't seen him nor would I ask him such outrageous questions." I turned and sat on the sofa, facing him.

"Hmm, interesting. So, you've learned a way to block us out and now our feelings don't matter to you?"

"If he didn't want me to know how to sever the connection, why would he teach me how?" He considered me for a moment.

"To protect you," he paused and smiled devilishly, "From me."

A rolling heat in my stomach gave way to a pull. I fingered the seam of the cushion to ground myself. A whirling, thick feeling started to surround me as the room became more dense with his intentions. My fingertips started to dig into the cushion as I struggled to keep him out of my head and emotions.

"Don't you remember me claiming you? You told me that you were mine." His voice filled my head, and I closed my eyes, trying to focus harder.

"While I was inside of you. You begged for me... moaned for me." The words dripped heavily into me, flashes of his hands on my hips before my eyes. I was reliving the sensation of his mouth on mine and his rough voice groaning in my ear as he climaxed, then the cavernous pit he left me with before traveling back to Cinder.

"Stop!" I stood up quickly, not realizing he had moved so much closer to me.

The hold over me broke and disappeared, the air thinning, but his scent still hung close to me, the heat of his body reaching my cheek. His eyes dark and duplicitous at what I had conjured. He wasn't surprised, but more amused, like I had gifted him a new tool to use in me. The back of his hand found my cheek as he softly caressed and traced my jaw.

"Isa, you are a more fascinating and dangerous instrument than I initially knew." I blinked with confusion at this.

"Why does that not actually feel to be a compliment?" I narrowed my eyes to him.

"Oh, but it is. Not many Mortals have been able to ward off an Incubo's draw. Especially one who has shared a bed with one... or two of us." His eyes traveled down my face, landing at my chest.

"That doesn't make me feel any more flattered." I tried to gulp in air, but only inhaled more of him as he inched closer.

"Would you rather me tell you that the thought of Amil putting his hands on you fills me with furious jealousy?" His hand moved down my face and neck, coming to rest on my shoulder.

"There is a difference between jealousy and being territorial." I remained still as his lips caressed the top of my cheek.

"Only the weak-minded possess the ability to lose what they believed to be theirs."

My eyes flitted closed as I started to feel his body press against mine, and everything else in the room blurred from my senses. A hand at the small of my back, the other cradling my jaw as his full lips pressed to my skin. Dragging down my face to the nape of my neck before parting and allowing his teeth to gently close around the delicate skin—a small gasp escaped my lips. Without knowing how they got there, my fingers entangled the back of his shirt, pulling him closer to me; his breath through his teeth heavy and hot over me before putting more pressure into his bite. My knees began to give way as a ragged hum from him sent vibrations down to my toes.

Within a moment, my back was pressed against the soft cushion. My legs were being hoisted across the sofa as he lay over top of me, finally releasing my neck to momentarily find my mouth. I lay beneath him and wondered how I let him put me here, but not wanting to be anywhere else.

"Talos," I whispered breathlessly, opening my eyes to him staring down at me, his eyes deep and hungry.

"Give me a few more moments and you'll only remember ever moaning my name. No one else's." I could feel his pull starting to consume me.

His hand slipped down onto my thigh, bringing the smooth fabric of my skirt up, pulling my panties aside, his thumb grazing against the moist heat there. His mouth crashed onto mine before he plunged two fingers into me, beckoning me to move against his palm. My hips struggled to escape his force and betrayed me as I gave in to his demand. My arms wrapped around his neck as he pulled his hand away before driving back inside, causing me to gasp and moan.

"Fight me, Isa. Give me your greatest attempt." His voice rough, ragged, and challenging.

I tried to focus on the chandelier hanging at the center of the room. The crystals caught the light and cast refracted light against the off-white, smooth ceiling. My eyes followed the silver loops and bends that met in the center of the ornate fixture. I tried to count the dangling gems. One, two, three. But he maneuvered his fingers again, knocking the room from my vision with slow circular motions in and around me. If only our clothing would dissipate so easily.

"Is that all the resistance you have?" I wanted to meet his challenge but wanted to chase my release more.

Suddenly, a new realization came to me. I slipped my fingers through his hair and locked eyes with him. Taking in a breath, I pressed his face down into my chest and downward towards my stomach, concentrating on the feel of his mouth through my clothing: first my blouse, over the rumpled skirt at my hips, then the silk of my panties. His eyes rolled up to me, waiting for my instruction, my command. I nodded and he pulled the fabric to the side, his mouth dipping down to replace his thumb, but his fingers not leaving where they were nestled inside of me. I moved my hips up slightly and slowly against his mouth.

The air rushed into my lungs, the room coming back into view around us. The details of the room focused as I let out a small whispered breath to encourage him. He swirled his tongue around and over me. I dragged his fingers through me rhythmically as I began to feel more tension mounting inside of me. His eyes not leaving mine as he watched me reach the edge of climax, he hummed his approval and pushed me over, shattering and cursing his name as he smiled against me.

He flattened his tongue, running it over me twice then withdrawing himself from me and replacing my clothing to where it should be. I sat up and smoothed out my skirt as he stood and licked his fingers before fixing his tie.

He turned and started to walk to the double doors without saying a word about what I had just been able to accomplish, but as he reached for the door knobs, he paused. "Amil will remain here to teach you further."

And with that he was gone, but I felt nothing as his form gave way to the doorway.

# CHAPTER TWENTY

The next morning I was awake before Althea. I had showered and dressed before going to wait for her in the sitting room. I walked past the double glass doors out to the balcony to see a low mist covering the grounds stretched out in front of the manor. A black car had pulled up the drive and quickly disappeared from view under the balcony, here to take Pytr off to the train station. A sound from behind me caught my attention, a muffled noise coming through the doors of the suite. Yamir might still be on duty or it could be a guard change this early in the morning. It wasn't seven o'clock yet, but I didn't know when they changed shifts.

I walked over to the door and cracked it open a hair and saw the back of someone in a dark suit right against the opening. Two hushed familiar voices, Talos' and Amil's, came in through the small space and I held my breath trying to hear exactly what was being said.

"You are not to have these lessons on duty. Althea comes first. Yamir and Klaus will be rotating shifts to shorten duration and keep everyone rested and alert. Understood." Talos' voice sounded harsh, angry.

"Yes, sir."

"I'll be back in three days. And I would prefer Isa not be turned completely against me when I get back."

"Sir, I—" Amil started.

"She is only here because I hired her to protect Althea. What is between her legs will not complicate your initiative or this union. Am I clear?" His voice raised slightly above a whisper and part of me wanted to shrink away from the door.

"Yes, Talos. Nothing will upset Lady Althea's union. You have my word."

"Your word has been weaker as of late. Do not make the same mistake in betraying my trust again, Amil, or you will not live long enough to see another assignment."

Amil didn't answer, and the shadowy form of Talos beyond him left swiftly. I pressed my palm into the door as I tried to close the door silently, but as soon as I took a step away it opened and Amil came inside.

"Thought I heard you listening. What are you doing awake so early?"

"I couldn't sleep." It wasn't a lie. I hadn't slept well with so much on my mind. "Good to see you're in one piece."

"I think I have you to thank for that. Apparently, your display of rebellion against Talos' pull impressed him enough to let me keep all my limbs."

He walked further into the room and past the sofas to look out the balcony windows. The sun started to rise higher against the line of trees around the property, casting golden light around his dark hair and over his olive skin. His cheekbone was casting a shadow on his cheek as he turned to me. My feet were moving before I realized as I joined him at the doors. Our eyes met before we heard the caravan of black cars and SUVs start up, and we watched them drive down the drive and out the gate.

He spoke without facing me, "They're moving up the wedding. Cornelius is going to tell Althea today."

"How soon?" I blinked at him, surprised that I was hearing this information from him and not Talos.

"Seven days." He paused before looking to me. "Hope you're ready for a busy week."

I was ready for this assignment to be over, I really was. But I wasn't sure that it would be that easy. I wanted to head to Amples to look for Argo. I wanted to be back in my own bed. And I especially wanted to be far away from these Incubo men who I've had to emotionally and mentally ward off. I was exhausted.

"I'll be outside most of the day. Be ready for a lesson later." He ran a hand down my arm, then held my palm in his fingers.

I nodded in reply. He leaned in and kissed my forehead before turning to leave. I wanted to stop him, to say something kind or express my thankfulness to him for wanting to help me in so many ways. To tell him how relieved I was to know that Talos hadn't fired him or killed him because of me. But the words wouldn't come, so instead:

"Amil," I called after him, meeting him in the middle of the room and pulling his hands into mine.

I closed my eyes and relaxed my defenses, felt my emotions pouring into my palms and tried to imagine them flowing into his. When I opened my eyes again to look to him, his eyes were jet black, the flame blazing clearly, staring into me as if I were a great wonder only to be seen once in a lifetime. I blinked and stepped out of our hold, but he closed the gap. His fingers raked into my hair and he pressed his body against mine, our lips meeting one another's.

Instantly, his pull bloomed behind my navel causing heat to ripple through me and come to life, the air around us thick as syrup. I took hold of the belt around his waist and pulled him as close as I could, but there was nowhere closer. Needing to feel him, every inch of him on me and inside of me, I pulled my arms up around his neck and pushed up onto the balls of my feet. He knew what I needed. I was fully open to him and his needs were mirroring my own. Or possibly amplifying his. I didn't care.

His arms wrapped around my waist and he effortlessly lifted me, and before my legs could even fall to his hips, we were at the threshold of my bedroom door. He pulled away, looking up to me with hunger in his expression.

I eagerly nodded before our mouths met again. One of his hands left my hip and opened my door. I stepped down and out of our embrace, and he followed and shut the door behind him. I picked up the hem of my blouse and pulled it over my head, tossing it to the floor, then stepped out of my skirt but left my dagger strapped in place at my thigh. He unbuttoned his shirt, eyes not leaving mine. Shrugging it off, he wrapped an arm around my waist, bringing me close and kissing me again. We backed up against the bed, the mattress hitting the back of my knees.

I sat before him, reaching up to unbuckle his belt then unfastening his slacks. The muscles in his taught stomach flinched as I grazed his skin, clothing dropping to the floor, his eagerness apparent. I took his length in my hand and looked up to him before opening my mouth and using my tongue to tease him, stroking him up and down as I whirled softly at the tip of him. His jaw dropped as he released a husky breath, closing his eyes and smoothing one hand through my hair as I took him fully in my mouth.

He let out a pleasurable curse and followed my motions with his hand. I watched him as he enjoyed each stroke, muscles tensing then relaxing as my lips pushed and pulled him. I listened to his silent requests to take him in deeper and followed his cues to quicken or slow my pace. Taking him deep into my throat, he held me still, the fauces closing around him and my lungs protesting after a few moments until he released and withdrew.

He pushed me onto my back to watch him take my under clothes off, kissing my stomach and hips. I roamed my eyes over the bulge of muscles of his arms and shoulders, every bit of him sculpted in lean, lethal muscle. There were several scars across his left arm and his chest, making him look more seasoned than I had thought before.

He bent down and scooped me up, my legs wrapping around his waist as we moved higher up over the linens of the bed, only pausing briefly at the top of the bed to look down at my naked body, admiring its curves against him. He pressed his chest into mine before entering me, giving slow and intense thrusts. I wrapped my legs around his waist to drive him deeper, savoring every touch of our skin, each kiss to my cheek and neck thoughtful.

My heart pounded against its confines, my core tightening and pleasure building as the pleased tone in his voice pressed in on my ears as he quickened his pace, causing me to groan against his shoulder.

His arms tightened around me, his body starting to tense. The build was deep inside of me before he toppled over the edge, a curse ripping from his lips in a deep, spent voice. He panted over me with slight disappointment in his satisfied expression. He kissed me again deeply, taking in a ragged breath before rolling over and off the bed.

"I'm sorry, I couldn't stop." He seemed embarrassed for finishing so quickly, but he wasn't the first, and I doubt he would be the last to do so.

"We should get back to work." I got off the bed and gathered my clothes, then turned towards the bathroom.

He grabbed my arm and turned me towards him, only wearing his undershorts. "That won't happen again. And next time I won't at all." Determination thick in his throat.

"Next time, huh?" I teased, as if I really had any complaints.

"If we didn't have to put our lives on the line for the next eight hours, I would spend the time between your thighs showing you how sorry I am." And that did it. Butterflies released into my stomach and a grin spread across my face.

He winked, then turned to finish getting dressed. I tried to swallow my pounding heartbeat and held my clothes close to my body. I padded to the bathroom to clean up and dress. Althea would be awake by now and likely waiting for me in the sitting room.

# CHAPTER TWENTY-ONE

After dressing, I opened the bathroom door to an empty room. Amil had gone, but there wasn't a pit in my stomach. No emptiness or barren hole where my guts should be. I wasn't sure if it was me becoming more aware of the Incubos' pull or if Amil was kind enough to sever the connection gently so it didn't affect me the way it had with Talos. Either way, I was grateful. I opened the bedroom door and found the sitting room still empty.

Walking out to the space between our bedroom doors, I debated whether or not to check on Althea. Breakfast hadn't been brought up yet and with her father being gone, I was sure she was feeling some kind of relief and possibly slept much deeper than she had the few nights before. I decided to grab my laptop and wait a little while longer on the sofa.

Some time passed as I checked emails, paid bills, and moved money around when I heard a small knock on the door. Amil had stepped back to allow the breakfast cart to be wheeled in by the young kitchen Fata. He stopped and looked around for a moment, unsure if it was his place to ask where Althea may have been. Which it wasn't, so I didn't volunteer to speak. Amil stood at the door waiting for him to exit, and he cleared his throat and the Fata shook his head and turned on his heels, the door to the suite closing behind him.

Moments later, Althea's door opened and her surprised face found mine.

"Oh, good morning Isa! Is everything okay?" She came and sat down on her sofa as I placed breakfast tea and pastries out on the low table.

"Yes, I couldn't sleep so I thought I'd get an early start on the day. Tea?"

She nodded and offered me a warm smile, her bubbly nature blooming once again now that the stress of her father being on the property was gone. I poured her some hot water and slid over a tray of buttery croissants.

"Can I ask you something?" Her voice was small, but I gave her my full attention. "Do you… um. You and Amil?"

"He's helping me learn to block out the male Incubo pull. It's been complicated." I didn't know how to explain it to her, or really to myself.

"I've known him a very long time, you know. He's like a friend to me and I see the way he looks at you." I really didn't want her to continue.

"Incubo and Mortals don't really mix well from the gossip I've heard."

"No, we don't. Which is why I'm trying to warn you. He has taken Mortal lovers in the past and it didn't end well for them."

I was speechless, and shock must have been hanging on my face because Althea chewed on her lip waiting for me to grasp the information she'd just dumped in my lap. I had known that Talos had a trail of disaster in his wake, but Amil hadn't given me the impression that he also had a torrid sordid past. I should have known, should have asked, but also should I really care?

The door to the suite opened and Cornelius stepped through

the doorway. Althea bounced up to her feet and bounded into his arms.

I shook my head, pushing my emotions aside.

"Good morning, dearest." He kissed her softly and then walked hand in hand to the sitting area.

"I'm so glad you stopped by this morning. I don't think we will have a moment for lunch today." Althea sat and pulled him down into the seat next to her.

Cornelius' face fell, his eyes on their joined hands on his knee. "Althea, I have to talk to you about something our fathers have decided. I know you're going to be upset, but I agree with them."

Her bubbles deflated and tears began welling up in her smoke eyes. I knew what he was going to tell her, but it didn't make the situation any less heartbreaking to watch. She had been planning and dreaming of her wedding day for so long, and her father made a choice and didn't even bother to tell her himself. But perhaps it was better that Cornelius was to be the one to tell her, he was the groom after all, but it wasn't going to be less of a blow.

"We have to move up the wedding day to next Saturday." He waited for her reaction, but her expression was blank and she was quiet for several long moments.

"Althea, my love. Please say something."

She stood up and walked to the windows looking over the lawn. She was quiet for another moment before turning around with a smile plastered to her face. Cornelius looked from her to me, then back to her as if wondering if I also saw that his fiancée had gone mad from shock.

"I better call the planner. There is so much to do and change. Most things were settled, but I'm sure we can move them up!" She turned and trotted off to her room.

"Um. I uh—" Cornelius turned to me, mouth agape.

I shrugged and looked to Althea's door as she swept back

into the sitting room with her notebook, wedding binder, and cell phone. She sat down next to Cornelius and started to dial a number on her phone.

"Darling... will you be alright? I have to get going for a few meetings." He stood slowly and waited, but Althea was now talking to someone in a friendly, rushed tone.

He walked out of the suite and glanced back one last time before closing the door, concern hanging on his face. I looked to Althea who was now listening intently to the person on her other line. She looked up to me with a look that resembled someone trying to keep the world from falling apart but not wanting to alarm anyone around them.

"Isa, could you do me a favor and summon the kitchen manager?" She cut to the person on the other line. "Yes, that's right. I want them here at six that morning until noon."

I stood and went to the door. I couldn't go myself, but Amil could fetch the kitchen staff. But now I was faced with the idea of having to speak to him after what Althea had said about his past indiscretions with Mortals. It wasn't any of my business, it didn't matter what he did in his personal life after all. I couldn't shake the feeling that he had withheld information from me and yet warned me about Talos.

Opening the door slowly, he turned and one edge of his mouth ticked upward. I stepped out into the hall, looking back to Althea who was too busy to notice. I closed the door and fully faced him.

"Althea needs the kitchen manager and likely the grounds keeper to be sent up. Would you mind sending for them?"

"I already called the kitchen, she'll be up soon. I'll get the other staff to come up after." I nodded and turned to the door. "Is everything alright?"

I paused "She's a bit frazzled at the moment, but I have no doubt she will have everything figured out in a few hours." I didn't look to him, andhe pressed a palm against the door to stop me from going inside.

"You seem off. I didn't realize you were so invested in Althea's wedding plans." His voice was low and not at all teasing.

"When you told me that Talos had had past encounters with Mortals that didn't end well, why didn't you say that you also had similar experiences with my kind?" The words fell from me more harshly than I intended.

He was speechless, he looked me up and down then opened his mouth to speak, but Althea reached open the door before a syllable could pass his lips.

"Isa, is the kitchen manager on her way yet?" Althea was still holding her phone to her ear and was looking more upset.

"I'm right here, dear!" The squat Fata was rushing down the hall towards us with the younger tall Fata at her heels.

Althea moved aside to let them in and grabbed my arm to pull me inside with her and the staff, leaving Amil in the hall to stew in our interrupted conversation. I still wasn't sure why I brought it up in the first place, and to spring it on him like that was asking a lot of someone that didn't owe me anything. I needed the reminder to keep my distance, to remember that this was just another job and these Incubo men were just a temporary obstacle.

The Fata were huddled around Althea taking down the new times and dates in order to have items finished for the wedding, each of them nodding their heads after each of her words. She waved me over to where they were all sitting to join in on the arrangements. I took in a deep breath before going to sit down. It was going to be a very long day.

# CHAPTER TWENTY-TWO

I was right. It had been a long day and, by the time the dinner cart was delivered, I was exhausted. Althea had summoned the wedding planner who brought three assistants with her to help rearrange the events and vendors. All but the guest list had been taken care of and it was going to be a long day of personal notes being written and messengered to each and every guest tomorrow. Althea took dinner in her room to eat while writing the first batch before retiring for the night. I decided to take her lead and eat in my room, just to have some peace. It didn't last long. As soon as I had finished and placed my plate on the kitchen cart, Amil walked through the suite doors.

"I wasn't sure if you still wanted a lesson, but Talos did request us to continue with them." He slipped his hands into his pockets and waited.

I didn't want another lesson. I didn't want to have to learn this new skill so proficiently. I wanted this assignment to be over so I didn't have to deal with any more Incubo males trying to ensnare me at every turn. But that wasn't the reality. Each and every skill in my arsenal was valuable, so I nodded and headed back into my room, holding the door open as an invitation.

He passed by me swiftly and leaned against the footboard of the bed, crossing his arms. I shut the door then pressed my back against it, waiting for him to speak. In a blink his body caged me against the door, hands on either side of me, his black eyes like daggers into me. Heat emitted off of him as the air thickened, choking me as I tried to focus. Before I could find something to hold on to, another wave from him hit me and my lungs crumpled. I gasped, throwing my hands to his chest, trying to push his tether out of my mind and off my body, but to no avail.

"This is mercy, Isa." His voice rasped in my ear. "This is only a fraction of what Talos could do to you. Now, sever the tie." He drove another wave of intangible force through his palms that shot up my arms.

I could feel something inside of me faltering, ready to burst open, and I didn't want to know what would happen if I didn't drive his power back. I pushed harder against him, trying to dig deep inside to push him out before finally feeling a cooling rush of air to my lungs. I cursed loudly, my voice ringing through the space between us as he took a step back.

"What the hell!" I steadied myself as he turned away from me, loosening his tie.

He ran his hands through his hair as he retreated back towards the bed. He slouched his jacket off and threw it over the footboard, turning and rolling his sleeves up.

"You wanted a lesson." His brows furrowed with a challenge in his tone.

He tossed the tie over his jacket before taking down the first two buttons of his shirt. Undone just enough to reveal some of his chest before sliding his hands in his pockets once again. He was anything but casual as he stood waiting, his body tense against the white dress shirt. The muscle in his jaw clenched as he raised his chin to the side. He was obviously bothered by our talk earlier and was already defensive. This wasn't going to be like our previous lessons. He was going to be visceral, raw, and ready to cause me pain for not giving him a chance to defend his character while on duty.

Fine. If it was a fight he wanted, it was a fight he would get. But I wasn't going to play by his rules.

I bolted to my nightstand. He tried to stop me, but I caught him off guard and slipped from his grasp. I grabbed the Alexandrite dagger, and as I turned around, it landed at the soft flesh of his throat. He put his hands up and backed away slowly, but I followed, only giving him one step of distance as I lowered my blade. Storm clouds filled his eyes again, chasing away the pitch black pools of rage, his irises coming back into view as we reached the middle of the room. Holding this weapon wasn't fair-minded, but neither was the display he had made.

"If you think Talos will give you warning, you're not as clever as either of us thought." He lowered his eyes to the dagger.

"I wouldn't think that of Talos, but I expected more from you. That won't happen again."

He spun away and tried to knock loose the dagger, but only managed to knock me off balance into the bedpost. Pushing off of it, I lunged and kicked out at his knee. He dropped to the floor and rolled onto his front, sweeping out his leg then grabbing for my wrist. Scuffling, my elbow smashed into his jaw before I rolled my body onto his back, pulling his hair to bring his chin up to slip the sleek blade against his throat. I drove my knee between his shoulders as he struggled from the weight of me on top of him. Both of us out of breath, adrenaline throbbing in my ear, I waited for his next move knowing full well that I wouldn't hesitate to let this blade first slice through his skin, then veins before letting him bleed out on the floor.

"I love feeling you on top of me, especially when your temper is peaked," he gruffly mocked.

Anger surged through me, heat seeming to sprout from the pressure on my legs. I released him from the blade before giving a shove further into the floor. I got up and crossed the room, catching my breath and cooling my temper partly in defense of another wave of his attack, but also knowing that a clouded mind can cost you your life in a fight. I didn't take my eyes off him as he hoisted himself up off the ground and smoothed the wrinkles of his shirt. One brow raised as a half impressed thought tugged at the side of his lips.

"This lesson is over." I didn't move but raised my chin to the door.

"Giving up already?" he scoffed without glancing where I directed.

I crossed my arms over and adjusted my weight to one hip. I shouldn't have the bitter taste of betrayal looking at his smug face. We hardly knew each other, and the time we had spent together had only been a mess of confusion. Even now, his words were challenging me in more ways than one: to give in to him, to let him into my head and body, or to admit that I wasn't strong enough to fend him off.

I took a deep breath as he stepped closer to me. My fingers wrapped around the dagger's hilt, the muscles in my arm tightly wound, ready to strike. Another step. His eyes began to darken.

Two more steps, my breath lodged in my throat.

One last step, he towered over me. His nimble fingers gently lifted my chin, his lips feather light over mine. I could feel myself slipping deeper into his pull as the never-ending black-ness stared down into me, threatening to engulf me fully. Another hand found my hip and pulled me closer.

"Say it," he breathed, "Say you submit and I will take you to that bed and you will never question who I really am again."

The familiar flicker in his eyes came to life. The far-off spark of a candle in a long dark hallway beckoned to me, inviting me in to be wrapped up in its warmth and safety. The words he wanted, words that I wanted so desperately to give to him, were clawing their way up my throat. All I had to do was open my mouth and let them free. I could be free. Worried tension melted away from my head and shoulders, seeping through me and settling behind my navel as his fingertips tightened on my hip. A silent ask to answer. A haze enveloped the both of us as if the room itself were waiting for my reply, my surrender.

But Banners do not surrender. We do not give in to anyone. We fight until our last breath. *We do not shy away from darkness, for we are the shadows. We do not have fear, for we are the terror. We know no danger, for we are vicious.* I could hear Zaida's voice calling to me from the darkness, pulling me away from the beacon and drawing me back from the void, reminding me what we were. Deadly.

My knee struck first, sharply cutting up into his groin, bringing him to his knees to where my dagger was waiting. This time leaving a rip in his shirt that was quickly damp with his blood. With the blade firmly pressed at the side of his neck, he rolled his pain-filled eyes up to mine. My chest heavily rose and fell as I fought back the gnawing pit growing in my stomach.

"I'd give you everything if you let me." I almost believed him.

"I bet you say that to all the pretty things you've broken to pieces and left to shrivel to dust." Anger filled me again as I watched his eyes start to clear, the spark gone.

"Who were they?" I pressed the blade against him harder, casting him a dark look. "Do you even remember their names?"

"This is nothing like them. You are different. Stronger." He didn't move, didn't pull away in defense.

"Is that supposed to be the excuse for what you did?"

A thin line of blood now trailed from the cut at his neck and disappeared down the open collar of his shirt, reappearing in a pooling stain at his chest.

"I'm not making excuses for my actions. I do regret them. And it has been a very long time since I've taken a Mortal to bed."

"You lied to me. Why should I believe you now?"

"Because you have always felt my heart. You know me inside and out."

"Bare emotions don't mean we know each other. What we've felt during these sessions has been nothing but heated moments manipulated to teach me defense." I cut deeply at his ego.

"Is that really how you feel? Show me then." He leaned into the blade, more blood spilling from the cut.

"I don't need to prove anything to you, Amil." I pulled the dagger away and took a step back for him to get to his feet. He was done fighting.

"The nights we have spent together in that bed, the moments we have spent intertwined within one another, that meant nothing to you?" His voice pulled at me, but I had to push back.

"You were a good lay, Amil, but that was it." I was lying now.

He was good in bed, only one of the few who knew what they were doing and cared if they pleased their partner. Between him and Talos, I didn't know who I would choose, but it was very close. They were both powerful in their own rights, but also attentive lovers that got off on giving what the other person desired. Using their abilities to sense what I wanted or needed to reach euphoria, they left me wanting more after each encounter. As for feelings, real feelings. I was still trying to figure out if what I felt for either man was real or just amplified lust that I was being fed. Amil was sweet, caring, and if given the chance would probably make a decent partner. But I didn't need a partner. I'd never had one. My line of work didn't permit for anything more than frivolous bedfellows.

"I know what you felt. You may not, but I can show you." He was suddenly and silently behind me, lifting my chin with one hand, lips pressed to my neck.

"Don't." I could barely speak as his pull mounted, his arm smoothing across my waist as he drew me into him.

"Let me show you, Isa." Warmth started to creep down my arm and up my neck.

I closed my eyes as the heat flowed through me, reaching deep inside of my core. Coaxing me, it stirred to life the fire behind my navel. But this wasn't anything more than lust and I knew it. I met his touch with a vision of ice, forcing his hold to retreat and sever from me. He should have known it would happen. Maybe he did because he didn't pull his hands away, but let the connection dissipate.

"This lesson is over." I pulled out of his arms, and he didn't stop me.

I reached the foot of the bed before turning back to him, a look of defeat and anguish hanging over him. I wasn't angry with him; I wasn't anything. But something heavy pressed against my chest. He sighed, approaching the bed to retrieve his things. The tear at his shirt was still wet and the trail of blood from his neck joining the pool.

"Are you going to be ok?" I crossed my arms and lifted my chin in a pointed gesture.

He looked down to the wound at his chest, then pressed a hand to his neck, pulling it away to evaluate the amount of blood left on his palm. "I should be fine tomorrow. I'll heal slower, but to your disappointment, I'm sure, I will heal."

I reached out to his hand, looking at the smudges of bright red against his dusky skin, then looked back to his eyes. "I don't want you hurt, Amil. Let me clean you up, it's the least I can do."

I didn't let him answer; he would have rejected my offer after the confrontation we had just had. I went to my dresser and pulled out a first aid kit then went to the bathroom to wet a cloth. When I came back to where I had left him at the foot of the bed, he had taken his shirt off. I couldn't help but stare at his bare chest. I cleaned the cut at his neck first until it stopped bleeding. The gash on his chest was deeper and longer, but didn't look like it needed stitching. I disinfected then placed bandages over the wounds. After cleaning my hands and packing away the kit, I stood in front of him.

"Thank you," he said humbly, standing up straight and turning to grab his things again.

"Stay."

He stopped, but didn't turn to face me. "Isa…"

"That's what I want. I want you to stay with me tonight."

I wasn't sure why, but I didn't want him to leave. For whatever reason, or whatever this was between us, I didn't want him to leave like this, and I knew he didn't want to leave either. He had made it very clear that he wanted me, but I was willing to wager that he didn't know why or what that meant any more than I did.

He didn't speak. Instead he undressed down to his undershorts and set his bloody clothes down on the chair near the dresser. I eyed the muscles of his back and shoulders as he moved to the side of the bed, favoring his injured side. I changed into sleeping clothes as he pulled the linens back on the other side of the bed, sliding between them. I watched as he lay back and stared silently at the gauze canopy above. Then I leaned over and turned the table side lamp off before climbing into bed and lying on my back, mimicking his pose.

"You're learning very quickly." He broke the silence.

"Are you complimenting me or are you disappointed?" I asked, looking over to him.

He turned towards me on his side and propped himself up on an elbow to look down on me. "Every bit of what you have accomplished is impressive. I don't think you fully grasp how unique this ability is. How difficult it is to master. I have not lied to you, Isa. You are different, stronger than any other Mortal I have ever met."

"You told me about Talos, and the Mortals he had used, but

didn't mention your own experiences. You may not have lied, but withholding information like that doesn't evoke trust." I scanned his face, there was sincerity and remorse there.

"It's been years since I've engaged with a Mortal. Partly to do with employment restrictions but also because of the toxicity that I bring. I knew that no matter what I was feeling towards them, they could never endure me. Until I met you," He paused, reaching out to touch me, but pulled back, "I only get a small glimpse of what my influence does to you, but believe me when I say that it is several times worse for me. The agony I feel when I leave a room you're sitting in feels like every bone in my body is breaking, trying to will each shard to return to your side."

I couldn't move, I didn't know what to say. He reached for me again, this time running his thumb over my bottom lip.

"The slightest graze of your skin against mine ignites my every nerve. Every inch of me becomes alert and starved for just one touch of your finger. The pitted feeling you get in your gut is a small aperture compared to the canyon that implodes within me."

My throat was dry; pain welled in my chest as he spoke such beautifully tragic words. Things no one else has ever said to me, how could they when I've rarely given them my true name. I rolled towards him and pressed my palm to his chest, a resonating heat brushing against my fingers. He took in a deep breath then audibly sighed, putting a hand over mine to hold me there. Our eyes met as his opened up into black pools, the distant ember's reflection inviting me down into their depths.

"Do your eyes always light up when you're...attracted to someone?" I breathed.

"No," he smoldered.

*No.*

No—that far off flame was for no one else but me. That spark first made its appearance on the train. The illumination in a black willing to consume me fully.

"How does it work? How is it you and Talos can affect me like you do?"

He hesitated for a moment as if he didn't want to answer. "I cannot speak for Talos, but I can sense your pulse quickening. I can feel the heat of your body rising, and it provokes something inside of me and ignites all my senses. I can tap into your most basic emotions. I can feel you on a cellular level: joy, pain… fear. At times without being able to control it, my desires overrun my sensibility and speak for me. This is when my feelings can bleed through our connection to amplify and influence yours. When you were more susceptible to Talos before we started training, I could feel you slipping under his mind. How he dulled, then hurt you."

A mix of anger and guilt flashed over his face. He likely blamed himself for not getting to me first or fast enough. As if he had allowed Talos to take advantage of me before he had met me.

"The energy that you experience emanating from me while we're training, when everything goes dark and your lungs are gripped, that is the magnitude of my will over your mind. When an Incubo does want to manipulate their intended prey, it could be pleasure they have never experienced before or it can be so excruciating that they feel as though they're dying."

"I don't understand." I shook my head gently, trying to process.

"It's not for Mortals to understand. And if it were my choice, you wouldn't experience it at all." A look of regret flushed his features.

"Show me. You said you could show me how you feel."

"Isa, did you not hear what I said about the full effect I could have on you? What my inner demons would put you through?" he asked, his tone gentle.

"You don't think I could withstand you?"

"I think you are the most formidable Mortal I have encountered in my lifetime. But that doesn't mean I want to see you suffer or be the one to inflict it."

"Would Talos?"

He grasped my point and reluctantly leaned in close to me to wrap his fingers around my jaw, and pulled me in closer, taking possession of me, his lips weightless against mine as he breathed into me. His eyes shifted in color, heating as I waited for the flicker of the kindly flame to beckon to me.

"Open up to me, Isa," My name slipped through his teeth and dripped from his mouth full of want. "Let me in."

A small crack to my guard as I took him into my lungs. A growing fever burned in my chest and belly as the whirl of him rushed into my mind. The room around us was darker, as if it had been swallowed up by the night sky. A fierce pounding in my head swelled as the growing presence of him filled my lungs. Pain shot through my heart, to the tips of my fingers and toes. I let out a small whimper, but if my throat allowed my voice to pass, I couldn't hear it over the sound of my heartbeat in my ear.

As quickly as the pain had started, ecstasy swept into my core. Wetness pooled between my thighs as my hips turned and pressed against him. He moved over me to settle his leg between mine and sank me into the mattress. The weight of him didn't feel heavy. I needed him to be closer. I wanted to feel him invade every bit of my body. I tilted my chin up to meet his lips, but he pulled away slightly, eyes not leaving mine as he gently pulled my knees up around him. Feeling him harden so close to where my body was crying out for him was torture.

I reached around to his back and pleaded with him silently to give into our desires, but he didn't budge. His breathing steadied, his focus impaling me as another emotion flooded my core. Sweet and cool, like ice over my arms and into my lungs. A firm gripping onto my womb. Tension and pressure pulsed through my nerves, building from nothing, but there nonetheless. Another wave of heat washed over me before he pressed his lips to mine. A moan rang in my ears as my back arched and release rippled from my core, sending jolts to my fingers and toes.

Breathing in sharply as he lifted his body off me to allow me to catch my breath, he propped back up on his elbow to watch me. I sat up and ran my hands over my face, then through my hair, waiting for the aftereffects to ebb away. My skin tingled and prickled against my clothing and the linens that all at once felt too restrictive. I pushed the blankets away, feeling suffocated, and pulled my legs crossed under me then turned my attention to him.

"You held back?"

Even though I had asked him to let me experience him at his most volatile, I was hesitant to experience the pain again.

"I had to, but you made it difficult." hunger pushed through his restrained demeanor.

"And those sensations, it's what you feel when we are together?"

"That's what I feel when you are sitting drinking coffee and I am at the door. What I am experiencing right now as we sit this close. Not touching you. That is much more intense, but it's worth every bit of agony."

"If it's agony, then why is it worth it?"

His eyes and fingers found a speck of dust on the linens, fingers picking at it.

"Because I have felt the unbearable pain and emptiness inside of you, and I would do anything to fill that void. To give you brief calm, a retreat from the shadows, and a moment of content."

Pain crushed my windpipe and tears blurred my vision. I wasn't alone, I had a family with The Black Banners, but for someone seemingly unbroken to want to make me whole even for a moment... even if the act in itself tore them to pieces and sacrificed their own happiness. I hadn't known that type of care and I wasn't sure how to respond or if I was even worthy of such affection. But before the storms of doubt could take hold of me completely, Amil sat up and pulled me to his lap. Gathering me up in his strong embrace, he cradled my body between his knees.

With his hand to my cheek, I lifted my chin. The sharp features of his face were illuminated by the moonlight coming in through the window. The warmth of his body pressing in on mine. He kissed me softly, sweetly, lovingly.

He held me close all night, our hands never leaving the other's skin, limbs tangled or draped over a leg or torso. Intimacy was something I'd never experienced before, and I wasn't sure I'd ever be able to after. As heartwarming as his words were, this time together was limited, ending quicker than we had both signed on for. The union would come and we would go our separate ways. But for the night, we would have this space.

# CHAPTER TWENTY-THREE

Morning arrived far too quickly, but I didn't wake up alone. Amil's chest pressed to my back, and every breath he took caressed against my skin. It was still early, the sun barely rising over the crest of the shrub line outside the window. Streams of light danced on the ceiling, uninhibited by curtains that I had forgotten about last night. I knew Amil had to get ready for the shift change, but the thought of him getting dressed and leaving nudged the inevitable burrowing to creep to the surface of my memory.

"I'll only be on the other side of the doors," a sleep filled gruff whispered in my ear.

"I didn't say anything." I couldn't suppress a guilty grin; I was caught feeling.

He kissed the top of my shoulder before rolling away to put his pants on. The bandages I'd placed on his wounds were still in place but looked to have done their purpose, only small patches of dried blood could be seen through them. He shrugged his ripped shirt on, then his jacket, not bothering to button either one; he was going back to his room to change before the shift change. Rounding the bed to me, he leaned down and ran his hand up the figure of my body under the linens and brushed a lock of hair from my cheek.

"If it were up to me, I would lie next to you in this bed all day just to hear you breathe my name as you slept." A kiss and he made his way to the door.

Before closing the door behind him he offered me a wink, but as he turned he spoke to someone in the sitting room, his voice pleasant and warm, "Good morning, Lady Althea. Isa will be out in a few moments. Can I get you anything?"

Fire. Lava. Pure searing power of the sun rose up my neck to my face. I pulled the blanket up over my head and curled into a ball of abashed mortification. I heard the door click, but open again only moments later. I peeked out to see Althea standing in my doorway, her hands on her hips and an aghast look hanging from her face.

"Isa! Do you not remember me warning you about Amil? And why was he bleeding?" She looked out the door as if she could still see him walking back to his room then back to me.

I sat up as she came closer, her expression grave. She had warned me about Amil to try and save me from falling to pieces like other Mortals before me. I didn't have to explain myself, but she needed me to assure her that I could manage my own emotions, at least better than previous Mortals before me.

"Althea, I—"

"We have a lot to do today," she interrupted and stormed out of the room.

Another wave of shame washed over me at disappointing someone who cared for me. I wasn't sure how I would make this right, but perhaps a shower would help me clear my mind. I padded to the bathroom, finding small droplets of blood here and there on the floor as I went. That would be interesting to explain to the housekeeper.

After showering and dressing, I found Althea in the sitting room with a few Fata staff members. They had brought breakfast in full banquet fashion. Large trays of meat, eggs, pastries, potatoes and so much more lined one wall of the room. Althea was joyously chatting with several of them, her smile bright and bubbly. She glanced at me, but that was the only acknowledgement she gave before continuing her conversation. The doors to the suite were wide open and several Fata breezed in and out of the doorway with plates in their hands.

A kitchen Fata approached me with an empty plate. "Here you go, ma'am"

I took the plate, a blank expression my only reply as they walked away. I went down the line of food, taking small samplings of everything and filling a cup with coffee. The low table had been replaced with a larger dining table with several chairs scattered around. They had pushed the couches several feet back to make room. I sat and ate my meal, watching each and every being come in and out of the suite to speak to Althea. She took each conversation or greeting as a personal request for her attention. This was her true element, being the center of an event and conversing with anyone who would listen.

After a long conversation with the kitchen manager's young assistant, Althea came to sit across the table from me with a cup of tea. There were only a few Fata roaming around, but they seem to be cleaning up and gathering up the spread to return the room to its normal state.

"I wanted to thank them for their hospitality and hard work," she said between sips of tea.

"That's very kind of you to think of them."

"Well, the next few days are going to be very stressful for everyone. It's the least I could do for all they will be enduring." A sour look crossed her as she met my eyes.

"I'm not criticizing you, Althea."

"Amil was here earlier. He grabbed a plate for Yamir and Klaus." She rolled her eyes in her cup.

"Althea, I did hear your warning about Amil, but you have

nothing to worry about. I am here to protect you and ensure that your wedding goes off without a hitch." I extended my hand across the table, holding my palm up to her.

She sighed, but laid her hand on mine before speaking, "I don't want to lose you to that… that—" she gave an exasperated sound.

"You can't lose me," I promised, and I meant it.

She smiled and gave a small nod. Not another word was spoken about the matter, but there was slight worry on her face when Amil checked in at his shift change several hours later.

The rest of the morning, however, was calm. We sat and watched as the suite went from makeshift dining area back to the lush sitting room. Talos would be back some time tomorrow and the wedding was only a few days away. Althea didn't have meeting after meeting planned. Instead, she spent most of the day reading and checking messages or answering phone calls. In the early evening the wedding planner and a band of her assistants arrived to go over the checklist of what needed to be done or delivered and what would be coming in the next couple days. I was amazed to see how quickly they were able to move everything up.

The only issue was the guest list. In their social circle it was expected for at least one hundred guests to be present at the reception, but with the sudden change, the list had dwindled down to a couple dozen. Many of her father's acquaintances would try to make it, but had not given an RSVP to the new date. Cornelius and his father began calling and sending messengers to their associates, but only a fair few would be available. Althea didn't mind this. She preferred a smaller audience and only agreed to invite guests she didn't know by request of her father or out of obligation to Cornelius' status as Lord.

Cornelius and Althea ate dinner together out on the balcony that evening. A small table with many candles had been set for them to enjoy time alone. I ate in my room while I sharpened my knives and checked emails. I hadn't heard from any other Banner in days since they set off for Amples to track down Argo. I took this as a sign that they hadn't found anything of substance yet, but if they didn't check in tomorrow, I would have to reach out. The anxiety of what that phone call would bring started to gnarl my stomach.

A small knock at my door brought my back. "Yes?" I called.

The door opened and Althea peeked in. "I wanted to say goodnight. Talos just gave me a call to let me know he would be arriving tomorrow afternoon."

I nodded. "Ok, sleep well. See you in the morning." She closed the door over and I heard her footsteps grow small as she went to her room.

Several minutes later, Amil arrived not bothering to knock on the door. Instead he gave me a warning pull before he entered. I stood at the side of the bed and held my Alexandrite pendant in my hand. Feeling the stone warm to my touch, the cool silver at my chest, I focused harder than I would have before, waiting for him to send a powerful wave my way.

I met him in the middle of the room and he began circling me slowly. "Breathe. Don't let your barriers down. Don't let them crumble." He ran a finger across my back as he passed, sending cool sparks through me.

I took in a deep breath and let it out slowly as he began pushing through my thoughts, the smallest tug behind my navel answering him. I squeezed my hand around the necklace harder, feeling the metal encasing the stone dig into my palm. The room began to brighten, the air thinning as he stopped in front of me.

A proud smile greeted me. "That was very good. It felt like you were in control the whole time."

He walked over to the dresser and took his jacket and tie off before rolling up his sleeves. I watched every movement of his fingers over his clothing and skin.

"Althea wasn't too happy to see me this morning." He cocked his head with a guilty grin.

"She's not too pleased that I didn't heed her warning about you," I shrugged.

"She cares deeply about you, and I can understand her worry. She's seen me at my most selfish." He slid his hands into his pockets.

I tried to find something interesting about my feet or the rug on the floor, not sure how to respond to their history.

"Are you ready for round two?" He took a few steps closer to me.

"I think I am, but don't hold back this time. Talos will be back tomorrow so we better have something to show for these lessons."

The devious smile on his face was telling. He rolled his eyes to mine, his bottom lip pressed between his teeth to stop his sass. His eyes already dark, the far off flame dancing its warm greeting and sending a small teasing pull. I blinked and he was only a breath away from me, his arm wrapped around my waist. He took in my scent and let out a gratifying sigh.

I held my ground as a heavy wave washed over me, the air around us becoming soup and the lights from the bedside tables becoming only shadows. My eyelids felt heavy and my knees weak as he pressed his chest into mine. I held my stone against my skin, flat against my palm between us, and recalled every color that shone when the light hit it. I focused on how beautiful it looked in full sunlight or the weight of it around my neck. I counted how many tiny silver rings held it together.

"I'd like to see you wearing only that necklace." A gruff voice echoed in my ear.

I smiled. "I'd like to see you wearing nothing but my dagger to your throat."

A throaty laugh broke the tether as he stepped away from me. "Well, I think Talos will be pleased... or intrigued by your progress."

He sat at the foot of the bed and crossed his arms over his chest, a more solemn expression than playful. I shifted my weight to one hip and fiddled with the dangling jewel at my chest, waiting for him to give more than his apprehensiveness.

"When he comes back, he's going to want to test you." He looked down to his crossed ankles.

"You're worried?" I didn't really need to ask, I could see it on his face.

"I'm worried that I've failed in preparing you for what he can truly draw out of you. He's much more powerful than I am." He refused to meet my eye.

I sat next to him, leaning back on my hands and letting out a sigh. I didn't know what to expect when Talos returned and checked on my progress. The skill would be precautionary, but I also didn't want to find out how underdeveloped it was under extraneous circumstances.

"Let's go again, this time give me everything you've got. Don't hold back." I sprang from the bed and crossed the room.

Amil rolled his eyes up to me, finally seeing me fully. "I can't."

"What do you mean you can't? That first session was more intense than you'd managed before. You said yourself that I held control the entire time," I assured him.

He stood and slipped his hands back into his pockets. "I'm tired, I should go."

Utter confusion gripped me as I stepped in front of him, blocking the door. "What's the matter, Amil?"

"Like I said, I'm tired. It's been a long day and the lesson has worn me out." He made to step around me, but I moved into his path again.

"If you're truly tired I will let you walk away, but if there is something you're not telling me or you're running away because you've lost your courage, then say so." I crossed my arms and planted my feet firmly.

"I'm not a coward, Isa."

"Then don't run away from me. Don't hold back. One last lesson before Talos returns and expects me to be able to fend him off at his full strength. Please."

He shook his head, but when his eyes found mine again they were filled with a deep void. A familiar clutch was behind my navel, but something deeper began to bubble up from underneath his familiar allure. I shut my eyes tight against the feeling of my lungs being constricted by the growing thickness of the room, but my throat began to close painfully. Every one of my nerves jolted to life at the faintest brush of my shirt against my skin, the seams of my pants feeling too rough. As if a rash were spreading from my core to my fingertips, I wanted to scratch and pull at my hair and fingernails. The whole world became too much of a stimulation that my brain could not focus on anything at one time. My limbs moved on their own accord, and I could feel the space around me changing and becoming my own personal hell.

I tried to scream, but the air trapped in my lungs was too precious to waste. Something far off was calling to me: a light, or a voice, or maybe even nothing at all but my own consciousness desperately trying to cling to me. I couldn't wait for that entity to find me, I needed to run towards it and hold on to it for dear life because I felt as though I were dying.

I heard my heart pounding in my ears and pressure filling my head as I focused as hard as I could on the dim glow finally coming into focus. Gasping greedily at the now thinning air of the room, when I finally started to see the bedroom furniture come back into focus, my hands and knees were holding me up from the floor. Amil crouched down on the balls of his feet several paces away from where we had started with his hands clasped out in front of him. His eyes had returned to their gloomy grey, but a disappointed look loomed on his brow.

I took another deep breath and got to my feet, realizing that I had taken most of my clothing off and strewn them about the room.

"What happened?" I wrapped my arms around myself as a crater opened up into my chest.

"I didn't hold back." He stood and took a step closer, but held our distance.

I walked over to my dresser and grabbed some sleeping clothes to cover myself. He turned away as I dressed but didn't attempt to leave again. He was right, of course. He didn't hold back during that round and it wasn't me who severed the tie. He had broken it so I wouldn't shatter to bits or go mad. If Talos was more powerful, then I surely would have been a puddle on the floor if he truly wanted me to be. He may be impressed with my progress, but I had a long way to go if I was going to be able to sever any pull placed upon me from other Incubo.

I flushed with shame and regret for asking Amil to not hold back and then needing him to stop without being able to end the session on my own. I could hardly look him in the eyes. "Maybe you're right. Maybe you should go."

"Is that what you really want, Isa?" He came to my side and put a hand on my shoulder.

I shrugged his hand away and walked to the side of the bed, trying to put distance and furniture between us. I took my necklace off, but held it in my hand, feeling the silver warm in my cupped hands. I glanced at the door, then back to him.

"Isa. I need to hear you tell me to leave. If I walk out that door without talking this through..." The ferventness in his tone could break me if I didn't look away, but I couldn't bring myself to give him what he needed.

"Amil. I—" But his lips crashed into mine, cutting off my words.

He wrapped his arms around me, lifting me and holding me in his embrace. His palms flat to my back as my legs wrapped around his waist and arms around his neck. I didn't want him to go; I didn't want to end the lesson this way. I didn't want the pain in my chest to be the only thing I had left from him tonight. He set me down and smoothed his hands down my arms and met my hands.

Our fingers intertwined, and our brows gently pressed together. His hips pressed to mine, and his breath fell onto my chest. The familiar tug in my stomach became tighter as each one of his exhales cascaded over my jaw. The smell of bergamot and persimmons gently coaxed me to remain anchored to where we stood and not walk away.

"I shouldn't have pushed you. I'm sorry." I knew I didn't need to apologize, but I was sorry. I could see how it hurt him to bring me to my knees in anguish.

"No. You were right, we have to keep pushing your ability if we are going to be able to show Talos that you've been utilizing these lessons and mastering this skill. We have to keep going."

He kissed my brow and led me back to the middle of the room where we went round after round for hours, gradually intensifying his power with each lesson until I was exhausted. I didn't remember him leaving or what time it had been when sleep overtook me.

# CHAPTER TWENTY-FOUR

The next thing I knew, sunshine was streaming through the cracks in the curtains and there were sounds of clanking silverware in the sitting room. The muscles in my shoulders, back, and neck were sore and tense from hours of bracing myself and from mentally blocking and dismantling Amil's attacks. He didn't show his full potential again, but said he'd been close and I had been able to build up momentum to either block or sever the connections. I peeked out into the sitting room to see Althea and Cornelius chatting and eating breakfast together. I closed the door quietly and lay back in bed and fell back to sleep in an instant.

I awoke some time later to the sound of my secure phone ringing, practically jumping out of my skin to hear its distinct chiming alerting me that it was a Banner calling. I fumbled out of bed to reach it on its charger, the I.D. unknown. I answered and waited for the familiar chorus of our creed, but I was met instead with heavy breathing and a dull hum in the background.

A husky voice on the other end creaked, "Your brother misses you, Isa. Won't you come rescue him?"

My heart jumped to my throat and my stomach dropped. "Tell me where he is and I will."

The mysterious man gave a low snicker. "A Black Banner needs an address? Not as smart of a group as I thought."

I needed to keep him on the phone as I ripped open my laptop and frantically instant messaged the rest of my siblings in Amples. One of them would be able to answer, one of them could track the call. One of them could find Argo.

"Tell me your price and you will have it in exchange for his safe return. Kill him and you get nothing but a death warrant."

I watched as Zaida's messenger showed she was typing back to me. The man's broken voice telling a colleague near him of my threat with haughtiness, as if I wouldn't hunt him down and rip his trachea out with my bare hands.

"My price, Isa," pausing and emphasizing my name mockingly, "is a free hit. I have a mark for you and when the job is done, you may have your brother back."

*Z: Keep him talking, we've tapped your phone and are downloading his location...*

"Must be someone high profile if you need a Banner." I spoke slowly and intentionally.

"We have a little issue here in Amples with beings forgetting their place in the food chain. We'd like to send a message."

A political hit. I've done dozens and they are typically higher priced with the risk of exposure and capture. I paused and waited as Zaida typed.

*Z: We got it. He's calling from several miles away from us, but we should be able to get there. We just have to hope they don't move him. Leaving now.*

"Who's the mark?" I didn't need this information if Zaida and the others could get to them first, but just in case they did move or the location was wrong it was better to comply.

"I'll text you the information. Goodbye, sister Isa."

"Wait. Put Argo on the phone so I know he's still alive."

A moment passed, but the line didn't go dead.

"Isa…" It was Argo, but his voice was hoarse and tired.

"Argo, are you ok?"

"They've got me…" his voice trailed off and a sound of something hard knocking the wind out of him met the silence.

"That's enough sibling time."

"If he dies, so do you. Give him food and water. And do not touch him again or you will be his mirror image of every single bruise and injury." Deadly heat rose up my neck as he chuckled at my threat.

"Of course," he laughed, and the line went dead.

Anger flooded my veins, my blood boiling under my skin as the mocking tone of the kidnapper rang in my ear. My hands shook as my stomach churned at the thought of Argo being held in the clutches of such a lowlife. How could he have been caught off guard after years and years of training—a decade of drills to watch our surroundings and escape capture. Argo was bullheaded, but he was one of the best of us. Now I would have to wait for contact, continue waiting and guessing if I'll see him or my other siblings alive again. Waiting here in this pampered manor: silken sheets, catered meals, and cushioned sofas while Argo likely is starved and beaten into submission.

I stared at the screen of my laptop, waiting for a message from Zaida or Markus or Talia or anyone to tell me they found Argo and killed the bastards who took him. After an hour of staring at my screen with no new messages from anyone, I finally gave up waiting and got dressed. Talos would be back soon, if he wasn't here already. When I walked into the sitting room, Althea was reclined and reading on her sofa, the sun high in the balcony windows.

"Did you sleep well?" came her voice over her pages.

"Yeah, it was a long night. Did I miss anything?" I sat down, my phone clenched in my hand.

"Neil came for breakfast, then for lunch. I told the kitchen to send up a plate, and it should be here in a few minutes. Do you want some coffee? You still look...exhausted." She paused, putting her book in her lap and leaning towards me to get a better look.

I gave a weak smile. "I'm fine, just had an upsetting call about my brother."

"Is he still missing?" Concern in her tone.

"Umm, yes. How did you know—"

"I heard you talking with Amil. Sorry to eavesdrop." She hugged her knees shyly.

"No, don't be. But yes, he's missing and I'm worried about him."

Her eyes dropped to the floor between us. "I'm sorry you can't go find him right now. I feel selfish for asking you to stay..." she trailed off.

"Althea, I will not leave your side until you are safely on your way to your honeymoon. I promise, I am where I need to be." I laid a hand on her arm and smiled when she met my eyes.

She gave a weary smile and patted my hand. There was a knock on the door before the plump kitchen manager came in with a tray.

"I brought you a bit of lunch. Lady Althea said you weren't feeling well so I brought you my famous Tattie Drottle."

She placed the tray in front of me and lifted the lid of the steaming bowl of potato and leek soup. Chunks of poached white fish settled in the middle of the bowl, a few thick slices of sourdough bread on the side.

"Thank you, it smells wonderful." I picked up the spoon and took a bite, the warm, chunky purée slipping down into my stomach and instantly warming me inside and out.

"The recipe has been in my family for generations. Nothing some potatoes and love can't fix." She winked at me then bustled out of the suite.

She wasn't completely wrong. The soup was filling, warm, and chased away my anxiety and dread while I enjoyed every last bite. The warmth of the meal settled in my stomach as Althea read quietly, but peeked up over her pages every so often to check on me as if I were as fragile as a bomb.

# CHAPTER TWENTY-FIVE

H ours later, with no text or message from Argo's kidnappers, Althea coaxed me into taking a walk around the grounds with her to check on the progress of the large white pavilion tent being set up on the lawn behind the manor. Much of the Lord's grounds staff were busily buzzing in and out of the pillowy panels with tables, chairs, and thousands of beautiful flowers in large silver and gold vases. The groundskeeper, who had been coordinating with Althea and her wedding planner, was directing several Fata with exaggerated hand gestures to where tall and overflowing garden urns should be placed on what looked to be the beginning of a walkway.

At the main entrance of the pavilion was a sizable archway where deep green vines and white jasmine flowers had weaved and climbed. Cut purple blooms were being attached to fill in any bare spaces. The walkway would be covered with a thick carpet-like aisle runner leading from the ceremony to the reception tent. From the sound of the commotion near the many chairs being piled up, the runner wouldn't be delivered until tomorrow morning, barely in time to be set up for the ceremony.

The sun high over our heads intensified the brightness of the pavilion and accessories scattered about the scene, each being passed in and out, faceless shadows against the canvas. Althea waved to the groundskeeper as we approached to discuss the progress, but I could hardly keep focus as they talked about flowers and monstrous urn decorations.

"Isa." Came a husky voice from behind me.

I turned around, expecting the caller to be farther away, but practically ran into Talos' chest. His shoulders towered over me causing me to squint as I peered up to him.

"Anything to report?" His request robotic.

I stumbled over my words, "No. I- nothing has happened since you left. Althea is speaking with the groundskeeper at the reception tent."

I turned to look to where Althea was standing with the Fata several yards away, miming their discussion of where the decorative flower arrangements should line the walkway into the reception. When Talos didn't move to approach them, I turned back around to find him staring down to me.

"And your training?"

"Amil has been training me in the evenings. He would be able to give you a better assessment on my progress." I restrained myself from rolling my eyes.

"No need for that, you will show me this evening. Meet me in my room at seven o'clock."

And with that he turned and headed back to the manor, the pit of anxiety deepening in my stomach, reminding me of the usual pit he left. Althea trotted back to my side, looking after Talos as he disappeared into the doorway.

"Talos is back. Did he say if my father would be bringing anyone from Cinder for the wedding?"

"No, I'm sorry, he had to go," I replied.

"Of course. Well, I better go do some phoning around. All

218

this work would be for nothing if some of our Cinder guests don't make the trek."

We headed back to the suite to find Yamir at the door instead of Amil. I gave him an inquisitive look, but he only smirked as he moved aside for us to enter. Althea went to her room to begin her calls and left me in the sitting room. I half expected her to ask me to help make the calls, but she didn't return. I went to my bedroom and put on the Alexandrite necklace then settled on the sofa and tried to practice my new skill. If Talos was going to test my skills, I would need to clear my head and focus. After the last encounter we had, he wasn't going to go easy on me. In his traveling, he had time to marinate on how much I had learned in his previous absence. He may have higher expectations than I was able to present to him. I wasn't sure what that would reflect poorly on most, my ability to learn or Amil's tutoring skills.

Without an Incubo to test my ability, I had to rely on my own confidence that I could concentrate enough to sever Talos from me at his full potential. My stomach tumbled when the thought of what he could be capable of flitted to the forefront of my mind. The tall kitchen Fata brought up dinner around six o'clock. I retrieved Althea and we ate together. She told me about the guests in Cinder who had pretended to be thrilled to hear from her and said that they would try to make it, but couldn't promise anything.

"I'm sorry you won't have a larger audience than originally planned," I said between bites of roasted quail.

"That's alright. Neil will be there and that is all that matters." She giggled and blushed.

"Althea, can I ask you something that might be too personal?"

"Have Neil and I had sex?" She scrunched her nose up at me, making me laugh.

"That wasn't what I was going to ask, but I had assumed you hadn't by the way Talos speaks of keeping your union 'pure.'"

She lifted a hand over the table and willed her water glass to rise weakly. When it reached her hand, she took a long drink before setting it back down and speaking again,

"It's another silly Incubo tradition. Once we announced our engagement we had to abstain from any relations to be sure that if pregnancy were to occur, it would be within wedlock. But like Incubo men, I have had my fair share of lovers."

"I'm sorry if I overstepped—"

"You didn't, Isa. It's just... never mind. I'm anxious for the wedding to be over. It's been fun organizing and planning, but I am so nervous." Her eyes became gloomy as she picked at her cuticles.

"Althea, I will be with you every step of the way." I laid my hand over hers in her lap to rest her worry and she smiled in return.

"What were you going to ask?"

"How powerful is Talos?" I turned my eyes down to my plate, shame heating my cheeks.

"I'm not sure. I think he is more powerful than my father, which is saying quite a bit," she spoke in a hushed tone, "I don't personally know the extent of his strength, but from what I'm told, he almost killed my father after my mother died."

"How? With Alexandrite?" I leaned in closer to her and watched as her eyes cleared to their normal spring sky pigment.

"No, he didn't need a weapon. Incubo men can focus and penetrate the minds of their opponents to create great pain. Not every one of them has the amount of mental strength that Talos or my father does, some can't at all. Amil can do this as well, but I've only seen him do this to Mortals. Sort of like the pull they have on you, but painful, like they're tearing your body apart from the inside." She hugged herself and sat back on the sofa.

"Amil tried to explain this to me—tried to show me."

Her eyes became wide and her voice filled with fear. "Did he hurt you, Isa?"

"Yes. But I asked him to. It was part of our training session." I tried to reassure her but her jaw tensed and brows furrowed.

"Isa, you don't know the enormity of the ability you've been cultivating. If any other Incubo find out that you have this skill and you're training with another Incubo, you could be putting yourself and him in grave danger."

"I won't tell them if you don't." I winked.

The tension in her jaw relaxed minimally at my jest, but she worried her lip for a moment before she spoke again,

"Please, promise me that you'll keep this between the four of us. I'm not like you. I wouldn't be able to save you if other beings came for you."

"Althea, you are a force to be reckoned with. I'd like to see any other Incubo wrangle wedding planners, florists, and the kitchen staff for a last minute wedding with a bounty on their head!" She giggled at that and fiddled her fingers in her lap.

"It's helped to have you here with me. I know this isn't what you signed on for, but having you here has given me the strength to push through every complication."

I gave her a warm smile and we finished our meal together before Althea excused herself to retreat to her room. Which left me waiting until it was time to meet with Talos. I was feeling less confident in my abilities after talking with Althea. But when seven arrived I went to Talos' room. Both Klaus and Yamir were at the suite door when I left. Neither spoke to me, but they shared a telling glance as I passed them in the doorway.

Talos' room was two doors down and had been left ajar. I laid a hand to my chest where my Alexandrite pendant lay against my skin. My knuckles tapped lightly, and the door opened wide an instant later revealing Amil on the other side of it. I passed him a questioning look, but he only looked to his feet and made space for me to enter. Talos was sitting at an upholstered bench at the end of his bed, his eyes following my every step.

"Are you ready to begin?" His voice shattered the silence of the dimly lit room.

# CHAPTER TWENTY-SIX

I glanced to Amil then back to find Talos standing too close to me, his broad chest obstructing the view of the room. The air around us started to thicken, darken, threaten; Talos' eyes were obsidian and dangerously pressed down on me. His hand lifted to my cheek and gently caressed down to my neck and collarbone. The familiar pull filled me as his lips dipped low to my ear. But there was something else there. Something sharp and jagged.

"I have missed you terribly, Isa. Have you missed me too?" His hushed voice fell over my shoulder, causing a chill down my spine.

"Talos…" I breathed.

He weaved his fingers through my hair, twisting it around each digit to take possession of me, and his wrist pulled back to bring my chin up to meet him. His lips parted against mine with a sickeningly sweet grin, and he inhaled deeply.

"Did Amil warn you?" His tone was low so only I could hear him. "Did he express his concern that I could crawl beneath your skin and nestle into your beautiful mind? That I could have you screaming in anguish and pleasure without so much as a touch?" He was toying with me, and his eyes flicked a warning to Amil in a silent check of his power over the both of us.

His scent reached me, begging to choke me, but I forced myself to think of Amil. To remember the etching of scars on his arms and chest, his cologne on my pillow and sheets lingering after we'd been together, and a dip in my stomach—not from Talos but from myself. Talos groaned into my lips, pulling my hair to raise my chin, opening my throat to his other hand. He gave my neck a gentle squeeze between his powerful fingers, dragging the image of Amil's face from my mind, demanding all of my attention be on him and his cocky grin.

"What warm and fuzzy feelings you have, Isa. But the taste of his sweat nor the memory of him buried deep inside you will save you from me. You're going to have to be enough to fend an Incubo off on your own." His voice smooth and outstretched through the air around us.

The thought of Amil being the one to ground me had gotten to him. He was threatened by the mere thought of Amil making me stronger. Amil wasn't here for me, but as punishment for developing feelings for me. He may have been instructed to step in if Talos lost control, but it was unlikely Talos would allow me to affect him enough for that to happen.

I would have to be more clever than Talos, a step ahead of him in every move he made. In lessons with Amil, he'd taught me that my greatest strength was to distract my opponent, to break free of the ensnarement. Talos knew he was powerful, he knew he could tear my mind to pieces if he wanted to, but he also had his weaknesses. Being second choice or being seen as unworthy would be enough to enrage him and wound his ego. So, I used what I had to my advantage and closed my eyes with a smile.

"Amil," I hummed a coo of affection.

Talos pulled away and took a step back to survey me. He gave a low amused huff as he began to circle me predatorily.

Amil stood unmoving at the door that was coming back into view as Talos passed. His face held no expression, but his fists were clenched at his sides. My hands hovered over the weapons at my hips, waiting for Talos to make his next assault. As I readied myself mentally, I ran a finger over the hilt of a knife. My throwing blades wouldn't kill Talos, but they would slow him down if needed.

"Do you know why I wanted Amil to continue these lessons, Isa?" Talos spoke from behind me.

"To better protect Althea if another Incubo had tried to use their influence to get through me." I proposed.

"That is partly why. But I also wanted you to have this skill for future assignments. This union is causing quite the stir and I need a secret weapon. A being who is as lethal as they are beautiful. Someone who would do anything for me. For Althea." He pressed his chest against my backside.

"Someone you thought you could control. Your very own Banner who you could keep as a pet," I finished his sentiment.

"You wouldn't be mistreated. I'd take very good care of you," he paused and grazed the top of my ear, moving in to whisper, "And we would take care of your brother."

"What do you know of my brother?" I said between bated breaths as he stepped in front of me.

"I heard a great deal about your missing Argo. The Banners aren't the only ones with operatives in Amples. Word gets around fast when a Black Banner has been captured. At the moment he's being auctioned off to the highest bidder." He casually shrugged.

"It's said that this particular Banner has a sibling willing to work for free to see he is returned alive. A sister who has had contact with his captors."

He'd found my weak spot. Burrowed down inside of me just like I had done to him to break his concentration.

"Imagine my surprise to hear that I already have his sibling within my reach. Agree to stay on with me after the wedding and I will personally see to it that Argo is safely delivered to you when we return to Cinder. I could save you the trouble of becoming someone else's kept pet." A cunning grin and a raise of a brow graced his face.

How clever he must have thought himself to be with his happenstance of knowing that Argo was, in fact, the brother I was missing. That I had agreed to do an assignment for free for his safety. But he didn't know about Zaida, Markus, or Deric, who had Argo's location. He didn't know everything about Argo being taken and held ransom, which only gave me a slight advantage.

"What would you want from me for such a generous offer?" I mocked.

"Just what I've asked, Isa. Your further employment for an extended period of time. And possibly a little more *personal* attention." He stepped closer, fingers lacing through my hair once more.

Inky black clouds massed in his eyes as he attempted to ensnare and persuade me into agreeing. His tongue ran over my bottom lip, then the top. My breath caught in my throat as he pressed his lips to mine softly, his hand flat to the back of my neck, pulling me in closer. The thought of Argo being saved by the Incubo I was presently working for would solve my immediate problem, but would open up inquiries on every one of my siblings and me.

The room dimmed against the whirl of power emanating from Talos. The pull behind my navel awakened and churned as his fingertips ignited my synapses with each of his strokes. A warm calm filled me as the urges brushed up against my ribs, calling to him. His kiss deepened, pulling me down into him with each stroke of his tongue to mine.

"Can you feel me pressing in on you? Reaching and filling you from the top of your head to the soles of your feet? I could fracture you," he rumbled dangerously into my hungry mouth between kisses, "But I could also envelop your every sensation. We could inspire the earth to break beneath us as I worship you in the dark, wither and crumble the taste of another's name on your lips. Permit me to permeate through you until you are sated in ways you could never imagine possible."

The air in my lungs went stale as my throat closed in on itself—I choked on his insinuation. Every bone within me threatened to break under the weight of his lightest touch over my skin. A mix of pain and wanting filled every crevice of my chest, pushing the last bit of air from me as his lips pulled away for our eyes to meet.

A flash image of Amil and I in my bed streaked across my mind, but I was too deep and the tie held fast. Talos didn't have this hold on me naturally, and he was desperately trying to coax me to shatter for him.

Zaida's voice echoed in my ears, begging me to break the tether, to push back. *Fight.* I squeezed the Alexandrite pendant in my palm, feeling it warm against my hand. The memory of when Zaida had given it to me, what she would do if she were in my position, came to mind. Would she take Talos' help to protect Argo?

No.

She wouldn't. She would have stabbed Talos before he could have wrapped his fingers around her throat. I managed to get my hand to one of my blades and quickly slashed Talos at his ribs. He cursed in pain, stumbling as he grabbed at his side. Fresh breath rushed into me as I backed away to regain space and my wits. He sat back down on the bench and looked up to me, but amusement dawned his face where I had expected rage. He took off his black jacket, bright red staining his white dress shirt. Amil shifted from one foot to the other by the door, but didn't look to me when I glanced his way.

"That was dirty, Isa," Talos teased.

"No one ever said Banners play fair." I breathed through the small well that had opened up with the tie severed so abruptly.

He scoffed as he stood again to approach me, the flesh of his wound slowly stitching itself back together before my eyes. I waited for his next attack; the tension in his shoulders or the tightening of his jaw would give him away.

"Do you know that you are the second Banner I have had the pleasure of engaging with?" He glanced to Amil. "The first didn't last more than five minutes when I questioned her."

I watched him as he crossed to the window and leaned against the pane, crossing his arms. He looked me over, waiting for me to respond, but was met with silence as I was still tracking the muscles of his jaw and arms.

"You remind me of her, not only in style of training, but the determination in your eyes. The way your pulse quickens when I get near you. The rise of your skin when I touch you...Tantalizing." He closed his eyes and turned his face to the ceiling, his mouth opening at the salaciousness of his own thoughts.

"You must really get off on the power you hold over Mortals," I interrupted.

"Not all Mortals, but you have been my favorite." He pushed off from the wall and took a few steps closer to me, his eyes returning to the black abyss.

He left space between us and cocked his head to the side, surveying me then looked to Amil, speaking to him in a playfully wicked voice, "Is she your favorite too, Amil? Is our darling Isa your new plaything?"

Amil didn't answer, didn't move.

"What's the matter, Talos? Don't like to share your toys?"

The edge of Talos' mouth perked as he turned his attention to me again. His voice took on a tone I'd not heard from him before. Bloodthirsty.

"Oh, I'd love to share you, my dear, Isa." Acid dripped from my name. "But for the moment, I could bring you to your knees.

Make you cry my name. Have you beg for me to touch you. Would you like to see?"

My heart started to pound in my chest, and each tympanic beat rang like thunder in my ears as he took a step closer. The room disappeared as darkness fell over me. My skin began to crawl, and ice filled my belly as I tried to gulp down air, but it felt as if my lungs were filling with sand. My knees hit the floor hard before my hands found the rug beneath me. The only sound I could hear was the crash of my own pulse in my veins; the sense of Talos wrapped around me. His scent crept up my nostrils and down my throat to meet the lodged scream. I searched around me for any sign of his weakness in the cloaked nightmare.

A knife. I needed a knife.

The fog shaded my teetering mind that was now on the brink of closing off all useful thoughts. The floor met me as I stumbled forward. My hand outstretched and grasped something hard, calming my vertigo momentarily in order for my hand to find my hip to palm a blade. But before I could decipher a direction to aim, searing pain shot up my spine; splitting anguish reached my temples. I heard my own scream ringing through the room.

A bright light brought the scene around us back into existence as the pain subsided. I looked around searching for the source of my agony and relief when I saw Amil holding Talos down on the floor. I pulled myself up to my knees to watch the struggle.

Talos kicked Amil off him and stood up quickly. Amil stepped back clutching his rib and stomach with pain on his face. They both stumbled to keep balance, mirroring ruthless expressions on their faces as they waited for the other to make a move.

Amil struck first with a fist to Talos' gut, knocking the wind out of him. He backed up and attempted to shield me, but Talos lunged forward to grab Amil by the waist and took him to the ground. They became a mass of fists and elbows in a heap on the floor. Each made impact after impact on the other, new blood being spilled from noses and lips.

I watched in horror as Talos picked Amil up as if he were a sack of flour and threw him against a wall. Amil's body crumpled and lay limp on the floor as Talos approached him, not ready to give up the fight. I stepped in his path, his eyes meeting mine. Dark pits of hellfire stared back at me as he took another step closer. He outstretched his hand, going for my neck. His draconian fury closed around my throat as my feet left the ground. Gasping and struggling to little avail, I raised an arm high and plunged my blade into his arm. He howled in pain and threw me across the room, landing on top of his bed.

Air pushed down my bruised esophagus as I scrambled to my feet and off the bed. Talos was swiftly in front of me again and I prepared myself for his next blow.

"You still have a lot to learn. If you take anything away from this evening, let it be to never step between two Incubo during an altercation," his words were harsh, but his eyes cloudy and disarmed.

Amil stirred with a groan and lifted himself up to his hands and knees, grimacing in pain with each movement. I stepped aside of Talos to Amil's side, but as I placed my hand on his shoulder he shrugged me off. He put a hand to the wall as he stood to steady himself before he spoke. He didn't look to me but to Talos. "I told you she wasn't ready."

My chest clenched and my swollen throat burned at his words, his lack of faith in me. His lack of faith in himself. If he hadn't had stopped me, I may have even been able to break the hold Talos had. He made the choice to step in where he hadn't been asked or instructed to. I turned away as anger and frustration manifested and tears threatened to fill my eyes. I turned to leave before I said something I would regret or throw a blade at one of their knees. Talos' cooled voice reached me before I made it to the door, giving me pause.

"My offer still stands. But your training will be continued by me after the wedding."

I didn't stop to answer or argue with him. I slammed the door behind me as I stormed down the hall back to the suite. Klaus and Yamir gave me puzzled looks as they watched me from their stations at the doors. A renewed flood of anger surged through me as I walked past them and straight to my bathroom to wash the stench of both Incubo off me.

# CHAPTER TWENTY-SEVEN

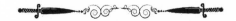

As I finished dressing I heard a knock at my bedroom door. I expected it to be Talos or Amil and thought it better to ignore them completely. I took a moment, but I decided to check to be sure it wasn't Althea stirred awake by the commotion or from nerves for the morning. I was wrong about all three.

Yamir's dark figure stood back a few steps in the dim sitting room. I looked him over, then behind him to Althea's door which was closed and, as far as I could tell, all was calm.

"What is it?" I whispered.

"I came to check on you." His clear voice cut through the space between us.

I opened the door further to see him in the light being cast from my side table lamp. He stood in his dark grey suit, vivid violet and gold thread embroidered flowers at the cuffs and lapels of his jacket. He was smartly dressed even though he was on night duty. I raised a brow to him and he sighed.

"Amil came by to see you but it didn't seem like you wanted company after your meeting."

"Thanks." I wasn't sure what to say but was grateful to not have to see Amil or Talos again so soon.

"Can I be blunt?" He shifted and slid his hands behind his back. I nodded.

"They are both imbeciles to be fighting over a Mortal, even one who has been trained as ferociously as you."

"Is that right? You think they're both so head over heels for me that they have resorted to bickering like children to have me to themselves?" I crossed my arms over my chest and cut him an unamused look.

"Offended that I don't see it too?" He said with a teasing tone and a wink.

"No, I think two Incubo men's attention is plenty."

"I don't like competition and you're not my type anyway." He gave me a fox-like grin as he gave me a brief once over.

"How ever will I recover from this utterly heartbreaking rejection, Yamir?" I joked.

"Well, if you decide to try and change my mind I'll be right outside."

My eyes rolled of their own accord at his comment. "Good to know."

"Isa, all jokes aside. If you need anything, they're not the only ones who have your back. You're part of the team, after all."

"Thank you, Yamir. I'll be fine." I relaxed my grip on my arms at his sincerity.

The golden flecks shimmered against his cloudy eyes as he nodded and turned to leave through the dimly lit sitting room. I hadn't realized it before, but I didn't need to have my guard up while he spoke to me. He didn't attempt to lure me in. We hadn't spoken much but there was something comforting about him checking on me after being shaken up and tossed around Talos' room.

An hour later I'd calmed myself down enough for bed. I

needed to be prepared for the long day that tomorrow would inevitably be. I walked through the assessment. The way Amil had behaved towards me. How Talos had goaded him into action. This wasn't just a test for me, but for Amil as well. To see if his loyalty to Talos and subsequently Althea's union would win out against whatever Amil felt for me.

And it seemed that he had failed as Talos had said.

I lay in bed for a long while playing the scene over and over until my brain and body succumbed to fitful sleep. I awoke too soon to Althea jumping onto my bed. Her giggle and broad smile let me know there was no need for alarm, but she was ready for the day to get started. I checked the clock, six o'clock in the morning, and she was wide awake. I smiled back to her as I sat up and rubbed the sleep from my eyes, my throat throbbing from the damage inflicted. The fight between Amil, Talos, and I the evening before still rang in my ears. The image of Talos throwing Amil to the wall then lying on the ground replayed over and over every time I closed my eyes until I was too exhausted to keep them open. But I knew I had to look remotely normal for Althea's sake; it was her special day and my last day on duty.

Althea beckoned me to get up, but not to bother getting dressed. The breakfast cart would be up any moment and the prep team would be in soon after to begin the primping for this afternoon. I reluctantly got out of the appealing bed and fetched my robe before meeting her in the sitting room. When the kitchen staff came into the room, I craned my neck out the door, but couldn't make heads or tails as to who was manning the suite. It was still very early, and Amil's shift didn't typically start until after seven and even if he were on duty he wouldn't be able to talk much. Not today anyway. There were to be too many beings in and out of this suite before the ceremony started.

The kitchen manager brought up a tray of breakfast meats,

eggs, and stacks of fluffy pancakes. Warm syrups, fresh juices, and fruits ladened the low table before us. No coffee or tea today because, "You don't need extra jitters or bathroom breaks today."

Fair enough.

Breakfast was wonderful and filling, surely to keep us energized for the long morning ahead. I was glad to not have had caffeine rushing through my veins during the dressing portion of our preparation. The team the wedding planner had brought with her consisted of the dress designer, two makeup artists, a photographer, and an outside florist who designed the bouquets and boutonnières. Each Fata or Incubo had to be patted down by the two-man security at the door before coming or going. The spacious sitting room of the suite was suffocating with so many busy beings about the suite.

I was dressed first, so I was able to step away from the crowd and into my room to strap the Alexandrite dagger and several throwing blades to my thighs. I tried my best to conceal them under the thin lace fabric, hoping the slight bulges wouldn't be too noticeable by eyes that should be focused elsewhere today.

After what felt like days, it was finally noon. The ceremony was to start in a half hour and most of the help within the suite was packing up to leave. Caravans of guests' vehicles were being directed outside the balcony window. Most were Incubo, family to the Royals or business colleagues. Althea explained that she didn't have many friends of her own, that most of the beings in her life were acquaintances.

"I'm very fortunate to have you here with me. You might be the closest friend I've ever had."

My heart burst at the thought. Of course, we had become friends during the last couple weeks, but it had been such a short time and under rather dangerous circumstances. I had to admit that outside of the Banners, I didn't have close friends either; Althea had found a special place in my heart.

"I'm honored that you consider me a friend, Althea. I feel the same way." I offered her a warm, sincere smile.

She gripped my hand in hers for a moment then took a deep breath. "Alright, it's time. How do I look?"

"Perfect." And she did.

Her dress was elegant and shaped to her every curve, and the veil trailed down her back but didn't take away from the laced back panel. Her hair was styled in flowing curls, her makeup subtle but accenting her features romantically. Her smoke filled eyes looked more ash-smoke, clear with her excitement and anticipation.

I opened the door to the suite for her, nodding to Yamir who was standing at the right of the door, and he nodded in under-standing. He signaled to someone at the end of the hall before sweeping his hand in a motion that the hall was clear and ready for Althea's departure. I turned and smiled to her again, and she flushed before walking towards the door, passing me and heading down the hall.

Stepping out, Amil had been hidden to the left of the doors. He grabbed my upper arm to silently hold me back a moment. Yamir followed Althea, but glanced back and gave us a look that surely meant "Make it quick."

Amil started to speak low and quickly, "The grounds have been swept several times, each guest has been searched and vetted, and every entrance to the grounds has coverage. This day should go smoothly, but don't let that relax you."

"I am in no way relaxed." I smirked, resting a hand to my hip. "How are you?"

He winced and placed a hand to his shoulder. "I've had worse altercations. You look beautiful. Even if you do have a knife shaped protuberance at your side."

He winked and gave me a half smile which I returned with an elbow jab to his ribs before turning and walking down the hall together. He was to escort me to the ceremony to make it still seem that I was only a friend of Althea's and not part of the security team. Amil, Yamir, and Talos were to be the first line of defense during the wedding. Several other Incubo under Talos would be walking the grounds during and after. I was to stay by Althea's side no matter what did or didn't happen, until the end of the night when she and Cornelius would make their way to their marriage bed in a different wing of the manor.

We reached the staircase and Amil stopped and cupped my arm. "Isa, I want you to know," a light flickered to life, searing through me, "that after tonight—"

"Amil," I interrupted. "I can't do this right now. I have a lot I'd like to say, but right now we have to make our way down flights of stairs and finish our assignment in one piece. Let's talk later; we will be off duty in about seven hours."

I smiled at him, but his face fell. Shaking it off, he nodded in agreement and we proceeded down the stairs to join the rest of the wedding party waiting in the entryway. Althea's father, Pytr, was speaking with Talos near the large heavy doors. Lord and Lady Welp were speaking with a young Incubo that looked to be a relative. He had a very similar bone structure to Stavros. Althea was at the foot of the stairs waiting for the rest of the group to get in positions, and she glanced up to me with a determined smile still draped over her. She widened her eyes as if to hurry Amil and I down the last few steps then looked to Yamir who would be trailing behind her and her father up to the altar.

Amil and I reached them and a moment later, Talos appearing next to me to address Althea. Pytr was close behind him, but stopped to chat with Stavros.

"My dear, you are breathtaking. I am honored to be witness to the wonderful young lady you have become and see you marry the man you truly love. I have never been more proud and humbled." The sincerity in his voice pulled at my heart and brought tears to Althea's eyes.

He handed her a tissue from a pack in his pocket, and she dabbed gingerly, trying to preserve the hours' worth of makeup applied to her face. He turned to me, dipped his chin in greeting before drawing me away from the group, but only a step behind Amil. Almost tucked behind a large potted plant, he looked around before speaking in a hushed and precise tone.

"I have your travel tickets ready for you to leave in the morning. I will take you to the station myself and you should be in Amples by evening. My operative will meet you at the station there and give you any information they have on where he's being held."

I didn't have time to ask any questions as the wedding planner came to the hall and began arranging the party into groups that would walk the aisle before Althea. Pytr held the crook of his arm out to Althea and she gracefully accepted it, her smile faltering only minimally. She wasn't going to let anything impede on her happiness today, and I admired that about her more than I could express.

The wedding planner bustled about lightly, moving each person here and there in order of importance to the ceremony and seating arrangements. She came to me, looked me up and down, eyes briefly landing at my thigh, but decided against dealing with my bulge, and moved on. Talos came to stand in front of me with a gorgeous young woman with long, jet black hair at his side. I was to walk ahead of Amil who would be walking up before Althea and Pytr. Yamir would head up the rear and stand at the edge of the seating area. No one was to stand with the bride and groom. It was custom for the Incubo to commit their bond to one another alone at the altar. I would be sitting as close as I could, which gave me the advantage of looking about without drawing attention to myself.

Music from out in the garden started to waft in. The string quartet played a beautifully haunting melody singing through the hall, signaling that it was time. I glanced back to Althea and her cheeks were aglow, her toothy smile infectious. I shifted my bouquet and turned, waiting for my turn to begin walking, fully viewing Talos and the woman on his arm. They leaned in to each other as he whispered something in her ear and she gave a small giggle. A venomous heat filled my belly, but I shook it off, focusing on the aroma and colors of the flowers I was holding at my front. I had no reason to feel anything towards him or his companion, especially with Amil standing to my back.

One by one, each person in the procession made their way out the back doors and into the sunlit garden. All manner of beings sat in white chairs draped with flowers and sprigs of eucalyptus. The Incubo standing at the end of the aisle was wearing a blue three-piece suit. To his left, Cornelius stood waiting with a proud look to his stature, his chest raised and spine lifted. He had also been primped with plenty of hair product to keep its style for the remainder of the day and night. The closely tailored, deep plum colored, three-piece tuxedo complimented the black shirt and tie. A single black orchid pinned to his lapel completed the midnight, dreamy attire.

As I approached, Talos and his consort were directed to the right at the front. They sat and whispered amongst themselves as I reached the end of the line. I was directed to a seat at the edge of the walkway opposite them and sitting next to me was a familiar face that I was shocked to find there: Lawrence, the younger white-blond haired Fata from our outing in the city. The one who tried to stop the bickering at Welp's offices. He was just as handsome as before, his dark mustard three-piece suit had small pops of royal blue blooms on the cuffs of the sleeves. An iris pinned to his lapel on one side and an amethyst handkerchief tucked into his pocket on the other. He flashed me a welcoming, amused smile as he adjusted himself in his seat, ensuring our knees or thighs wouldn't accidentally touch. I returned with a nod and sat down, placing the bouquet in my lap, but slipping one hand to my thigh, ready to pull a blade if need be.

"It is interesting seeing you here. Isabella, was it?" He leaned close and whispered.

Amil passed me by, giving me a glance before moving to where he was to sit across the aisle. I didn't turn to Lawrence nor did I answer him because Althea and her father were walking down the aisle now, and I wanted to be sure all my attention was on the crowd behind them. Yamir's eyes found mine for a brief moment before also scanning around. No movement. Nothing alarming.

Pytr kissed his daughter's hand before handing it over to Cornelius. The two beamed at each other as Pytr found his seat next to Talos. The love I had witnessed in small doses through our stay here all amounted to this moment. A welling in my chest began to ache and a tear threatened to escape me. A deep bluish swatch of fabric appeared on the top of my hand, and I blinked a glance at Lawrence, bringing the silk to my eye to dab my eyelashes.

"Thank you," I said, handing back the handkerchief.

"You hold on to it. You may need it more than I do. Wouldn't want anything to stain your exquisite dress." A foxlike expression ran across his lips before he turned his attention back to the happy couple.

I tucked the handkerchief under my bouquet and waited for the ceremony to begin as everyone in the crowd settled and quieted. The Incubo standing before Althea and Cornelius cleared his throat and ruffled a small notebook in his hands before beginning his speech, "Friends. Family. Confidants. Love has truly blessed these two Incubo here today and we are all here to bear witness to their union and a new union of power amongst our kind."

There was a subtle shifting next to me, Lawrence closing the distance between our thighs. "How long have you been working with the Welps? You know, you're not the first." I didn't turn my head, but I held my breath waiting for him to continue.

"Did you know her? The last Banner Cornelius hired to take his future father-in-law's life?" He waited for my shock, but he wouldn't get it.

"I don't know what you're talking about. Lawrence, right?" I said under my breath.

"Oh lovely, you do not need to keep this act up. I am the one who helped Cornelius acquire a Banner. I wouldn't be a good politician if I didn't recognize an assassin when they disarmed me." He slipped his arm behind me, draping it over the back of my chair, and leaned in closer for me to hear.

"You have much better aim than she did, I'm afraid. But perhaps this wedding will be more exciting than I thought it would be."

"I suggest you keep what you think you know to yourself."

He turned his attention back to the ceremony, but didn't move his body away. I wasn't sure why he would reveal himself as Cornelius' accomplice in the attempted assassination of Pytr, but his presence and his willingness to discuss it so freely put me on edge. I glanced to Amil across the aisle, but he was scanning the guests in his section and didn't give me notice. Lawrence shifted as he tucked his hands inside of his jacket to a concealed pocket. I gripped the dagger at my thigh. It would only be one breath if he decided to make a mistake. His ribs were still open to me, his arm could easily be pinned to the chair. But he pulled out a pair of glasses, set them on his face before glancing to me with a sly grin as if he knew I was watching him—aware of his every movement, knowing that my body would be tuned into his for the remainder of the ceremony.

I let out a heavy breath and heard the officiant continue his speech on unity and love: the unique circumstances that brought the bride and groom to be joined together for the remainder of their lives, wishing them all the happiness and luck on starting their new life and a family. Finally it was time for Althea and Cornelius to exchange vows, starting with Cornelius. He shifted from one foot to the other, but if he was nervous, he didn't show it as he continued to beam at his bride. His eyes looked to be filled with the translucent smoke screen that I'd come to associate with admiration or love, nothing I'd seen from Amil or Talos when they looked at me.

"My dearest, Althea. You are the calm in every storm. The only light in the darkness. Standing here with you today feels to be a dream, but one that I would gladly live through every single day if I awoke to you by my side."

A single tear began to swell in his eye. He tried to blink it away, but it rebelliously fell to his cheek before he continued, "I will spend the rest of my life trying to make you smile. I vow to keep you safe. To keep you close to me even when we are far apart. I will always be your comfort and safe place to lay your head at the end of the day. With this ring, I vow to love and live for you. My darling."

He placed a simple gold band around her finger then replaced the large-stoned engagement ring. Althea was positively glowing as she smiled up to him. She took a deep breath before starting her own vows.

"Cornelius, you are more than anything I ever imagined in a partner. Your kindness, generosity, and valor are remarkable. But what I love the most about you is that you worry about the big things—for your people, their wellbeing, their livelihood. You are what I see in the future. Not just for me, but for our kind, and I am proud to be standing beside you through that change. I vow to not only be your wife, but your partner in all things. To stand by your side in hard and prosperous times. To love your people as my own and care as much as you do. With this ring, I vow to love and live for you."

She placed a gold band on his finger and pressed her lips on top of it. Some in the audience gave audible swoons, but the air was still thick with discontent as someone across the aisle shifted several times before standing and walking off to the side.

I couldn't be sure, but he looked like one of the men who was also at the meeting with Lawrence. One of the men who was also trying to get away from Damon, the Incubo who held the gun that day. I thought it odd that either would be invited, but perhaps it was a gesture of good faith between them and the Lords. Possibly seats needed to be filled and this was one last effort to solidify bonds before the union was complete and power shifted.

Amil watched after him, and I watched Amil. Lawrence leaned in closer to me again, his breath hitting my neck as he loudly whispered, "Political drama. Nothing like it to ruin a wedding, don't you think, Banner?"

"I suppose." I didn't turn into his gaze, but could feel him waiting for more from me.

At the altar, Althea and Cornelius were none the wiser about the sudden departure of a guest. The speaker was addressing them, completing their union before announcing them husband and wife. Cornelius swept Althea into his arms before turning at his waist and dipping her into a romantic kiss. Everyone in the audience stood, clapping and cheering for the newlyweds. I remained seated to be shielded as I looked around for any other guests trying to slip away.

I looked up to where Amil had been, but couldn't see him in the thick of the crowd. Instead, Talos' eyes caught mine from across the aisle, the smoke of his eyes catching me so off guard that I flicked my eyes to where Althea and Cornelius had stepped hand in hand at the mouth of the walkway, beginning their descent from the altar and through the parted sea of faces. Each row of guests turned towards them as they passed, cheers and applause following them until they reached the doors into the manor.

The guests began to make their way to the large white pavilion, fully assembled just in time. I hesitated, unsure if I should go to Althea to be by her side until it was time for her and Cornelius to be brought to the pavilion for their reception.

I didn't have to wonder for long. Talos appeared in front of me as I made to take a step towards the manor. He gave a sideward glance to Lawrence, who had gotten to his feet next to me. Talos looked him up and down with a pungent wrinkle of his nose before bringing his attention back to me. The beautiful woman on Talos' arm put on a bright smile as she waved aimlessly at those passing by.

"Althea and Cornelius will be along shortly. They must consummate their marriage, then will join the festivities." He said this so casually, as if it were such common knowledge and practice.

I gawked at him, looking from him to the doors that Althea and Cornelius had passed through moments ago. Lawrence took a step closer to me, his hands sliding into his pockets. "A truly archaic ritual, but for the royals." He shrugged knowingly.

"Interesting assessment, Mr...?" Talos extended a hand for Lawrence lazily, not remotely interested in who this stranger was or why he was intruding on our conversation.

"Lawrence Codwell, I am on council with the Lords." He didn't extend his hand, merely glanced to the crowd at Talos' back.

"The same council that tried to stop this union?" Talos retracted his hand, laying it on the knuckles of hand at his elbow.

"Simple differences of opinions on how these lands should be managed, but I don't see a reason it should darken a beautiful ceremony and likely an open bar. Isn't that right, Isabella?" He turned his attention to me and was met with a look of confusion.

Talos gave an exasperated sigh. "Isabella, this is the Countess Marmond of Amples. Jessica, this is the dear friend of Lady Althea I was discussing with you earlier."

He nodded to me, bringing the countess' attention to our conversation and to me. She grinned widely as she assessed me then the handsome Fata next to me. She was taller than me even without her jewel studded stilettos—her long black hair looked like strands of silk in the afternoon sun. Her perfectly mani-cured hand met the space between us expectantly to Lawrence. He took it, but only inclined his head slightly before letting go, and her gleam seemed to diminish slightly at his curt greeting. I was getting the impression he didn't have a fondness for the royals or any Incubo. A twitch of a grin threatened my cheek at his blatant arrogance and the fire that would surely be growing within Talos.

"It's nice to meet you both. Talos has told me very little about you Isabella, but my condolences to your circumstances. I will do my best to assist in any way I can." She didn't sound sincere, but her bell-like voice dipped when it was expected to. She had practice talking to beings she felt were beneath her.

"Thank you, Countess." I gave Talos a pointed glance but tried to sound thankful. Offending her wouldn't make my trip to Amples any easier.

"Lady Althea and I are cousins; we practically grew up together. I've missed her. We haven't seen each other in so long. Did she tell you I was her telekinesis tutor? Has she been practicing?"

"Yes, she has. Every day," I lied, and she smiled brightly.

"Talos, darling, shall we? The new couple will surely be arriving soon, and we should be there to greet them." She turned to Lawrence and I to finish her statement.

"Of course." He patted her hand then turned his attention to me. "Isabella, we will speak later."

Then he looked to Lawrence. "Mr. Codwell, enjoy the festivities."

He didn't wait for Lawrence to respond. He turned away and signaled to Amil and Yamir to follow. Amil's eyes met mine for a moment. He was checking in and must have recognized Lawrence as well. A hand at the base of my spine shook my attention away from Amil and onto its owner.

"May I be your escort? Out of all in attendance, you are by far the most interesting." He meant this as flattery but was clearly boasting about his own contemptuousness.

He held out his arm, and I had to make a decision. It would be a good cover for me to have an escort to field other guests' questions and curiosities, not to mention he knew what I was. If he knew what was good for his own wellbeing, he wouldn't get in my way if I needed to move quickly.

So, I took his arm and we made our way down the pathway to the elegant white pavilion, the large urn planters filled with rich purple blooms and pops of green. Eucalyptus and sweet lilac welcomed each group as they passed and entered the jasmine covered archway.

"Rather extravagant for a Lord that didn't pay his taxes last quarter, wouldn't you say?" Lawrence mocked as we came to a table just inside that was laden with tall flutes of champagne.

He picked a glass up and handed it to me, then grabbed one for himself before moving us deeper inside. I took a sip to avoid engaging, the financial affairs of the Lords was not something I had any business commenting on. He led me to a table with two other couples who were already seated. One of the men I recognized from the meetings as well but couldn't recall his name. He had been the one that dove for cover when Damon drew his gun. He didn't not notice me, but greeted Lawrence with great pleasure on his red cheeks.

"Ah! Lawrence Codwell, good to see you here my boy!" His flute was empty in front of him and there was another in his hand, half gone.

"Andrei, you look as if you've already begun celebrating for all of us," Lawrence mused, "And where is your lovely wife, Patricia?"

Lawrence's eyes flitted to the beautiful woman sitting next to Andrei. She was much younger and much too beautiful to be with Andrei, who may have been handsome when he was a decade or so younger, but was now balding and plump. The young woman's dark skin was draped in a gold gown, her curls reminding me of Zaida's but much longer and fuller. She eyed Lawrence and gave a sly smile before answering for Andrei.

"I am his dutiful escort for this event. Patricia was not feeling well and you know that a powerful man like Andrei cannot be presented without a companion." She turned her face to Andrei and gave him silent approval, revealing her pointed ears.

She was a Fata and likely a Temptress. Lawrence returned with a smirk and pulled out a chair, gesturing for me to sit. I did so to keep attention off me. I looked across the tiled dance floor and found Talos sitting with the countess, her lips close to his cheek as she spoke into his ear. A small smile twitched at the corner of his mouth, a hand on her knee that was peeking through the table linens.

I tore my attention away and checked each table that I could see fully. Each group was greeting each other, raising a glass and toasting the new couple. Servers were walking around with bottles and hors d'oeuvres, passing through my line of sight. One approached our table, bringing me back to a conversation I had missed most of between the Temptress, Andrei, and the other couple sat at the table. Lawrence was reclined in his seat, tipping his glass up to empty it before holding out for the server to fill, his arm outstretched in front of me.

"Would you like a refill, madam?" the server spoke to me. I'd drained half my glass without realizing it.

I held it out for him to fill, then he proceeded to fill others before making his leave for the next table. I listened to the Temptress tell a story of her recent trip to Arta, her experience with the locals and how wonderful it would be to live here. She, like me, was from Cinder. Temptresses often stayed in larger cities for work and travel, but not often.

"You are from Cinder, aren't you Isabella?" Lawrence chimed in, meaning to start an offshoot of conversation away from the group.

"I am." He knew this long before we ever spoke.

"Do you have family there as well?" His cunning was presenting, and I had to answer to keep up the appearance of being his date.

"I do."

The Temptress, Irena, was watching me carefully. I could see that she was noting my body language; skilled Temptresses were taught to be better communicators and conversationalists. For her to be a Fata and a Temptress was rare and may have given her an advantage that I may not have had while I pretended to be one on assignments. Her dark eyes were dazzling, veins of gold dashed against obsidian. All the men at the table were invested in gaining her attention, if only for a moment. The jealousy of Andrei having such a beautiful woman with him was noted several times. The women at the table didn't seem to mind at all, but were also entranced by her. They asked her question after question just to hear her speak. Without a missed syllable she bounced from one person to the other, confident, warm, and inviting.

"She is a very talented Temptress, unlike your Banner friend I'm sorry to say." Lawrence's hushed tone came close to my ear.

I hadn't noticed how close he had moved to me, his arm hanging on the back of my chair and his knee pressing to my thigh. His chest became a wall against the other tablemates. I took a long sip of my glass before finally giving into his relent-lessness.

"Perhaps she needed more lessons. We don't always have access to Temptress education." I laid one hand on my blade at my thigh.

"Have you played the Temptress often, Isabella?" The way this false name fell from his tongue was a sing-song tease.

"Enough to know that Irena is very well trained but has also come by these skills naturally. She is clearly beautiful and also knows how to hold the attention of others as if they were made of glass."

"And you? Do you not hold the attention of men, or do you rely on other abilities?" A finger lightly grazed my back.

"If you know what I am, you are taking a great risk in goading me." I lowered my eyes to his lapel and placed a hand there before meeting his eyes again.

He took a slow breath that pushed against my palm. The pulse at his neck ticked as he took another paced intake of air. A tactic often used to slow panic, I'd learned it as a defense to giving away nerves.

"Banners are said to be as dangerous as they are beautiful. So, as I may have put myself in your crosshairs, it is exactly where I want to be. This is a very rare opportunity, as you may imagine, and I would be doing a great disservice to myself to allow it to pass by."

"You speak as if I'm an oddity to experience." I twirled a finger at his pinned iris.

"Like anything worth experiencing, it may seduce you, but may also take your life."

"Do you think I am trying to seduce you, Lawrence?" I raised a brow.

"If I could only be so lucky, Isa." He drew out my name.

My real name.

"How do you know of the Black Banners so well? How did you help Cornelius hire one of us to kill Pytr?" I was speaking only above a whisper, his eyes trained on my lips.

He opened his mouth to speak, but hesitated, the points of his mouth creating small dimples in his cheeks. "Come with me right now and I will tell you everything. And...I may even be able to save your life."

Confusion struck my face as many things happened all at once. The crowd all stood and began cheering. Our table was swallowed up by standing bodies, Lawrence's cool demeanor slipping into a deadly glacier. I turned to see Althea and Cornelius entering the pavilion, hand in hand above their heads. A loud bang then a scream.

I darted for Althea, and before I could take a breath, I was laying my body over hers. The bulk of Amil's back was lying next to me over Cornelius. Blade in hand, I raised my head to find Talos but couldn't see him over the mass of beings rushing every which way to escape. I kicked off my heels and got ready to run.

"Althea!" Her face under me was in shock. I got to my feet and pulled her up with me, pushing her shoulder low to keep her shielded.

I fisted the shoulder of Amil's jacket, and he rolled off Cornelius. A yell of pain came from the heap of men, but I couldn't distinguish who. I pulled Amil to his feet and pushed him towards the door with Althea. Cornelius would either be dead or at our heels, but our duty was to Althea only and we needed to move.

As we reached the jasmine archway, another clap of thunder sounded somewhere out in the lawn and I saw a group of beings fall to the ground. Many covered their heads, screaming. Someone was hurt, their pain ringing through the thick air. The smell of blood was mingling with the aroma of flowers. Amil led us to the side of the manor, and he pressed his back to the wall and pulled Althea in next to him. Meeting them there, I looked to the high windows and roof. If someone was shooting, it was likely they were perched high up to not be seen.

"Do you see anyone?" Amil's head swept the grounds, looking for the shooter.

"No, I don't know where the shots are coming from—" Another pop, another round of screaming.

The body of a man was splayed on the green grass, blood pooling at his back where the bullet had exited. He was yards away, but I could see the precision of the wound. Through the throngs of terrified bodies, Talos had caught sight of us and was running towards us; he had Cornelius by the arm, dragging behind him. Althea turned and called for Talos. Pleading for him to run faster.

I pushed off the wall to meet them. "Keep her there!" I yelled over the screaming to Amil.

I reached a hand out to Cornelius, but before I could take hold of his shoulder, a bullet hit his chest and he dropped back, flat to the ground. Talos didn't stop running, instead he hooked an arm around my waist and carried me back to the manor wall where Althea was screaming. Her face red and smeared with tear-washed makeup. Amil held her tight to restrain her from bolting out into the chaos. Her eyes black and streaked with bright, angry red slashes crossing through their emptiness, their hot gaze not leaving the sight of her new husband's lifeless body.

"Althea, we need to get you under cover. We need to leave now." Talos had stepped in front of her, commanding her attention. After a moment she quieted her sobs and drew her focus to him.

"I can't leave him here!" the pain in her voice cracked open.

"There is nothing you can do. They are using Alexandrite bullets; we have to get you to safety."

# CHAPTER TWENTY-EIGHT

Alexandrite bullets. I had never heard of such a thing. Whoever was behind this came for the Incubo and didn't care who got in their way. My mind went to the last moment before the shooting started—to the look on Lawrence's face. He knew something was about to happen; he had almost warned me by trying to save me. But where was he now?

I didn't have time to look around or even to bring this up. Talos had grabbed Althea up in his arms and was giving Amil directions. Yamir was nowhere to be seen, none of the other guards were. Did they not make it out?

Amil nodded at his instructions and moved down the wall to the back entrance. We stayed several steps behind him as he looked into the manor. It was clear and we moved forward. We had to get to the cars parked out front and the safest way was through the house. Other wedding guests ran past, frantic to find a place to hide. We reached the main entrance to the manor to find two bodies lying in pools of blood. They were Pytr's men, but Pytr was not in sight. The large, wooden front doors cast open on a scene of vehicles trying to flee all at once. Two

SUVs had smashed into each other, smoke rising from one of the engines. A woman screamed and another body dropped, but there was no sound of a shot.

I had my dagger in one hand and reached for a throwing blade for the other. Out of the corner of my eye, the shadow of someone moving towards us from the stairs caught the first taste of steel. I threw the blade before grabbing another. The impact of it to the person's shoulder stopped them. We were met with a yelp of pain before they landed at our feet. Amil grabbed him and pulled him up. He wasn't wearing a suit or staff uniform, dressed in all black and holding a gun with a silencer on the end. We may have stopped one attacker, but there were more swarming through the throngs of fretful attendees. Amil tossed the attacker's gun aside, then another scream accompanied by another body dropping came from somewhere within the manor.

"How many more are there?" Amil barked at our would-be assassin.

This Fata wasn't going to answer. He smirked at Amil and spat in his face, trying to provoke him. Amil wiped his face and landed a punch to the man's jaw, an audible crack at the contact. His body crumpled on the ground, and Amil swiftly kicked him in the gut before pulling him back to his feet.

"I will not ask you a third time. How many more are there?" he spoke through gritted teeth.

The man laughed, blood staining his teeth. His jaw offset, but adrenaline was allowing him to ignore the break. "You will not make it out of here with yours *and* her life."

He looked from Amil, to Talos, and then to Althea, his shrill laugh rising above the screams and yells of the last guests spilling out of the manor. Throwing the man to the ground, Amil took his gun out and let out one bullet to his gut. It wouldn't kill him, but it would stop him from following us.

Several more shots came from outside, the shooter from the roof or high window was picking beings off as they tried to make their run for their vehicles. We needed to get somewhere with an advantage for when the terrorists found us because it wasn't a matter of if. They were coming for Althea; she would hold the power over this land now that Cornelius was dead and his father's body was likely lying out on the lawn as well.

I tilted my chin, silently gesturing for us to head up the stairs to the second floor. Amil ascended first, Althea clung to Talos, and I brought up the rear. Off the stairs there was a large library. Behind heavy oak doors, each wall was lined floor to ceiling with books. Unlike the many studies in the manor, this library didn't have a desk or much furniture besides a lounge in the middle of the room. Amil quickly moved the long couch in front of the door to block it. It would only give us moments if we were found here, but an extra moment would be worth it.

"Althea, are you hurt?" Talos had sat her down in the farthest corner of the room away from the windows and door.

"Cornelius. He's... He's gone," she whimpered, and my heart hurt for her realization.

"Yes, but we are still here and he would want you to be safe," he spoke to her softly, calmly.

I looked to Amil who was standing near the door. He was taking his jacket off and rolling up his sleeves. There was a bloody hole at his shoulder, but the wound looked clean and possibly healing already. He turned to me. "Are you alright?"

I nodded and assessed the blades I had left. I had my dagger palmed, but would need to be careful or find a way back to the suite to restock. As if he knew, Amil came to my side. "You can't go out there."

"You forget that this is what I actually do for a living." I flashed him a smile, but he only looked more worried. Althea's low sobs from the corner of the room were muffled thanks to the books surrounding us.

"For now we wait, there is no reason to go now." He was right, but we also couldn't wait here for the attackers to find us.

I went to the window. It looked out onto the front lawn where several bodies were scattered around the once pristine driveway. There was no way to tell how many of them were Fata or Incubo, the pools of liquid rust around each of them all looked the same. It looked as if several cars had been able to make it out before the massacre reached them.

Some hours passed, and the sun started to set outside the window. Althea had fallen asleep in her ripped wedding dress in the corner, her head laid in Talos' lap and his jacket draped over her. We hadn't heard anything from outside the library for a long while, the last of the guests either dead or had found escape. None of us had spoken, at first out of necessity, but then out of not having anything to say.

The eeriness of the manor was suffocating, and it felt as if we were merely waiting to be attacked. One of us needed to go out into the hall. We needed to get Althea to a safe place and sitting like lame ducks wasn't going to keep us safe for much longer.

"I'm going to go look for the shooters. I'll stop off in the suite first to grab a few knives, then I'll find them." I made for the door, but Amil stepped in front of me.

"Amil, move out of the way. I'm not waiting around here for them to find us. For all we know they are waiting outside for us to come out."

"You're right, they might be right outside the door. I'm not letting you go out there to be killed because you're bored." His chest inflated and his fists clenched to his sides, becoming an impassable wall.

"Fine."

I took the dagger to the hem of my dress, ripping a long strip and wrapping it around my hand. Before he could stop me, I turned and rushed towards the window, throwing my whole

255

weight into the clear sheet and hearing it crack away into the chilled night air. I reached out a hand and caught the window pane, glass clinging to delicate fabric and drawing blood, but not nearly as badly as it could have. The outside wall hit my side, my shoulder taking most of the impact. I pressed my feet to the top of the window below and kicked as hard as I could.

Glass breaking and a scuffling noise from somewhere inside the manor gave way to alerts. They were coming, but they didn't know whom to expect. I dropped into the room, glass scraping the back of my thighs and back. My feet began bleeding from the shards on the floor. I scrambled to the edge of the room to assess where in the manor I was and how hurt.

It looked like a study, but one that wasn't used often. Sheets covered the oversized couch and the top of the desk was void of items. I dove under the desk and was able to get three large shards of glass out of the soles of my feet. If there were smaller pieces, they would have to wait.

There was the distinct clacking of expensive Italian loafers in the hall beyond the door, then the subtle turn and clink of the iron doorknob. I held my breath as someone took a few steps into the room and paused before the strewn broken glass on the rug.

"Come out, come out wherever you are, Isa." came the familiar voice of Lawrence.

He was still here at the manor and obviously in on the whole attack. I waited for him to take a few steps closer, round the desk if he dared, before I made a move. The less force I had to exert on my injured feet the better, but he stopped a few steps away from the front of the desk. I had to make the next few moves count or I'd end up just like the last Banner this Fata knew.

I saw my opportunity when I heard him shuffle some glass around. A thin throwing blade ready to be released as I sprang out from under the desk and over it before lunging for the open door. His arms outstretched to me, but only received a blade to his ribs. The sting of glass dug deeper into my feet, and I slid onto the cool marble flooring of the hallway.

I dashed to the stairs, making my way to the suite, past dark and empty corridors, then the library that Althea, Talos, and Amil were still locked behind. With me out, the intruders would have a new target to focus on, and they would have to kill me before going after Althea again. Or at least that was my hope.

When I finally got to the doors of the suite, they were flung wide open, the sitting room furniture tossed this way and that, our bedroom doors disturbed. I held the Alexandrite dagger firmly, taking slow and meticulous steps into my room. I heard nothing from inside, but also had no idea how many beings Lawrence had with him roaming around the manor, he could easily have staged the upheaval in the suite to throw me off guard.

I picked up a loose cushion and tossed it at the door, but no noise came from inside as the door opened fully. Without turning on the lights in my room, I went to the chest of drawers to grab more knives and my torso weapon guard, trying my best not to make excessive velcro noise before going to the night-stand and grabbing the small gun I rarely used. They must not have cared about looking through the drawers because aside from the linens being thrown off the bed, there was nothing amiss.

Buckling the gun to my hip and double checking my knives, I went to the bathroom with a change of clothes and more killing-appropriate footwear. I locked the door behind me, blocked the crease at the bottom of the door with towels before turning the light on. Upon examination, the cuts to the soles of my feet weren't deep, only small slivers of glass remained and were easy enough to remove. I changed my clothing. My dress was ripped, torn, and far too constricting for what had to be done to survive the rest of the night.

After several minutes, I listened to the rooms beyond the bathroom door for any sign that someone had followed me or thought to check for me. I had no idea if Lawrence had survived the knife to his side, or if he could heal as quickly as an Incubo would. I didn't know what type of Fata he was or what his true abilities were, but I was hoping that quick healing wasn't one of them. I packed my crossover bag with my computer, wallet, and my secure line phone. I wouldn't be able to return for my other possessions and needed to take any identifying equipment with me. I pulled the Alexandrite necklace over my head and tucked it between my breasts for safe keeping. It was the only item I didn't want to replace. I would have to go to Althea's room to pack her a small bag.

After several long minutes of silence, I turned the lights in the bathroom off and let my eyes adjust to the dark before opening the door. My bedroom was empty, but there was a light on in the sitting room where it had been dark before. I crept slowly towards the bedroom door and listened.

Nothing. Not a sound, not a breath from the sitting room. Perhaps they came by and turned the light on to keep track of rooms they had searched.

"Come on out, my lovely."

He had lived, but it wouldn't be for much longer.

I stepped out into the sitting room. Lawrence lounged in a chair that had been placed in the middle of the still mangled room. On either side of him were men dressed in all black, holding large firearms. I could only see their eyes through their battle gear, and they were either Fata or Mortal and my bets were on Fata. For whatever reason, they had orchestrated this attack on the day of the wedding to send a message of their kind's strength, but also to end whatever strife they had with the Incubo who had been lording over their land for too long.

I waited for him to speak, but he just looked me up and down, taking me in as he straightened his jacket.

"Should we get this over with or do you need another moment to gawk?" My voice unexpectedly cracked, but held stern.

He hummed out a lazy laugh. "Oh lovely, I don't wish you any harm. This war has nothing to do with you or your kind. I mean, as fascinated as I am to meet another Banner, I don't expect you to stay and protect the Incubo."

"I was hired to do just that." I took a few small steps along the wall towards the door, now standing fully in front of him and his dogs.

"I know. To keep Althea living until her blessed wedding day. You have succeeded." He slowly clapped his hands mockingly. "Congratulations."

"I'm not going to let you hurt her. She may have made it to her wedding day, but she will walk out of this manor alive."

"And the others? Talos and Amil's bodies are still unaccounted for, and I'm assuming they are still huddled somewhere. Tucked away in a cozy corner, waiting for you to come rescue them." He grinned wolfishly and adjusted his cufflinks.

I noticed the tear in his jacket, wet from blood where I had stabbed him earlier, but it had already begun to dry, the skin underneath smooth and only stained from where he had healed. I flicked my eyes back to his, hunger and raw devilishness stared back at me.

"I saw the way Amil watched you today and on the first day we met. He is quite fond of you. Talos on the other hand," he shrugged knowingly, "He'd likely leave you here to rot with the rest of the guests if it meant getting Althea to temporary safety."

"Talos hired me to do a job, he doesn't have to care about my wellbeing."

"And what if I wanted to hire you? I have good standings

with the Banners. Because of me, several of you have gotten paid handsomely for assignments."

"Except for the one you suggested to Cornelius."

"Yes, well. That was unfortunate." He stood and slid his hands into his pockets before taking a step closer to me.

"Your recommendation cost her her life. That's a little more than unfortunate and doesn't give me much faith in your employment opportunity." I took another half step to the door; he took another step to me.

"I thought she would be a means to an end. That her either fulfilling her mission or being found out would end this silly union. But adjustments had to be made when she was captured. However, that brought you here. And I am so glad it did." Another devouring grin revealed his too perfect teeth.

"What about me makes you so pleased?" I narrowed my eyes to him as he moved a few prowling steps closer.

"From what I hear, you have a particular skill that comes in handy among the Incubo you've been surrounded by, a nifty trick that Amil has been helping you cultivate."

"How—" I was stunned.

"The walls of the mighty Lords' manor have ears, lovely." His voice low and deadly, his cunning strides finally brought him close enough to me that he raised a hand and caressed my cheek with the back of his long fingers, resting on my chin a moment before falling.

"And how is this skill valuable to you, may I ask? You've already won by killing the Lords and leaving Althea a widow on her wedding day."

"This union was only part of a bigger battle between Fata and Incubo. Mortals like yourself have always been kept in the dark about the underground goings on between the two of us. But it is becoming increasingly difficult to not let the blood spill in the streets of Arta, or Amples, or even your dear Cinder.

Wouldn't you like to be one of the beings that helps stop a massacre of innocents?"

I didn't know if what he said held any weight. Before running into Talos on that elevator, I knew little about Incubo, but Fata were not such a mystery. They seemed to get along just fine on the surface. And who was I to start questioning that now because this Fata, who just murdered a whole wedding event, stood before me speaking as if it were truth.

It was all so hard to digest, my body sore and beginning to nag at me. Every pinch of glass fragment embedded in my skin screamed as I shifted my weight, exhausted from a day's worth of stress and very little sustenance. His words swam in my head and the smell of his cologne started to engulf me. The sweet smell of pine and juniper seeped into my lungs, a distant after-note of black pepper caught in my throat.

"This could all be over with your help. A Banner with your significant skill set would be an ace in our pocket."

"I don't want any part of your war. I just want to finish this assignment and never see another Incubo again if I can help it." I backed away, avoiding the broken pieces of wood from the low table that had sat between the couch arrangement.

"That won't be an easy feat. Two of them have had their teeth sunk into you; you're marked as their plaything. I could help you with that too if you let me."

"And how would you do such a thing? Erase an invisible mark of territory, as if there is such a thing."

"You don't think I smelled him on you the moment you walked into that boardroom? Or the other one when you came down the aisle? You reek of them. They have wrapped themselves around you so tight, no other Incubo or Fata would come near you if they knew what was good for them."

"And yet..." I looked him up and down, my brow raised.

"Ah, but I mean to free you from them. Harness what they have taught you and liberate us all from them forever." He stepped closer to me again, closing the small steps I had made between us.

He was a foot taller than I was, and I had to careen my neck to meet his eyes. I could understand why he needed my help; I was trained by Incubos to refuse their own kind. To push their control off me, and I could possibly teach others, but this wasn't my war, or any Mortal's war. If it were, we would be easy recruitment to whichever beings got to us first. But this could have been all about this land, the cattle or farmers inhabiting this area.

"What do you get out of this when this war ends, Lawrence? You seem pretty eager to be the forerunner of this attack."

A familiar sense of thickness started to swell in the room and a haze began filling my vision as Lawrence's gaze traveled down my face and landed on my lips. A hand hooked onto my hip as he angled his mouth closer. I took a slow breath in and focused on anything I could: the pain in the balls of my feet, the bits of wood shattered all around us, and pushed against the bond that was threatening to take me over. I looked around for the source, possibly one of the men with him was actually Incubo. Maybe Amil had finally come to see what had become of me since jumping out the library window. But I saw no sign of Amil's flickering flame. No dark clouded eyes from Lawrence's faceless men.

No. It wasn't until I met Lawrence's gaze once more that I found the source of this new intrusion. Lawrence's eyes filled with ashy smoke, wisps of silver dancing over his irises as he bore down on me.

"How?" I choked out as I tried to stop him from shaking my concentration.

"Show me your pretty trick and I'll tell you." His slender fingers raked up my side and pulled me gently to him.

I took as deep of a breath as I could and closed my eyes, imagining Amil. If I could push him away by way of the sense of another man like I had done before, it would be a quick sever. He didn't budge, instead he rested his lips against my forehead where I could feel him grin against my skin.

Anger rose up in me, fire set ablaze on every inch. I thought about the last time Talos had touched me, throwing me across the room without the slightest effort. A harsh strength brewed in my chest. Thrumming waves moved through me as I clenched my fists and felt the dagger's hilt warming in my palm.

I tried to bring all my focused energy on the jeweled weapon, remembering the beautiful gleam in the light, the impossible sharpness of its edge. How easily it could cut through Lawrence if I got the opportunity to strike and get away from his likely trigger-happy friends. The thought of plunging it deep into his chest or dragging it across his throat pushed air into my lungs quicker, the brightness of the room coming back into focus as he took a step away, but not removing his hands from me.

"That is very impressive, but I am only half Incubo. My powers of coercion are not as grand as my father's were." He pulled away and returned his hands to his pockets as he walked back towards the armed men.

"Incubo and Fata can not breed, you're lying." My eyes went from him, to his men, then around the room quickly before following his path as he turned to face me once more.

"That is what everyone seems to think, but it happens much more often than you'd believe. But, the cross breeding of Incubo, the most powerful beings among us, and the Fata who are seen as weak farmers or kitchen keepers, is highly discouraged. Not to mention, hard to accomplish. I would say that there are about thirty of us born in the last one hundred years that I know of. Many more are aborted or could pass as Incubo and adopted into families who could not have children of their own. Very hush hush." He put a finger to his lips in a mock shushing, then dragged it across his mouth.

"If you're part Incubo, why do you hate them so much? Why start a war with them?"

"Because they are monsters that seek to ruin everything they touch. They only care about their own kind and the rest of us facilitate their lavish lifestyle. Take this manor for example. Dozens of Fata work for the Lords, but they are minimally paid and treated as ghosts among the living. Hardly spoken to, but expected to be at their beck and call."

I didn't speak as he walked around some rubble. I didn't know where to go from here. I needed to find a way to dispatch his men before turning on him. Or to get to him quickly so his men wouldn't try to attack first. Either way, I was stuck listening to his rant on the status quo.

"But you...yes, you would be quite a nuisance to them. I imagine if more than just Talos or Amil knew of your fascinating trick you would be captured then auctioned off to the highest bidder. Come to think of it, if you don't agree to help me, I might just do that myself. A Black Banner with the power to disarm an Incubo influence? Oh yes. That is quite a prize." He turned to face me, his eyes clouded once more with the threat of my freedom.

"Is that what you'd want of me? To give me to someone else?" I asked lazily, calming my voice as much as I could to mask my unease as he began circling closer to me like a predictor sizing up its prey.

"No, lovely. I want you for myself." He lightly grazed a finger from one shoulder to the other and paused as he leaned in close to my ear, his chest flattening to my back. "I'd show you the true worth of a partner against all enemies."

"A partner in a war I didn't start and don't want any part of," I whispered slowly over my shoulder to draw him in closer.

"You would be my secret weapon. My most dangerous ace in the hole. The pinnacle pawn in my strategic placement for dismantlement of the royals and Incubo kind." His lips dragged over my cheek and down my neck as he spoke.

My core quaked, and I could feel him trying to pull me back into him as the air thickened once more and the room felt as if it were getting darker. My vision clouded and I was only able to focus on his mouth and the warm draw of breath on my skin.

"I would reward you beautifully. Not only with riches, but with the power you have earned. And you could dispatch Talos and Amil in any fashion you'd like."

"Are you threatened by them? That they have both had me first?" I groaned and shifted my hips against him.

He drew in a deep, harsh breath against my cheek. "I'm not threatened by over-exasperated Incubo men who have to use their influential snares to seduce others into bed with them. I would have had you begging on your knees for me to touch you without such vails."

His hands found my hips, fingertips digging in only inches away from my blades. A throaty want escaped him as he pulled me closer against the bulge in his slacks, but to prove his point, he severed the pull. The air was thinning and the room became bright once more. Both his men watched us closely from across the room, waiting for the cue to either shoot me or find Talos and the others. This would be my only chance, and I would have to play it very carefully. I raised a hand and weaved my fingers in Lawrence's hair, keeping my eyes on one of his men, giving him a slight smile. I parted my lips and ran my tongue along them slowly. The surprise in his eyes and the slight lowering of his gun told me what I wanted.

I laid a hand over one of Lawrence's at my hip and slowly pushed against him, grinding my hips, breathing deeply to over accentuate my heaving breasts, arching my back and leaning my head against Lawrence's shoulder. Both his men slowly lowered their weapons while they watched as Lawrence began breathing heavily and moaning against my neck. I could feel him pulsing against my back side, his hips following mine. I pulled gently on his hair to keep him in place and smiled dangerously at his men, watching them for the right moment.

Lawrence stilled my hips and let out a pleasure filled exhale, his slacks now so tight as he throbbed against me. I smiled triumphantly to his men who both blushed and flustered. They turned their attention away from us. This was it!

In one quick moment, I grabbed two blades from my vest and threw them. They landed at each of their throats as they gasped for air and grasped at their now bleeding necks.

Both sunk to their knees as I wrapped my arm around Lawrence's neck, holding him to me as he flailed. I sprang up and over, kicked off the wall, and tore him down onto his back and kicked a leg out over his chest. He coughed as he tried to catch the wind I had knocked out of him, realizing I had a knife to his throat.

"Isa!" He rasped underneath me, his hands gripping my arm, trying to pull me away.

He was strong, but didn't have the strength of an Incubo. He also didn't have their speed or quick thinking. He did have their unnatural attraction to me which had not only clouded his eyes, but his judgement of my next moves. He bucked under me, trying to throw me to the side, his hands groping the ground around him trying to find something to assist him.

"I decline your offer, Lawrence," I calmly said as I watched my blade slice across his neck.

His eyes widened. He gasped, and with his last feat of strength, pushed me off of him and onto the ground next to him. He sat up and got onto all fours and crawled, blood dripping with each movement. I stood and stepped away, waiting for him to collapse and take his final breath. But his body stilled for only a moment before he stood and rushed towards me, shoving me back onto the ground with his hands around my neck. He squeezed, and I could feel the structure of my windpipe faltering under him. His legs straddled over my chest, pinning me down and blocking me from my knives. I tried to think, but my brain was pounding as oxygen depleted.

I started to see bright white flickers, the sound of my pulse pounding in my ears drowning out all other movements in the room. This was it. I had failed Althea, and myself. The last bit of fight I had was slowly abandoning me as I struggled to draw anything that resembled a breath. Darkness was creeping over and through me.

All at once, my body was being flung across the floor as I landed on my side and gasped for precious air. My throat opened up against the pain as I choked down as much as I could. My eyes watered as I blinked around to where Lawrence was and for what had caused him to stop.

I heard where he was before I could see him—the mass of another body on top of him, landing punch after punch. A set of hands grabbed me off the floor and hoisted me to my feet. Then another took me into their arms, trying to rush me out of the room, but I pulled against them.

"Isa, we have to go! Please! Come with me!" It was Althea, they had found us and saved my life.

I looked back to the grappling to see Talos on top of Lawrence, beating him to a bloody mess and seething with anger. Amil stood only feet from me and Althea, guarding us in case Lawrence found the upper hand somehow. But from the looks of it, that was unlikely. My heart was still pounding against my sternum as it returned to its living rhythm, thankful and ashamed at the same time.

The Alexandrite blade either didn't work on Lawrence and he healed rapidly, or he had fought through his bleeding. Both men on the ground wailed in pain as blows were landed and bodies were tossed this way and that. I didn't know how long each would be able to last, if I should jump in, or if I was even able.

Amil turned towards us, his eyes smoldering with anger and grief, his expression punishing, but thankful to see me breathing. He grabbed my shoulders and brought his forehead to mine and breathed me in.

"Go. We can handle this. Go find a car out front and get Althea out of here. Go to the train station. Do not stop for anything or anyone. Go!" He pushed us out the door and slammed it.

# CHAPTER TWENTY-NINE

I could hear feet pounding against the stone stairs down the hall as we left the suite. I palmed two blades, ready for the newcomers to round the corner. Althea was behind me, her hand on my back, as we began our quick pace down the hall. I handed my bag to Althea to hold, giving me more range of motion.

A flash of black-covered movement landed at the top of the stairs as I let a blade loose. Upon impact, the target fell back and tumbled down the stairway, tripping their companion and causing them to fall a few steps back as well. When we reached the top of the stairs I let another blade fly, making contact with the second would-be assassin's arm, disorienting them.

I leaped with feet flying before me, landing on their chest, my hands on a step as I watched their broken body fall to the bottom of the staircase unmoving. I peered up to Althea, her eyes wide and full of fearsome clouds. Tears streamed down her stained cheeks as she found my eyes. I motioned for her to follow me as I stood and reached for another blade, ready for whoever Lawrence had waiting for us. I had no doubt the manor was crawling with men at every entry point. We would have to find another way out. With their leader likely dead, they would not just let us walk out the door.

We reached the bottom of the stairs and ducked into an alcove. The first floor was cast in complete darkness, but we could easily be found if someone walked by looking for the source of commotion from above. There were several doors heading out to the back lawn, but only one out to the front of the manor. They would be heavily surveying the cars that were still parked out in the drive, likely to lure us out with our guards down. I peeked around the corner, but didn't see or hear anyone, and there was no sound coming from above us.

"What do we do?" Althea breathed as close to me as she could to my ear.

"Stay close to me, do not run unless I tell you to. Here, can you manage to stab anyone who comes too close?" I handed her a thin throwing blade, her hands trembling as she took it and nodded her head.

She took a deep strong breath, gathering all the bravery she could muster. I knew she had never been trained in hand-to-hand combat, but she knew that she would have to go down fighting. Watching her carefully, she closed her eyes and drew another deep breath and, when she opened them again, they were dark, full of rage and survival. A small pebble of pride swelled in my chest for her. We were going to get out of here together. I nodded to her and began moving along the wall down the hall to the kitchen. We might get lucky and find a servants' entrance that may have been overlooked.

The vision of Talos and Lawrence tussling on the floor of the suite and the fear in Amil's voice crossed my mind as we approached a door at the end of the hall. I tried to push it aside, but my stomach turned over. Would I ever see either of them again?

Did it matter if what Lawrence had said was true?

At the door, we paused and waited to hear if there were any

obvious signs that someone would be waiting on the other side, but none came. I turned to Althea, giving her the sign that it was clear, when I saw movement swiftly coming towards us at the end of the hall. I pulled Althea behind me and waited for the source to come closer, but they had stopped in the shadows between windows, stalking us, waiting for us to make the first move.

I took one deep breath and made a move to the right towards the windowed side of the hall and flung drapes closed as I went. A predatory growl came from the darkness—now cast along half the hall. Reaching Althea once more, I pulled her towards the window closest to the door, placing her in the corner as silently as I could before reaching my hand to the door's knob and flinging it open. Dashing across the opening to the other side, I waited for the shape of a body to pass my view towards the dim light coming from the room beyond.

Moments later, footsteps crossed my path as I threw my arms out, knives thudding against the torso of who had been hunting us. They dropped to the floor with a sickening crack of their skull against the marble. A small squeal of terror came from Althea's corner. Laying my hand over the fallen body, I found their throat and sliced for good measure. A wet choking confirming I'd made the right choice.

"Althea," I steadied my hushed voice, "walk very slowly to me at the door, once inside wait behind it."

She did as she was told. I tracked her muffled steps as she slowly slid into the compartment behind the open door. I waited for any sound or movement, my back against the wall next to the open doorway. Mere moments passed as someone came thundering down the hall, their figure barely visible before reaching the purposefully darkened area. I waited, crouching low and ready to strike, one blade poised.

Heavy breathing approached in the dark, a dim flicker of a cufflink or possibly a gun was my alert. Springing to my feet, I kicked off the wall and over the newcomer's shoulder. Their feet beneath them gave way as they landed hard on their knees, yelping in pain as I dragged my blade from ear to ear, blood spilling hot and fast over my hand.

Letting the mass fall to the ground before me, I ran through the doorway, shutting it quickly and grabbing Althea's wrist as we dashed through the dining room and into the kitchen. Moonlight from outside gleamed off the stainless steel appliances and work surfaces, pots and pans filled with food for the reception that had ended so abruptly hours ago. Trays of food stacked in tall wheeled carts lined one half of the kitchen, leaving enough space to get to the back door.

Signaling Althea to stoop down with me as we slowly made our way to the door, the sound of boots shifting and shuffling outside, I counted at least three pairs as I caught my breath. Althea sat at the wall next to me, breathing heavily and trying to stifle her crying. I looked around the kitchen for anything to give us an advantage. I could easily take two men at once, but I had no idea how many would be waiting for us.

A frantic hand pawed my arm, Althea silently attempting to get my attention. A pair of black reconnaissance boots had stepped into the kitchen doorway, their owner shielded from view by the large work tables. We sunk into the wall as much as we could and waited.

One step in.

Two more towards the back door. Towards our hiding place.

Putting a finger to my lips then asking her to stay put, I crept along the floor onto the bottom shelf of one of the work tables, stealthily maneuvering around large bowls that would give my location away if shifted. Palming a knife, I edged closer to the boots before retracting my arm to give me some extra leverage, then I brought the blade down into the middle of the supple leather. Straight through to bone.

He wailed in pain, falling to his side and holding onto his

wound. A curse hissed through his teeth and his eyes darted around to look for the source of the attack. When his eyes landed on my smug expression, he called out. He was the trap and he had no idea. Taking a handful of his hair in my hand, I slammed his skull against the tile floor with a crunch, shutting him up.

The back door flung wide open and the other three predicted men stomped inside looking for the commotion, finding their now bleeding unconscious counterpart. They were too distracted to see Althea hidden behind the open door and the deadly creature lurking at ankle level with blades primed and ready for the fun to begin. The first slice to the closest calf dropped the owner to his knees. The blade plunged into his groin, aiming for his artery.

Gushes of blood pooled and flooded the floor, causing the other two men to back up towards the door. I rolled out from under the table and sprang up onto the top of the table, kicking out and connecting to a jaw. I spun around and let a knife carve a home in the eye of the remaining man before he could make out the figure before him. He was dead before he hit the ground.

A groan from the man I'd knocked out gave way to a scream of warning to whoever was outside waiting. A tall figure appeared at the doorway, but no one came after him. His broad shoulders were almost the width of the opening; he nearly had to duck his head to come inside. He had no fear, no reluctance to enter what had been the room of three of his friends' deaths. I pulled the gun from its holster. My last resort.

Still standing on top of the work table, I waited for him to come closer. Waited for this mountain's first move. To my surprise, he flicked the light on in the kitchen, shining bright, white fluorescent light in every nook and cranny around us. He was Fata and the largest I had ever encountered, as if he were bred to defend or upheave monarchies.

Atop his wide shoulders of solid muscles, he had a chiseled

jaw and long white hair. His skin had an unnatural, creamy blue smoke hue, like he'd spent a lot of time among the cigar-smoking big wigs—too long sulking in alleyways as his employers intimidated store owners and casino workers. He had the confidence of someone who had never lost a fight or been covered in his own blood, naturally gifted in brute strength and endurance.

His bright eyes were sharp on me, trained to watch the flexion of muscles and anticipate his opponent's moves. Inhaling deeply, I studied his movements. Every being had their weaknesses and this giant was no different. We stared at each other for a long moment, neither wanting to give away any glimpse of instability.

"Well, aren't you a pretty little thing. Come to protect the big bad Incubo all on your lonesome?" His voice was like cool glass.

"They don't need my protection. I'm just trying to leave this stone prison with my life." I adjusted a finger on the trigger, waiting.

He couldn't know Althea was somewhere close by. Keeping his attention solely on me would at least buy her a few minutes to escape if he successfully dispatched me. I shifted my feet, the delayed pain from the glass shards returning with the reposition of pressure. He saw the smallest of a wince cross my face and smiled. He thought he'd found his mark.

He took a step to me and paused before lunging for my ankles. Jumping out of his grip, I saw the door behind him close and the top of Althea's head rush towards him. He let out a howl of pain and turned around to land the back of his hand to her delicate cheek, tossing her across the floor.

Not wasting a moment of his attention being shifted, I squeezed the trigger and one bullet buried itself behind his ear. He fell to the floor, knocking into the table and causing me to topple over onto my hands and knees.

I hopped down from the table and went to Althea's side. A

bruise already forming from her right temple to jaw, her lip bleeding from a small cut.

I held her at arm's length, looking her over. "Are you alright? Can you run?"

Her tear and smoke eyes filled locked onto mine. "I can't leave without Talos."

"You don't have to." A labored voice came from the doorway.

# CHAPTER THIRTY

Amil stood in the doorway holding up a clearly worn out and bleeding Talos. Both men looked as if they'd been dragged through hell just to get one floor down from the suite. Talos raised his head to see us, but dropped it in relief when he saw Althea still whole and breathing.

Looking around the room, Amil smirked. "Had a bit of fun of your own I see."

I returned a smile. "I've had enough fun. We need to leave now before more of them find us."

He nodded and hoisted Talos up to alert him it was time to move again. Talos grunted and took a few steps. I wasn't large or tall enough to help Amil carry Talos, but I could be their eyes and ears. I searched the drawers of the kitchen manager's desk for her keys. They still expected us to escape to the cars out front, assuming we would have a car waiting for us after the reception. I pulled out a weathered key ring with several keys and an older model car key fob. Holding them tightly in my hand, I went to the back door and cracked it open to see if the coast was clear. Althea stood behind me with a hand to my shoulder.

I saw nothing out in the darkness and wasn't sure where staff would have parked, but we only had a slim chance of making it out of the front entrance, especially with Talos in his condition. I looked to Amil, his chest heaving under the great weight of his own injuries and Talos' half consciousness. Turning my attention to Althea, I gave her a nod and motioned my chin out the door. We slipped through the narrow crack and along the outer wall of the manor and headed away from where we knew the garden was to the right.

We came to a narrow walking path lined with cobblestones, smoothed by shipments and deliveries. It gave passage to a river stone parking lot where only three cars had remained. We hadn't seen any of the bodies of guests or staff on our way to the kitchen so there was no way of knowing if any of them had made it out, or if this set of keys was only the spare to the kitchen manager's vehicle, but there was only one way to find out.

"Go to the door as quietly as you can. Tell Amil to bring Talos to this corner and I will go get the car. Be ready to jump in as soon as I find it."

"Be careful. Here." She handed me the blood caked blade that I had given her earlier.

She turned and quickly made her way back to the door. I turned and took one step out from behind the wall. No one came out of the vast darkness so I made a dash to the first car closest to the manor. It was only a few yards away, but it would only take inches to catch me off guard. I pressed my back against the driver side door and flipped the key from the fob. Wrong car.

The two other cars were on opposite sides of the lot. One, a large red van, and the other a smaller sporty looking car. I hoped beyond hope that the van was the right vehicle and made a run for it. Halfway across the lot I heard the crunching of rock under boots and turned my head to see two men rushing for me. I slowed my pace and waited for them to catch up before crouching down and dropping them both with a swift round kick to their heels. With their backs flat on the ground, I took one of my last blades from my vest to accompany Althea's gift in my other hand and plunged into their chests. Leaving both embedded deep, I reached the van. The key slipped into the door lock and opened.

A flutter of movement from the corner of the manor caught my eye. It was Althea waving that they were ready. I looked around one last time before igniting the engine. It roared to life, the wheels shifting and crunching as I sped to where Althea, Amil, and a fully unconscious Talos waited. I unlocked the doors as I closed the short distance and the door was thrown open. Althea piled in first to pull Talos in next. Amil hopped in as I started down the service drive, and he shut the door and landed in the passenger seat.

Two men appeared out of a line of bushes as we passed, sending bullets whizzing and nearly hitting the van. Amil took his own firearm out, rolled his window down, and with ease dropped both men with precision. I swerved to avoid their fallen bodies and headed to the front entryway. One large black SUV stood in our path, but no men were visible. I looked to Amil, then to the back seat to where Talos was awkwardly draped over Althea's lap.

"We can't get out and check; we won't be able to fend anyone off." I squinted my eyes, trying to will my vision to see through the SUV's dark windows to no avail.

"I have an idea, but you're going to have to trust me." His face stone hard, calculating the risk he was about to take.

I did trust him. More than I may have ever trusted anyone outside my fellow Banners. I nodded.

"Be ready, and just keep driving no matter what happens." He didn't wait for my response, he opened the door and was instantly at the front of the SUV.

He pushed against the front bumper and it began to budge. His Incubo speed and strength were in full force when we needed it the most. I watched as he pushed the vehicle farther out of the road, but a rustle in the large boxy trees caught my sight. I screamed to warn him, but he had already seen the two men jumping down from the high branches. One landed a few feet from the front of the van, the other right next to Amil. I looked back to Althea, her terrified face white as snow in the lonely moonlight. I turned back to see Amil had landed one man to his knees, the other closing in on him. I couldn't leave the van so I did the only thing I could think to do, I pressed my foot to the gas and rammed into the figure blocking the road. Amil tossed both bodies to the side of the road and jumped back into the car.

"Drive!" He hardly had to tell me, I had floored my foot the moment the mass of his body entered the car and sped away from the manor as fast as the van could take us.

# CHAPTER THIRTY-ONE

We drove in silence for a long while, the only sound was the cooing of Althea to Talos and her soft sobs for the love she had lost a few hours ago. Amil was on high alert until we reached the main roadway and other vehicles shared the road with us. I made my way to the train station, but only vaguely remembered the direction we had come from on our trip here.

"There, stop up here at this hotel. We need to rest and ditch this car." Amil pointed to a shabby looking hotel.

Turning into the lot, I parked at the front office and waited as Amil ran in to reserve our room. When he came back, he opened the back door and helped Talos to sit up and closed the door.

"Drive to the end of the building, our room is the last one." I did as he told me but did not park.

He pulled Talos out of the van and into the room. The window emitted a warm orange light as his and Althea's figures moved behind the thin curtains. He came back out after a few moments, telling me to park behind the hotel and to throw the keys in the seat as if we had abandoned it here and hopefully giving the illusion we had moved on and not stayed the night.

When I returned to the room, Althea was in the small bathroom washing up. Talos was lying on one of the queen sized beds only missing his shoes and jacket. Amil sat on the edge of the second bed. He ran his gaze over me, stood, and hesitated to come any closer. I took a few steps closer and waited for him to decide whether to close the distance. He did.

"Are you in one piece?" His hand cupped my cheek.

"I'm fine. What happened to Talos?" I glanced over to the Talos shaped mound.

"Lawrence had the upper hand for a bit, and a few men came in right after you left. Nothing we couldn't handle, until someone threw a chair and it hit Talos over the head, knocking a little bit of sense out of him in the process." He gave a morbid grin.

"How did you know where to find us?" His eyes locked on mine, a pull reaching deep into my stomach and he didn't have to answer.

A groan came from over my shoulder as Talos shifted and rolled over, and, as if on cue, Althea emerged from the bathroom with several hot wash cloths to clean Talos' many cuts. I moved away from Amil and he retreated to the bathroom to get cleaned up. I moved to sit on the bed and began taking my blade vest off, then my shoes. My socks clung to me by dried patches of blood where glass was protruding from my skin.

Althea glanced to me, then quickly went back to her work on Talos. "You should soak your feet, the tub looks fairly clean."

"That's not a bad idea. Can I get you anything?" I didn't know how I would be able to make her night easier, but the way she stroked possibly the last person she held dear constricted my throat.

"No, I just want to sleep."

She finished cleaning and put the dirty cloths on the floor, then walked around the bed and curled up next to Talos, closing her eyes and releasing held tears.

I wanted to comfort her, but didn't know how. Zaida would have known the right words to say, or the right way to stroke her hair to give her a small bit of hope that tomorrow wouldn't be the worst day of her life all over again. Aching now for the comfort of my family and for my body to stop screaming from exhaustion, I walked to the bathroom door. I could hear water from the shower spraying and gave a soft knock before opening it just a crack.

"Do you mind if I wash up?" I called to Amil, hearing water fall heavily as he washed.

"Come on in," he said over the sound of the shower.

I turned on the tap and ran a hand under to test the temperature, grabbed a washcloth and began trying to wash splatters of blood and dirt from my face and hands. The shower's heat fogged the mirror, but I could still see remnants of my hair and makeup that had been done this morning. I rolled my head from side to side, releasing tension and worry as I heard Amil shut the water off and slide the curtain back.

Amil stepped out of the tub, and I could see the bullet wound at his shoulder, still fresh with large bruises at his ribs. The cuts had already started to heal on his knuckles and arms as he dried off with a towel that was far too small. I hadn't realized how relieved I was to see him again in one piece. He and Talos making it out of the manor relatively intact was a miracle. The look was either apparent on my face or I was too tired to block my emotions from him because he stopped mid-swipe of his leg to look up at me.

"I'm glad you didn't listen to me."

"What do you mean?" I crossed my arms and leaned against the sink cabinet as he finished drying himself.

"I told you to leave and not stop. To go out the front and head to the train station."

"No offense, but you had a terrible exit strategy." I gave him a smug grin as he wrapped the small towel around his waist.

"Well, lucky for me, you're as quick on your feet as you are adaptive. You saved my life today. I don't know how I could ever thank you."

"Get us back to Cinder and that will be enough."

"What about Amples? Your brother?"

He looked pained and tired, even with the freshness of a shower. He looked like he could use a long sleep and a good meal. We all could.

"I need to regroup with my other siblings and take Althea somewhere safe. I will go get my brother, but first I have to get back to Cinder."

He nodded, took my face in his hands, and pressed his lips to the top of my head before wrapping his damp arms around me. With my cheek pressed to his still damp chest, I could hear his ragged lungs drawing air painfully, likely from a few broken ribs. I took a deep breath and pulled away.

"In the morning we'll find another car and make the drive to Cinder. We can't risk the train." He silently agreed and left me to clean my own wounds.

After, I lay down in the bed we would be sharing and stared at Althea across the gap that separated the two beds. She had a few minor scrapes and a cut on her swollen lip, nothing that wouldn't heal overnight. The internal wounds she had sustained today would last her a lifetime. The pain she had endured in the last several hours would haunt her dreams until the day she takes her last breath. But, I had every bit of faith that she could overcome it all; the strength she had mustered to save my life was astonishing.

We have shared something most beings would never experience—trusting the other person with their life, surviving so that the other could see another day. She had never asked for anything more than to be happily married to a partner she loved deeply, but that was taken from her within minutes. Even though she may not have been officially declared a Lady of Arta, she was still a royal and Lawrence was not the only Fata willing to slit her throat for that power.

Going to retrieve Argo from Amples would be my first task after I returned to Cinder; my fellow Black Banners would have a lot to catch up on when I arrived home. Talos said he had secured information on Argo's whereabouts. Saving Talos' life would have to be payment for that kindness, but I had a feeling it wouldn't be so easy to convince him of this unspoken agreement. In the morning I would call Zaida, tell her I was coming home and to be ready to leave within a few days.

Amil shifted in the bed next to me and pulled me into his embrace. He took in a painful lung-full of my scent and sighed in relief. His hard body warmed my back and cradled me close. I didn't know how we would make it to Cinder. Or how I would explain to my brothers and sisters that three Incubo were now under my protection from a Fata militia trying to overthrow an underground royal family that we hadn't known existed. But as I lay there and listened to the shallow breathing of Amil next to me, and the unison sound of sleep from the other side of the room, I knew I had no choice but to pick a side to fight for in this war.

TO BE CONTINUED...

# THANK YOU

*Thank you to my friends and husband for supporting my dream. I could not have done this without great support and friendship. When I set out on this journey, I didn't know where it would take me. I couldn't have imagined how much growth I would have seen in myself and in the world around me. I'm so grateful to be able to bring this dream to life and feel it in my hands.*

Made in the USA
Columbia, SC
07 December 2021

50643218R00174